CONNECTIONS

CONNECTIONS

BY

S.J. RITCHEY

Published by
Bookstand Publishing
Morgan Hill, CA 95037
3250_2

Copyright © 2011 by S.J. Ritchey
All rights reserved. No part of this publication may be reproduced or transmitted in any form or by any means, electronic or mechanical, including photocopy, recording, or any information storage and retrieval system, without permission in writing from the copyright owner.

ISBN 978-1-58909-861-9

Printed in the United States of America

ACKNOWLEDGMENTS

Sincere appreciation is expressed to members of Blue River Writers, including Judy Beale, Carter Elliott and Paul Poff, for their helpful critiques and unwavering support. A special thanks to my wife, Elizabeth, for her review of the manuscript and her ability to discover errors.

This is a work of fiction. References to names, places and institutions are the product of the author's imagination, does not reflect their active involvement, or is unintentional.

CHAPTER ONE

The dispatcher in the Pine County Sheriff's office jerked awake when the telephone jangled at one a.m. Saturday morning. He mumbled the usual greeting, "How can I help you?" Unsure of how long he'd dozed, he rubbed sleep from his eyes and reached for the coffee mug. "This is Jack Abrams. I live at 224 Nugent Street." A slight pause and the caller continued, "Deputy, I'm calling because my daughter, Kathy, hasn't come home from the high school game. It's not like her to be late." The dispatcher could hear sobbing in the background, probably the mother or other kids.

The quick sip of stale, cold coffee offered little relief from his daze, but he responded, "Give me a bit of description." He pulled a pad closer, prepared to take notes.

Abrams responded, "She's five-five, weight about one hundred and fifteen, blonde hair, wearing the high school cheerleaders uniform. All her high school friends will know her."

Now fully alert, the dispatcher said, "We'll check around. Everything in town is closed now, so she can't be at one of the joints frequented by the teenagers." The local high school had played their second home game of the 1989-90 football season. There were young people on the streets for a couple of hours, driving around in the family car or walking the streets, trying to connect with buddies or members of the opposite sex. There were only two places in Pineville open after the games, unless she had gone out of town. Neither had reported anything unusual last night.

"I know. We looked for her in the places we thought she might be, but no one had seen her. We're worried something has happened to her."

"I'll notify the patrol cars to look for her. Was she planning to go somewhere after the game? We could start there, any friends she might be with?"

"No, she told her mother she was coming straight home. Had her plans changed, she would've called us."

"Was she driving a car?"

"She always walks. We thought she was safe. Friends usually walk with her until she's very near home."

Abrams continued, "Kathy is active in student government and, as I said, is a cheerleader, so everyone at the school knows her."

"Mr. Abrams, we'll keep our eyes peeled."

The dispatcher called the single patrol to alert them about the potential missing girl. He thought she'd turn up, probably went to another kid's house and forgot to call in. Youngsters weren't responsible these days. Anyway, nothing ever happened in Pineville.

He reheated his coffee in the microwave and remained alert for a while, but slowly drifted back to a dull watch, doing routine paper work and dozing, watching the clock creep slowly toward the end of another boring shift.

The next afternoon two ten-year old boys who'd been fishing and playing around Pine creek on the bright September Saturday afternoon stumbled upon a body in the town park used by residents for picnics and cookouts during the spring and summer. Holding their fishing rods, they circled the body, stretched prone in the ankle-high grass, looked at the dead girl and each other for a moment, then dashed home. One of the mothers called the Sheriff's office.

The deputies who went to the scene confirmed it was likely the Abrams girl. The description matched the information they'd received. Doubling as a forensic team in the small community, they took photographs and did the usual measurements of the position of the body, noting the grass around her had been trampled and evidence a car had been near. Her clothes, a high-school uniform with a short skirt, were intact and neatly arranged, but her panties and shorts had been tossed next to her torso. A sweater rested a couple of feet away as though someone had tossed it at her. At least two different footprints suggested she'd been attacked or dropped by a group. An ambulance transported the body to the morgue.

Jack Abrams came to identify the body, standing in a daze by his lifeless daughter whom he'd loved and nurtured for years, now inert on the steel gurney. He touched her face one more time, then turned away. He nodded, "Yes, it's her."

The Medical Examiner suspected sexual assault, but the vagina had not been penetrated. Deep bruises on her neck, thighs and back suggested she'd been hit or thrown around. After a thorough examination, he concluded death had resulted from a broken neck, likely from a blow to her face or neck. He collected samples of semen around the pubic area, skin fragments from under the fingernails, several hairs eased from her scalp, and strands of light brown hair clutched in the fingers of her right hand. He concluded someone had set out to rape her and in his excitement had been unable to carry out his intent. Then in his rage had crushed her neck. He stored the samples, expecting to be quizzed later about such evidence by the Sheriff and the County Attorney. And three days ago he'd read a short article in one of his medical journals about the potential of connecting criminals to their deeds by DNA. He didn't know much about the genetically associated compound, and as far as he knew, it had never been employed in a U.S. court system. Nevertheless, he'd stay on the safe side and hold the evidence for a while.

Based on the statements of several high school students, Kathy had walked away from the stadium on Friday night with Robert Jarvis. Sheriff Ross Talbot obtained a warrant, searched the home of Joshua Bull where the boy lived. On his green and gold school letter jacket, they found two long blond hairs, apparently from the victim, but matching would confirm that notion. Robert told the Sheriff he had walked with Kathy to the corner of Elm and Ninth after the game, but they parted there and he hadn't seen her since. Robert was arrested and charged with sexual assault and murder. When told Kathy had been killed, he shook his head, not accepting, his face contorted, and tears streamed down his cheeks.

When Mike Block, a younger deputy suggested the evidence was weak and there was no obvious way Jarvis had moved the body to the park, two miles from Elm and Ninth, Sheriff Talbot exploded. "We've got enough. The black bastard killed her. We'll worry later about how he got her all the way to the park." Talbot shrugged, "Maybe they walked there and he killed her when she wouldn't fuck him. You know damn well he intended to screw her. He'd already ripped off her undergarments."

"There's no blood at the scene, except on her. Looks like she was killed somewhere else."

"Then he did it and brought her there."

"Doesn't make sense. They both live on the other side of town. Plus Jarvis had no car, not even a bicycle. It seems unlikely, if not impossible."

"He did it. The hairs on his jacket prove he was with her. He admits walking with her."

"Why would he admit being with her if he's guilty. It doesn't follow."

The Sheriff retorted, "I'll talk to the County Attorney. See what he thinks." He stared at the deputy. "Also, why did the bastard get so upset, cried like a baby, when he was told. That was an act to cover up."

"I interpreted his reaction to mean he really cared for her. You have to admit, it's unusual for a criminal to demonstrate such distress."

Approximately the same time the body was being transported to the morgue, Harold Brown, a well-known lawyer in the town, set out to clean his Buick, a bi-weekly ritual. As he vacuumed the floor and seats, he noticed a deep dark stain on the rear seat. Although the mark resembled blood, he thought little about it, passing it off as a cut hand by one of the kids hauled around by Gil, his seventeen year-old son. They were always drinking soda, perhaps stronger things. He'd found broken glass several times in the past and hadn't worried about it.

He applied an organic solvent to remove the stain, but an unsightly mark remained in spite of his efforts. Harold was irritated at his son for allowing the seat to be marred, but passed it off as teenage lack of responsibility.

When the evening news on the local television highlighted the murder of Kathy Abrams, Harold became concerned. He knew Abrams, a good man, and his wife must be absolutely distraught by the death of their daughter. The newscaster revealed the site of the murder and suggested a car had been involved because of the remote location. Harold's hands and brow broke into sweat as he recalled the stain on the back seat of the Buick. Visions of forensic types examining the blotch raced through his thinking. He decided to get the advice of his boss, the senior partner in the law firm where he'd worked for fifteen years. If this turned out to be a real problem, Ledbetter would know how to shove it under the rug or bamboozle the town officials. He would do anything to protect the image of his firm and the people who worked there.

He telephoned Ledbetter to tell him of his concern.

On Monday morning Sheriff Talbot discussed the crime with the County Attorney, James Williams, known by most as 'Red' because of his hair color. Williams, a local boy, had gone to Southern Illinois, then to law school in Chicago, before settling back in Pine County. He had been the C.A. for ten years and no one seemed eager to run against him. He'd found a lifetime position. Everybody seemed content with his performance.

Talbot reviewed quickly the evidence and the circumstances of the crime for Williams, then said, "We're convinced the Jarvis kid did it, but one of my deputies wants to look further. He argues Jarvis couldn't have moved the body to the park without a car."

Red scratched his head, shifted his feet, and said, "It is a reasonable question, but the hair and their being placed together are solid pieces against him." He walked around his desk from where they were standing. "Have you checked with the Medical Examiner? Any evidence of rape or tissue samples, such as semen or hair, from the scene?"

Talbot looked down. "Not yet. I thought we had enough with the hair and people seeing them together after the game."

"Maybe you're right. We can get a conviction. A black boy and a white girl being together doesn't set well around here."

"Then, I'll let it ride until I hear from you." At the door Talbot turned back to ask, "Has Ned Ledbetter talked to you?"

"He called me at home late Saturday night."

"Me too."

On Monday after the crime Harold Brown and Ned Ledbetter met in the office of the senior law partner. Brown started the conversation, "According to the late news Saturday, Sheriff Talbot has arrested Robert Jarvis for murder and attempted rape. He's being held pending bail. I didn't know that when I called you."

"I heard, but who's Jarvis?"

"One of the high school football players. Apparently he and Kathy Abrams had a thing going. My son who's in classes with them, told me they were seen together often around the school."

Ledbetter's florid face lighted. "Now I recall. He's the star running back. Being courted by some of the major schools. He's black, right?"

"Yes. He lives with his grandfather, Joshua Bull."

Ledbetter said, "I've been thinking about this thing. This news will make our problem a lot easier. Juries in this county look askance when the issue involves mixing of races. Locals don't like it." He adjusted his pants, pulling them up over his bulging midsection.

He continued. "Sit tight. I've talked to the County Attorney and to Talbot. They both owe me big, so I can control them to a large degree. The only unknown now is the defense attorney."

Brown said, "Bull probably can't afford to hire a lawyer. The court will appoint someone."

Ledbetter walked over to the windows and looked into the town square. "Maybe we can influence the appointment."

"As I told you Saturday evening, I don't want anything to come out about my son and that stain in the back seat of my car."

Ledbetter knocked on Brown's door in mid-afternoon. "I've an idea to bounce off you."

"About the Jarvis case?"

"I'm considering recommending to Judge Peabody the appointment of Jerry Preston as the defense attorney. He's new and inexperienced, still a bit naive. We can guide him, make sure he focuses on the evidence presented by the prosecution and not start turning over rocks."

Brown smiled. "Good idea, but you really mean control him."

"I wouldn't want to put it quite in those terms."

"All we have to do is convince Peabody."

Ledbetter called Judge Charles Peabody and arranged for a meeting the following day. Ned knew Peabody was relatively new to Pine County and would have scant information about local attorneys and firms. He could make the approach as though the Ledbetter firm was doing the county a favor by eating the expense of a defense counsel.

In Peabody's office, Ledbetter said, "I hear Robert Jarvis has requested a court appointed attorney for his defense." Ledbetter had called the court clerk to make certain his information was correct.

"He has. You have an interest in representing him?"

"Not personally, but I'd like to recommend Jerry Preston from my firm. He's a bright young guy who could use the experience. He'll do a good job for Jarvis."

Peabody smiled. "And give your firm some publicity."

Ledbetter laughed. "It'd be a small contribution to the justice system." His face became hard. "You know the court fee doesn't nearly match what we'd get for his time on other matters."

Peabody turned over a folder on the desk. "Tell you what. Bring me Preston's resume. I'll consider him."

Ledbetter stood, knowing he'd won. "You'll have it by tomorrow morning. As I said, he's inexperienced, but he had a fine record in law school at Northwestern."

By the end of the next day, Peabody had confirmed the appointment of Jerry Preston as the defense counsel for Jarvis. The judge felt comfortable with the assignment of a young lawyer. All the preliminary information provided by the County Attorney and the Sheriff suggested the case was clear cut. All the evidence pointed to Jarvis. Preston wouldn't have to dig in preparation. He'd make a solid impression with the public and the press—bright, young, nice looking. This case could be completed cleanly and quickly. Not many of those these days.

Brown's round face beamed when he saw Ledbetter. "You did it. No hitch?"

Ledbetter grinned, taking pleasure in controlling people and events, and knowing his manipulations usually paid off for the firm, as well as for him personally. "Nah, Peabody went along without a question."

Ledbetter walked across the office to the coffee on the credenza. "Only problem now is making sure your son and those buddies of his don't become talkative. Get them together. Scare the hell out of them. Threaten them with whatever it takes to maintain silence." He placed one of his huge hands on Brown's shoulder. "You know, Harold, if there's a leak, we'll all be in trouble—big trouble, like obstruction of justice." He squeezed the shoulder. "You understand. Make sure those boys do."

Harold rubbed his shoulder as he left the room. Ledbetter was still a strong guy, even if he'd become flabby and less agile.

CHAPTER TWO

Irritated by the ringing telephone, Fred Ferriday waited for the caller to give up. When the ringing persisted, he stalked away from his lab bench, leaving a set of slides in disarray next to the small projector, to the end of the large research laboratory. He lifted the instrument from the wall mounted base, his eyes on a graduate student pouring dilute nitric acid into a beaker, hoping the neophyte didn't slop the stuff onto his shoes.

"Ferriday speaking."

"Dr. Ferriday, you don't know me, but I'm Jerry Preston, a lawyer representing a client who requested I get in touch with you."

Fred wasn't surprised by the opening. He had been called more frequently since the recent news articles about his research on the potential use of DNA in criminal investigations. He'd never dreamed his biology lab would become such a focus of interest by the media. Lawyers and criminals seeking ways to escape the justice system frequently called. Sometimes people needed real assistance but he was still learning the intricacies of the rapidly developing forensic tool. He'd regarded his recent publication about the stability of DNA as a preliminary notice of the future.

He responded, "I'm not sure I can help." He pulled a lab stool closer and perched, his long legs stretched across the aisle.

Preston interrupted, "It's complicated. I'd like to visit and explain."

"Mr. Preston, I can't give you much time. I'm in the middle of an important experiment and can't neglect the work." The beginning of the 1989-90 academic year at the University of Illinois had brought the usual flurry of starting classes, faculty meetings, and student advising that took time from Fred's research, teaching, and consulting, but he didn't explain that to Preston.

"You will when I tell you the situation." He went on without interruption, "You see, it involves Joshua Bull, an old acquaintance of yours, and a murder charge against his grandson."

Fred said, "I recall Joshua." He ran a hand across the top of his head, ruffling the short, but thinning, brown hair sprinkled with an increasing tinge of gray.

"You were buddies in your younger days in Pine County. Joshua says you'll remember."

"Well, I'll be damned. But I can't imagine how I could be useful. It's been so long since I've seen him, or even been in Pine County." Forty years ago he and Joshua, a Black boy his age, had played together in the woods and fields of southern Illinois farmland. Must have been about 1948. They'd been good friends, but circumstances and people drove them apart. When he thought about those times, Fred remembered the bitterness and the frustrations. But, there had been a lot of joys and good things too.

Preston insisted, "I'd like to come tomorrow afternoon and discuss the situation with you. What about two-thirty at your office?"

"Try to be here by two. I have a meeting at three with the Vice-President. I don't want to be late or have to cut our meeting short."

"I'll make it. Thanks, Dr. Ferriday."

Fred returned to the organization of the slides but visions of his youth in Pineville edged into his mind.

Fred was hanging a stained white lab coat on the back of the office door when Preston knocked promptly at two the following afternoon. He moved several books and a stack of journals from the nearest side chair. They shook hands and went through the usual introductions.

Fred pointed to a chair next to the desk. "Have a seat."

Preston placed his briefcase on the hardwood floor and dropped into the oak seat, shifting to get more comfortable. "Thanks again for seeing me. I know you don't have much time, so I'll summarize as quickly as possible."

Fred broke in. "First, tell me how Joshua is doing. I thought about him last night after your call."

"Joshua isn't well, but he manages okay. His wife died two years ago, so he seems lonely, but I don't know him well " He reached in the case and pulled out a newspaper and handed it to Fred. "Here's a starting point."

Fred scanned the headline from a St. Louis paper and the article following. A local girl, an All-American type, had been assaulted and killed after a high school football game. All the physical evidence pointed to a member of the team. He had been arrested and charged with first degree murder. The young man, Robert Jarvis, a star athlete, a good student, and black, remained in custody of the local law enforcement officials.

Fred returned the paper. "So how's Joshua connected?"

"Jarvis is his grandson. He's lived with the Bulls since he was eight. The father disappeared after the mother, Joshua's daughter, died in an accident at the local textile plant. He apparently couldn't cope with being a single parent and took the easy way out. Joshua and his wife became the parents for all practical purposes. Now it's just Joshua and Robert."

"I take it Joshua believes his grandson is innocent."

"Yes, although a lot of evidence made public suggests otherwise."

"What do you think?"

"Dr Ferriday, the court appointed me to represent the client when Mr. Bull couldn't afford an attorney. I don't know about the innocence or guilt. But I've been impressed by the sincerity of Joshua Bull. It's obvious he believes with all his heart and soul his grandson is not guilty. He'll testify Robert was with him when the crime occurred. But the Sheriff and the County Attorney don't believe him. It's clear they want resolution as fast as possible. I doubt the testimony of the grandfather will carry much weight when there's conflicting arguments." Preston shifted his feet, crossed his legs before continuing, "To be candid, the fact that the defendant is black and the victim was white has stirred the emotions of the community. I hate to admit it, but Pine County still has more than its share of racist leanings."

Fred said, "I'd hoped it had changed over the years."

"It probably has to some extent, but I'm new to the area. I've learned the feelings are there, maybe more subtle, almost invisible at times, but everyone understands." Jerry

Preston looked young, medium height, nice features, neat appearance in a solid brown suit and polished loafers. Fred thought he'd not seen much of life yet.

"I'm sorry Joshua has to live with that, but I still don't understand how I might be useful."

Preston took a deep breath. "Joshua is an intelligent man, not educated, but smart. His sister read in a St. Louis newspaper you'd gotten some recognition for your work with DNA testing and your research formed the basis for demonstrating a suspect accused of rape hadn't been involved. Now both Joshua and his sister have the idea DNA evidence would clear his grandson. And he believes you'll help him."

Fred remained thoughtful, looking at Preston, who continued, "I've tried to convince him that a world class scientist such as you wouldn't be free to spend time on this case, but he insisted I meet with you. He wants you to come to Pineville and talk with him."

Fred turned in the chair to stare out the window at the oaks, still green in the early autumn, shading walks in the middle of campus, thinking about his commitments for the next week. Turning back to look at Preston, he said, "It'll be hard with my commitments. I've got to be in London next Wednesday to present a paper as part of an international conference. I can't cancel at this late date."

Preston said, "Joshua will be terribly disappointed. He's counting on you."

For some reason he couldn't explain at the moment, Fred felt pressure to respond positively to his boyhood buddy. "Tell you what. I'll drive down this weekend, talk with Joshua and the grandson, and we'll see from there

17

how it might go." He paused. "I don't know if you've had experience with DNA evidence. It's quite new and hasn't been used widely but it doesn't impress rural juries very much. They often view it as a bunch of mumbo-jumbo dreamed up by high powered attorneys and egg-headed academic types. It's still too new to be readily accepted. But there usually is other evidence that helps make the case."

Preston said, "I've never been part of a defense when murder is the charge. You're correct, I know essentially nothing about DNA except the items I've read in papers and law journals. But we have nothing else at this time and we're grasping at straws. The DNA information might not be worth anything, but who knows at this point."

Fred stood, glancing at his watch to signal he had to go to the meeting with the Vice-President. "I'll come on Saturday morning, but I've got to be back here by late Sunday. Make sure Joshua and the young man are available Saturday afternoon, if you would."

He reached for his suit coat and walked out with Preston.

In the hall, Fred said, "I'd appreciate your making a reservation at a local motel for Saturday night. I no longer recall the possibilities."

Preston smiled and said, "I'll be glad to do that. The Pineville is on the west side of the town square and is likely the best option. I stayed there when I visited for an interview."

Fred left his house in Urbana at six on Saturday morning. Driving south on U.S. 45 through small towns and past huge farms brought back memories of his first trip on the route when he came to the university as a freshmen roughly thirty years ago. A lot had happened since then. Four years on a football scholarship, war in Vietnam, graduate school at Wisconsin, marriage, increasing reputation as a scientist, travel all over the world, returning to Illinois as a faculty member when an endowed professorship was offered. Good times, sad times. The worst had been watching his wife Martha deteriorate in the clutches of cancer. Now he'd been alone for two years and work had claimed everything in his life. South of Mattoon, he took Route 70 in a southwesterly direction toward St. Louis, then later went south on a small state road directly into Pineville. To his surprise he remembered the routes, but the scenes had changed dramatically with less open space, many more businesses and houses, and more traffic on the two-lane roads.

A sign on the town limits indicated a population of twelve thousand, but he didn't know how dated the information was. He drove into the central part of Pineville before he recognized any familiar land marks. The square hadn't changed much. Built late in the last century, it was still dominated by the courthouse and administrative offices of the county, surrounded by four blocks of small shops and two or three restaurants. None of the names were as he remembered, probably all had changed ownership.

He found the Pineville Motel on the west side of town, checked in with the older man at the desk, found his room, dropped his bag on the floor by the double bed, and called Jerry Preston. "Mr. Preston, I'm checked in. Ready to go as soon as you are."

"Pick you up in fifteen minutes. We'll visit the grandson in the county jail, then see Joshua."

The jail, in the basement of the courthouse, needed repair. Peeling flakes of paint on the door frame revealed the bare wood beneath. The floor boards creaked under their weight as they entered the Sheriff's area. The burly deputy at the desk grunted and nodded as they interrupted his watching the Cardinals on a small television, but led them down a dark narrow hall toward the cell, their footsteps echoing in the chamber.

Fred asked, to pacify the deputy, "How're they doing?"

"Behind 5 to 4 in top of the sixth. Bad year."

Fred attempted to crack the officer's stern demeanor. "Looks like the Reds and Oakland in the World Series."

"You're likely correct," the deputy responded, but his tone was less gruff.

They stopped at a door to a cell. Preston called out, "Robert, someone I want you to meet."

A muscular young man, six-two, two hundred pounds, dressed in an orange jumpsuit put a book on the small table and came toward them as Preston said, "This is your grandfather's friend, Dr. Ferriday. He's come to talk to you and Joshua about the trial."

Robert glanced at Preston and Fred, then watched the deputy walk away. "I guess I should thank you, but I suspect there's not much anyone can do." His face reflected his sadness, his eyes dull and without hope.

Fred reached through the bars to shake Robert's hand. "Who knows what might happen between now and the actual trial. I'll talk with your grandfather, but tell me about yourself. I knew Joshua a long time ago."

"He told me about you. He's proud you were friends." Robert paused. "I'm a senior at Pine County high school, planned to graduate in May and go to college. But that's all gone now." His shoulders slumped even more as he dismissed the future.

"Mr. Preston says you're quite an athlete."

For the first time, Robert spoke with slight animation in his voice. "I've played all the sports in school. Several universities have sent people to watch the football games and I've received quite a few letters offering me a slot on their team. Before this happened, I'd planned on visiting Illinois and Notre Dame, maybe Michigan and Tennessee." He shrugged and turned his hands upward in resignation.

"Did you know the victim? I think her name was Kathy Abrams."

Robert's expression became even more sad. "Everybody knows everyone in the school. Kathy and I were in classes together. She was a cheer leader, homecoming queen, editor of the school paper. One of those who's into every activity."

"Were you good friends?"

Robert looked away, around the small square space of the cell. "We talked a lot, sat together on the team bus to out of town games, things like that." Fred thought there was a trace of tears and Robert didn't care to reveal the depth of their relationship, if they'd had any.

"Did you date or meet at social events?"

Anger rose in Robert's voice, stern, almost challenging Fred to disagree, as he said, "We couldn't do that in this town. There's an understanding. Blacks and whites don't date." His hands gripped the bars firmly, the knuckles discolored.

Robert's tone suggested a deep seated frustration, causing Fred to think there might be more here than anyone knows about. Maybe the two kids had strong feelings for each other, but were afraid to reveal them in the environment of this small community with racial barriers clearly understood by locals, but never articulated to outsiders. Fred recalled from his youth many small towns in the southern part of the state enforcing unwritten laws that blacks could not be in the town limits after dark. Surely that was no longer true but he couldn't be certain.

Fred wanted to know the young man better, but he had no reason to raise questions relevant to the actual crime. His potential role was that of a friend or as an expert witness. He said, "Robert, I don't know what'll happen, but I'm to see your grandfather now. He'll let me know his expectations and what my involvement may be. But I'll see you again, I'm sure."

"Dr. Ferriday, all I can tell you is I didn't do it. I don't have any idea who would do those things to Kathy, but I didn't." Robert's voice quavered. His hands gripped the steel bars as though he intended to rip them out of the concrete.

Fred said, "Mr. Preston and I'll make sure you're treated fairly."

As they walked out into the bright sunlight of the fall afternoon, Fred observed, "Some things change slowly in communities like this."

They found Joshua sitting in a wooden high-back rocker on the front porch of a small frame house on the outskirts of town, where Elm street became a state maintained highway. As they gained the wire fence around the property, Joshua struggled from his position and grasped the porch railing, staring at them intently. Once they were through the open gate, Fred called, "Joshua, it's Fred Ferriday. How're you doing?"

Joshua had reached the top of the steps when Fred took his hand in greeting. "Thanks for coming. I knew you would when you understood the mess I'm in." Joshua turned to retrace his steps to the rocker. "Pull up a chair or use the swing." He looked again at Fred, a broad grin creasing his face. "I would've known you on the street. You haven't changed much, maybe lost some hair, see a few wrinkles. It's been almost forty years since we hung out in those woods." Joshua seemed to remember the lanky youth, six-two and a hundred and eighty-five pounds whom he'd seen on the streets of Pineville a few days before Fred went to university.

"I thought about those times driving down today. Life goes quickly doesn't it."

"I don't know. Sometimes life drags a lot." Life had not treated Joshua very well. He was stooped, overweight, hair completely gray, quite different from the trim, husky teenager Fred had known.

Fred wanted to reminisce, but he remembered his time commitment and thought they should focus on the purpose of his visit. "Josh, I've seen your grandson. He seems like a good young man, bright, intelligent, respectful. How'd he get in this situation?"

Joshua rubbed a gnarled hand across his face. "Don't know altogether. But I'm scared about what might happen. This can still be a mean place for us."

Jerry Preston said, "Mr. Bull, tell Fred what you believe is the truth. What you know."

Joshua shifted in the rocker, moved to and fro a few times, rubbed his hands together. "It happened a week ago Friday. Robert played football at the high school stadium, then came home. The eleven o'clock TV news had just started when he came in. We talked a bit about the game and he had a soft drink, then went to bed. The police came to arrest him the next night. He'd just got home from his week-end job. Police said he'd murdered this girl. They won't believe me about the time or anything else."

He rocked back and forth several times, gazing across the corn field ready for harvest. "The police say she was beaten, then killed. They say she and Robert left together after the game and strands of her hair were on his jacket."

Jerry asked, "How'd Robert get home on that Friday?"

"Walked. Most times he rides his bike, but a tire went flat, so he walked."

"Three miles is a long walk after playing a football game."

"He's a strong boy." Joshua shifted again. "My sister in St Louis read in the paper about your award and called me because she remembered our times together when we were kids. That got me thinking about the things found at the scene. It could be the kind of evidence that shows who really did the thing. I couldn't get the police to try to find out more. So I talked Mr. Preston into calling you."

Fred turned to Preston. "I assume appropriate samples were collected in case the investigators decide to employ techniques of matching sperm and other tissues or fluids?"

"They were. The Medical Examiner has them."

"But nothing has been done with the samples?"

"Correct. The Sheriff contends they have enough evidence without wasting money on further testing. The County Attorney supports him."

"But the defense can demand those tests be done or obtain samples for their own analysis."

Preston seemed uncomfortable. "The Sheriff and the County Attorney have resisted the release of any samples. I'll have to get the judge to force them with a court order."

Preston's excuses caused Fred to suspect that Preston's heart was not in the case. Why had he not persisted in obtaining important evidence if he represented Robert and planned to mount an aggressive defense? He would press him later about his apathy. Maybe there were other circumstances involved in the delay.

Fred turned to Joshua. "You know if Robert and the girl were friends?"

Joshua scratched his head. "Think so, but Robert won't tell me how he feels about her. He's sad about what happened. He cried, the first time I saw him do that since he was a little boy."

"Would some of their classmates know about their relationship?"

"Maybe. Don't know for sure."

"Does Robert have a close friend? Someone he might tell how he feels or who's around him enough to understand the relationship. You know, Joshua, young people don't always tell their elders everything. But a good buddy might know."

"His closest friend would be Earl Sloan. He comes around the house sometimes. He's the only other black on the football team."

Again Fred reminded himself of his potential role and turned to Jerry. "But those are your questions. I shouldn't be interfering."

When Preston didn't respond, Fred asked, "So have you talked to Earl yet? He might know something that would be useful."

Jerry looked away. "No, I haven't yet. I was assigned only a few days ago."

"Has a trial date been set?"

"The preliminary hearing is next Wednesday. I anticipate the Judge will establish a date at that time."

"What happens at the preliminary?"

"The prosecutor presents the evidence in a summary way, enough so the Judge can determine if there's sufficient cause to schedule a trial and hold over the defendant."

"Can Robert be released on bail?"

"The Judge will set terms at the preliminary. I'll request minimum bail, but I'm sure the prosecutor will demand the max, since it's a murder charge."

Joshua said, "I won't be able to put up bail money."

Preston shifted on the swing and said, "I have a meeting in St. Louis tonight, so I need to leave soon. Maybe you can visit again in the morning, but I can't be here."

Fred shook Joshua's hand as they stood. "Josh, I need to get back early tomorrow, but I'll keep in contact. I probably can't do anything if the lab tests aren't completed. It's up to Mr. Preston to make sure that happens. I'll be disappointed if they're not done because they might reveal that Robert is not guilty. But you need to understand those tests might also prove beyond any doubt that he's guilty."

Joshua, still holding Fred's hand, said, "I know he didn't do it."

"I'll talk to you later. It's good to see you after all these years."

As they drove away, Jerry said, "I think you believe I'm not interested, but I am. I've gotten a lot of pressure to let things progress as the prosecutor desires. My boss, the head of the firm where I'm employed, has told me everything will be okay."

"I'm not so sure. It's strange there hasn't been more follow through by the Sheriff in searching for additional evidence."

"I've been assured everything will turn out okay."

"But you don't know. Those guys may be willing to sacrifice this young man."

"What are you suggesting?"

"Something is not right here. I've been in town only a couple of hours and discover important leads aren't being pursued. Frankly, I'm shocked. No, I'm more than shocked. I'm mad as hell. Where's your integrity and the integrity of your firm?"

"Dr. Ferriday, that's too strong. You're being unfair."

"I don't think so."

Preston didn't respond. Fred said, "I have no idea on earth what I can do about this, but I'll find out. I wish I didn't have to travel next week, so I could do some calling to law firms who would take this more seriously and who could tell me what the hell is going on in Pine County. Frankly, Preston, this sounds like the eighteen hundreds."

"Fred, I've been overwhelmed by the reactions. I'm new in this county. I'm depending on advice of senior people in my firm to guide me. They're telling me to not rock the boat."

Fred thought Jerry might be naive or lacking in courage, but decided to push him a bit more. "I tell you what. I want you to aggressively work for Robert. If I believe for one minute you're not doing your very best for him, I'm going to raise hell in the state capitol." Fred didn't know what he could do, but he knew Jerry would not be certain of his connections.

When Jerry stopped at the motel, Fred said, as he stepped out of the car, "I'll call you as soon as I'm back. A week from Monday." He held the door open, leaning down to see Preston. "I'll be disappointed if there's no progress with those samples by the time I return." He slammed the door harder than necessary.

CHAPTER THREE

Never completely satisfied with his efforts, Fred focused on his manuscript during the flight to London. He altered a phrase at times to make it more precise and changed a word he thought was clearer. Scheduled to present research his laboratory had done on the stability of DNA under a range of conditions in the past two years, he wanted to put a lot of details in his head before he stood in front of an international audience of top scientists. He looked forward to meeting those scientists who'd opened the door for genetic fingerprinting in 1984, an event that triggered Fred's imagination and led to his own investigations in perfecting the forensic tool. He'd read all of their papers and had talked with a couple by telephone in the past two years. Now, four years after the breakthrough in which a murderer had been prosecuted based on the biological evidence gleaned through mass screening of a village population, the use of DNA profiling had been gradually accepted as a viable tool in discovering the truth about crimes. But the courts and the public, particularly those who were always leery of new scientific advances, still questioned the authenticity of the biological method. Plus, there was still much to be learned about the methodology and the potential applications, not just in forensics but in the implications related to genetics of different species, including the human.

Interruptions frustrated his concentration. He'd paid extra from his personal account for a first class seat to gain additional leg room and privacy, but relief from the normal service of drinks, dinner and more drinks could not be achieved. He had forced himself to put the final pieces of the paper together Sunday night after returning from Pineville, but he couldn't close his mind to the dilemma confronting Joshua and Robert. Two hours after takeoff from O'Hare, he gave up, turned off the reading light, and attempted to sleep.

He drowsed sporadically remembering Joshua Bull and their times together. Joshua lived in a tenant house on the farm adjacent to Fred's family's place. He discovered Joshua in the woods one summer day when they were both eight. Neither had other friends. Four miles from the center of Pineville, they were isolated and out of touch with the kids who lived in town. Soon they became best buddies, roaming the woods, building small dams in the creek, and chasing squirrels and raccoons. In his semi-sleep state, Fred smiled at their innocence. Two kids playing games, oblivious to the taboos associated with race. They did not know yet.

Their mutual activities cemented the relationship throughout the summer months. An understanding, never spoken, became routine. They met each day by the huge elm at the corner of the corn field as soon as their daily chores were completed. Both wondered about not seeing the other in school, but neither asked.

One day Fred and Joshua attempted a new venture using the small pine trees on the edge of the woods. They climbed toward the top until the tree could no longer support their weight, and held tightly as it bent to the ground. When they were standing on the ground and released it, the tree would rebound upward to its original standing position. When Fred's turn came again, he selected the largest pine in the cluster. He climbed from limb to limb, moving steadily toward the top, but this tree failed to bend as the others. Joshua urged him to keep going, yelling encouragement from below. With a loud crack the uppermost portion of the trunk snapped off. Fred crashed to the ground, still clutching the tree top.

Fred thought he was dead, trying to regain his breath after falling solidly on his back. Joshua leaned over him after pulling off the pine branches. "Fred, you okay?"

For a minute, Fred couldn't respond. He felt like he was going to suffocate. Joshua was rubbing his face and brow. As some air returned to his lungs, Fred struggled to a sitting position. "I'm okay, I think. But, wow, I hurt everywhere."

"Maybe something's broken. See if you can stand up."

Fred hadn't thought about that possibility. Notions of splints and casts frightened him. "I should get home, just in case."

"You walk okay?"

Fred, with Joshua's assistance, scrambled to his feet, but felt very unsteady. "Maybe you could walk with me. I don't feel too good."

Together they started toward Fred's home. By the time they were in sight of the house, Fred could manage without leaning on Joshua and the pain had abated. He decided nothing important could be badly damaged or he wouldn't have been able to move as well as he could.

Weeding a flower bed in the back yard, Fred's mother watched them arrive. She stopped her hoeing, shifted her straw hat, watching the two boys as they planned their next meeting.

In a few minutes, Joshua departed for his house and she came to Fred, who hadn't told her about falling from the tree. She said, using a tone he didn't often hear, "Who was that boy?"

"Joshua Bull. He lives in one of the tenant houses on Grimes' place."

"It's not a good idea to play with him." Her features were stern, her expression he saw only when he was in big trouble.

Fred protested in surprise. "But why, he's my friend. We get along good and have fun."

She poked a finger into his chest. "Fred, I want you to stop seeing him. That's all you need to know. Don't play with him again." She returned to her chore.

Fred didn't know how to react. He let the matter slide for the moment, but knew he wouldn't stop playing with Joshua.

Jostled awake by the stewardess who offered another pillow, Fred adjusted the blanket and stared into the blackness of the night for several minutes before his mind returned to the days when he and Joshua roamed the woods. He recalled the den they'd made by cutting away the middle of a huge growth of small shrubs, leaving a vacant space surrounded by bush. They put up four poles and covered the sides and top with burlap Fred had taken from the feed room in the barn. They spent long hours in their cozy hide-away, talking and dreaming about all the things little boys think about. It became their retreat from the rest of the world.

They would lose track of time as they raced through the woods, waded in a small stream, then returned to the hide-out. One day a young girl approached the den and called, "Joshua, mother needs you at home."

Both boys edged through the passageway to look at her. Joshua explained, "This is my sister. Her name is Louise."

Louise, younger than the boys, turned away, saying, "You need to come home before mother gets really mad. The chores are waiting."

Fred watched them leave, thinking Louise was quite pretty, although she was likely only four.

Soon school began and homework and his chores took most of his time, but for the first time, Fred's awareness that Joshua didn't attend the same school bothered him. He realized there were no Blacks in his school. When he asked about the situation, his parents informed him that Blacks went to a separate school. They didn't elaborate, but passed it off as a matter of nothing special.

Fred and Joshua continued to find each other on weekend days during the fall. Fred asked Joshua why he went to a different school. Joshua's only comment was that's the way things had to be in Pine county.

As winter approached and the pasture turned brown, one of Fred's chores included throwing loose hay from the barn loft and distributing it to hay racks along the side of the barn. The cows pulled the hay from the rack without getting it wet and dirty. One Saturday, Fred asked Joshua to come help with the hay; then he could play a while longer,

33

having forgotten his mother's disapproval. They climbed the ladder to the loft and threw down a large pile of hay to the ground below.

Fred said, "Let me show you a good trick." With that, he dropped his pitchfork onto the loft floor, and leaped through the opening into the middle of the haystack below, letting out a yell as he landed.

With some encouragement, Joshua followed and sank deeply into the loose material. "That's fun. Let's do it again."

Back up the ladder to the loft, twelve feet above the floor. Fred leaped, then scurried out of the pile to make room for his buddy. Joshua ran forward and jumped, but missed the middle of the stack and fell heavily on the fringe. The thud told Fred his friend was hurt. Joshua groaned and rolled on the ground, but didn't get up, clasping his stomach. He rolled from side to side, gasping heavily.

Fred rushed over, placed his arms around Joshua's shoulders and began to lift him. "You okay?"

Joshua couldn't speak for three or four minutes, then he grinned a bit. "Knocked the wind out of me. Be okay in a while."

They were squatting against the wall when Fred's father walked near. He asked, "What happened?"

Fred said, "Joshua missed the pile when he jumped from the loft. He'll be okay in a minute."

The father stood looking, frowning, his face darker than usual. "Joshua, you should go home. I don't want you and Fred playing together anymore. Don't come back here again."

Shaken by the ultimatum, his eyes staring at the ground, his shoulders slumped, Joshua started toward home. Fred followed, planning to walk part of the way with him, but when they reached the gate to the large field, his father called, "Fred, come back. I want to talk to you." The sternness in his voice reminded Fred of his mother's tone the day she'd told him not to see Joshua again.

Fred's father said, "It's not good to play with Joshua."

"But why, dad? I don't understand."

"Your mother told you to stop. Now I'm telling you. We mean it. Never again."

"Tell me why not. I like him. We get along good. And he's the only boy my age near here."

His father placed his hand on Fred's shoulder and looked down at him. "It's not good for whites and blacks to become too close. I don't care if he's your buddy. It has to stop. That's final. Don't let me catch you two together again or I'll punish you."

A week later, Fred met Joshua at the den. Fred said, "How're you doing? Get over the fall okay?"

"Yeah. Really sore for a couple of days, but I'm okay."

Fred struggled to find the words to tell Joshua about his father's threat. With a slight tremor in his voice, he mumbled, "I'm in trouble with my folks. I can't see you anymore."

Joshua seemed to understand better. "I told my mom what your father said in the barn. She got mad, but warned me not to go back to your place and stop meeting you in our den."

Fred said, "I don't understand this stuff about blacks and whites. My parents get upset when I ask why I can't play with you."

"I know, but that's the way it is in Pine county."

The two boys looked at each other. Some inner force pulled them together. They hugged each other tightly, then turned and walked back into their separate worlds. Both had tears in their eyes.

Fred was awake now, thinking about his renewed relationship with Joshua Bull. After that day in the den, they'd never met again. Fred had sneaked back to the den several times, but Joshua never returned. On rare occasions, they saw each other in town and paused to talk briefly. Each felt awkward, unable to say what they truly felt. It became easier to just nod and move along. As they matured and interacted with others in the town, they became more aware of the racial divides, separate but so-called equal schools, boundaries not voiced among the adults, and the barriers each accepted as matter-of-fact.

During Fred's senior year in high school, he encountered Joshua on the main street during the Christmas break from classes. Looking around to see where his parents were and not seeing them close, Fred said, "Joshua, how're things?"

Joshua grinned, bright teeth shining in his dark face, "Doing okay. I'm working at the textile mill. I may get married next summer."

"That's good. Who's the girl?"

"Mary Jo Peters. She was in my grade."

"You dropped out of school?"

"Yeah. No reason to keep going. I knew as much as the teachers. How about you?"

"I'll graduate in May. I'm going to the University of Illinois in the fall. They've offered me a football scholarship."

"You must be a good player. I've heard about you and how far you can throw the ball, but I've never been to a game at your high school. You understand."

Joshua saw Fred's parents coming out of the hardware store. Averting his face and turning away, he said, "Good luck to you."

Fred and Joshua touched hands. They parted without looking back.

Fred had not heard from him again until Preston called. Before he graduated from Illinois, his parents sold the farm and moved to St. Louis and Fred had no reason to visit Pineville.

Fred roused himself from his memories as steaming towels were brought. Aromas of breakfast exuded from the galley. He wondered how Joshua's life had gone. He had acknowledged during the visit to Pineville that he wanted to renew acquaintances and discover how his friend had survived all these years. Life at the mill and in the small community must have been difficult. Joshua had lived in a different world than Fred.

Fred exchanged his athletic ability for a sound education at an excellent university. At an early age, his interests led him toward the biological sciences. Roaming the woods, streams and fields around the farm opened vistas and whetted his appetite for understanding how nature worked.

He became fascinated by animals, bugs and birds—their living, surviving harsh climatic conditions, reproducing, and their interactions. A major in biology opened the door for graduate study in biochemistry. He had done well at every level of education.

As the first glimmer of the morning sun appeared, Fred was contrasting in his thoughts the educational experiences between Joshua and himself. Now he understood what the separate schools had done, or at least exacerbated. It likely meant that Joshua never had an equal opportunity for being challenged and gaining in knowledge and confidence. Fred admitted to himself that he had been fortunate in so many ways. If he had not been able to obtain a scholarship to play football, it would have been difficult to go to college. His parents, struggling on the farm, could not have afforded the tuition. Perhaps he would have qualified for an academic stipend of some kind, but the support would never have equaled the athletic grant.

Fred's thoughts returned to the recent meeting with Joshua. He accepted the lingering affection for his boyhood pal, although there was no residual common interest. Joshua was calling on him for help in this time of need. Maybe he had no other avenue of potential assistance. Maybe he was desperately searching for support and had inadvertently been led to Fred's name in the paper. Fred had been disturbed by his own feelings during his conversation with Joshua and the whole environment surrounding the charges against Robert. He felt betrayed and bewildered in some respects. But the overwhelming emotion was that of debt, pulling him to Joshua and, in turn, to Robert by some inexorable force. During the drive back to Urbana from Pineville, he had concluded that somehow he would become more deeply involved in the situation in Pine County than he really desired or had time to commit. Somehow rational thinking was being swamped by strong emotions, almost beyond his control.

The announcement from the flight deck that the descent into Heathrow had begun brought Fred back to his more immediate responsibilities. By the time they landed, Fred had scanned the manuscript of his talk scheduled for mid-afternoon. He thought when that duty was fulfilled, he could relax and catch up on sleep. He would be expected to participate in other aspects of the conference, but the pressure of being a central player would be behind him. As he gathered his carry-on bag from the overhead compartment, he vowed to focus on his work for the next three days. Pine County and Joshua would have to take a back seat in his thinking.

By the time Fred returned home near midnight Friday, he was exhausted. The long flights, coupled with strange surroundings and a cold hotel room, were cripplers. He collapsed as soon as he could strip off his clothes and find pajamas.

A bright autumn sun streaming through the cracks in the blind aroused him from the deep sleep. He managed to get moving, although in a state of semi-alertness, to set the coffee maker, and headed for the shower. While scanning the Saturday morning headlines, he decided that he would go to the office, respond to any important mail, then call Jerry Preston in Pineville.

Jerry responded on the third ring. "This is Fred Ferriday. Got in late last night and decided to check on any recent developments."

"Not much to report. Robert is still being held, pending someone willing to support bail. Trial is set for December 9th."

"You mean he'll be in jail for three months. Just waiting for a hearing."

"At the preliminary the Judge ruled there was sufficient evidence to hold him over for a trial."

"What about the samples from the scene?"

"Still working on that. The Judge wanted to talk with the County Attorney."

"But the prosecutor won't do anything. That evidence might jeopardize his case."

"I know."

Fred said, "Jerry, I'm afraid Robert is not going to receive a fair hearing. It's hard for me to accept the position of the prosecutor, who is less interested in the truth than in winning a case. Bolsters his chance for reelection."

Jerry didn't respond immediately, but Fred could hear him breathing through the receiver. Finally he said, "Dr. Ferriday, I've come to believe that county politics is forcing both the Sheriff and the prosecutor to take positions counter to discovering the truth. Someone or some group doesn't want the actual facts revealed. Someone with real power has something to hide."

Fred didn't know how to respond. He doubted Jerry's accusation and decided to focus where he might help. "What does it take to get Robert released?"

"Bail was set at fifty thousand. It would mean a bond of five thousand."

"I'll do that. It's crazy to have that kid locked up. He needs to be in school."

"You understand if he runs, you'll lose your money."

"I'll take that chance. What do I have to do?"

"Send a certified check to me. I'll work with the bondsman to get Robert released."

Fred promised to send the check first thing Monday. He'd have to go to the bank and transfer money from savings, but he had the funds. As he opened the mail from the past week, he wondered about getting in too deep. The easy thing would be to let it all drop and hope that justice would prevail. But he owed Joshua more than that.

CHAPTER FOUR

With the precarious status of Robert constantly on his mind and concerned about justice for his friend's grandson, Fred decided on Sunday to rearrange his commitments for the coming week and return to Pineville on Friday. That meant a rushed week, altered meetings with several graduate students, one less day to devote to his laboratory work, and less time for reading manuscripts submitted to the journal of which he was the editor. Nevertheless, after hours of inner turmoil, he acknowledged he wouldn't be completely efficient again until this business with Joshua and Robert had been settled.

He departed early Friday morning and was in Pineville, signed into the motel, by noon. In his previous visits he hadn't noticed how badly the place was run-down, faucets leaking, bed sagging, but it would suffice for the short stay. He called Jerry Preston.

"Jerry, it's Fred Ferriday. Can you spare some time this afternoon? I'd like to come by to talk to you and the head of your firm."

Jerry vacillated momentarily. "I can see you anytime. But I can't be certain about Mr. Ledbetter, though. He's awfully busy."

"Please set up an appointment if at all possible. I'll come along to your office in a few minutes."

The offices of Ledbetter, Kline and Brown were on Vine street, two blocks east of the main square. Fred parked in a visitor's slot behind the building, entered a rear door, ignored the elevator and climbed two sets of stairs to the young attorney's office. Jerry Preston seemed uncertain and despondent, his usual smile absent, when Fred entered his small cubbyhole tucked away on the back side of the second floor. Jerry had a couple dozen books stacked on wooden shelves and an ancient oak desk. A desk lamp supplemented the dim overhead lights. An IBM computer station represented the modern era..

They shook hands and Fred dropped into a straight-back oak chair in front of the desk.

"I'm surprised you came today," said Jerry, "assume your trip to England went well?"

Fred nodded. "It went fast, but okay. It's good to be able to interact with people on the cutting edge of the things you're working on. You always get new insights." He looked around again. "Jerry, I've thought about this situation all week. When an issue bothers me, I have to try to do something. I've always been that way."

Jerry stood and eased toward the door. "I arranged for a few minutes with Ned Ledbetter. We'd better go now. He leaves early most Fridays."

As they walked down the carpeted stairs to the main offices, Fred said, "I'd like to visit Joshua and see Robert's friend while I'm here. Could you track Earl Sloan for me and set up a time? Maybe tonight or tomorrow morning would work for him."

"I'll call his home while you're in with Ledbetter." Jerry reaction suggested he'd never seen such an aggressive guy, a real take charge personality. Maybe that's why he's a leader in whatever he does—biology, football.

The main office of the firm was plush compared to anything else Fred had seen in Pineville, suggesting money and power. Computers, becoming an essential tool in modern office, nested in walnut work stations. Along two walls, leather chairs made visitors comfortable. Three secretaries concentrated on their computer terminals. The young woman, quite pretty, at the first desk greeted them. "I'm Susan. I expect you're Dr. Ferriday." She nodded at Jerry.

Fred's assent brought the tall, shapely brunette, dressed in a navy suit, around the large reception desk and work station. She smiled, "Mr. Ledbetter can see you now." She led him to the closed door, knocked softly, and stuck her head in. "Dr. Ferriday is here, if you're ready for him."

Ledbetter was a large man, well over six feet, broad shoulders, bulging mid-section. The brown custom-tailored wool suit helped his appearance but failed to camouflage his bulging mid-section. He stepped toward Fred with his hand stuck out. "It's good to see you. Come in and sit down. Would you like coffee?"

"Coffee would be nice. Straight black is fine."

By the time Ledbetter had arranged himself on the leather couch, and Fred was seated across a coffee table from him, the receptionist returned with the refreshments. Ledbetter said, "Thanks, Susan." Fred noted that Ledbetter's eyes followed her trim figure as she left the room.

Ledbetter swallowed some coffee, and said, "Well, how can I help you?" His voice, harsh and direct, exuded belligerence.

Fred placed his cup and saucer on the table. He told Ledbetter about his call from Preston, his visit to Pineville two weeks before, and his concern about the Jarvis case. "Frankly, Mr. Ledbetter, I'm worried for Robert Jarvis. Everyone seems ready to accept his guilt. No one is trying to discover the truth about what happened."

Ledbetter's mouth smiled, but his eyes remained hostile. "Why do you think he's not guilty? The Sheriff and the County Attorney indicate there's no doubt. I admit they jumped to that conclusion pretty quickly, but they seem certain they're on the right track."

"I don't know personally that he's not, but his grandfather is prepared to testify that the young man couldn't have committed the crime because of the timing. I tend to believe him. Then there's the issue of the location of the body—it was too far from the town center to have been moved by a young man without a car."

Ledbetter's face suggested disdain. He ignored the concern about the site and said, "Of course, he'd testify to that effect. But he won't have much credibility. Everybody expects him to defend his grandson."

Fred responded, "I agree that's a natural reaction, but I don't think he'd lie."

"Of course he would attempt to put a good light on his grandson's behavior." Ledbetter paused slightly, no longer faking a smile. "People will always defend their own, no matter the circumstances."

"I've known Joshua Bull since he was a small boy," said Fred. "I believe he's sincere."

"So you're from around here?"

"I grew up on a farm west of town and went to Pine County High School. I knew Joshua during those times since our homes were near each other."

Ledbetter's face hardened even more, any semblance of friendliness erased. "So you understood the place of blacks in these communities. Some things change slowly."

Fred decided not to pursue that line, but said instead, "I really came to see you about Jerry Preston. I'm concerned he's not being aggressive enough in seeking release of tissue samples from the crime scene and in his overall efforts to defend Robert. There appears to be little or no effort to seek additional evidence. I'd think your firm would be interested in Jerry Preston doing a credible job, in seeking justice and a fair trial."

Ledbetter's ruddy features reddened a bit more. "Jerry gets his guidance from me. He'll do what's necessary. I'll make sure that happens. And I'll make sure there will be a fair hearing." He grinned, a crooked contortion of his features. "I don't wish to have this firm in the bad graces of the courts."

Fred pushed his agenda a bit more. "But I take it you're convinced that Robert is the guilty person and that additional evidence would only cloud the case."

Ledbetter shifted and leaned forward to stare at Fred. "You're right. If you pushed me to a vote, I'd lean that way. The evidence suggests strongly that Jarvis committed the crime. But what I don't understand is your interest in this. You haven't been in Pine County in a long time." The tone had changed to an open challenge.

"Joshua Bull contacted me when he realized that Robert would be treated as guilty prior to an actual trial. My guess is he had no one else to turn to for help and he saw my name in the paper. He was grasping for straws and I happened to come into his sights." Fred sipped from the coffee, now cold.

Ledbetter struggled to his feet, his bulk apparent as he wrestled out of the seat. "I'm afraid there's nothing we can do except follow the events as they enter the picture. Jerry Preston will defend the boy based on the evidence. I'll make sure of that."

Fred, now standing, said, "Thanks for your time, but I'm disappointed. I'd hoped to gain your support for a more vigorous effort on Robert's behalf. I'd expect Preston to exert a greater effort in getting the result of those samples into consideration." He walked out, frustration growing more deeply, accepting he'd run up against a stone wall in spite of Ledbetter's insistence he'd push Preston. The underlying connotations in Ledbetter's tone and body language suggested otherwise.

As he passed the reception desk, Susan smiled and said, "Mr. Preston left this note for you. He had another meeting." Fred wondered if Jerry really was busy or was avoiding further confrontation.

Fred settled into a long evening in the motel room after a tasteless dinner in a restaurant on the square recommended by the desk clerk. He tried to work on a manuscript, but couldn't concentrate, watched television for a short while, then decided to walk out for a bit. Exercise would help him sleep.

As he closed the door, he glanced toward his car, parked three spaces down from the room entrance. He saw a pamphlet tucked under the windshield wiper blade and decided to retrieve it. Probably some advertisement for a local event. He pulled the paper from underneath the driver's side wiper. In the outside lights of the motel, he could make out the scribbled message. *For your own safety, stay out of the Jarvis case.*

His nerves jumped, his hands suddenly clammy. Automatically, he looked around the parking area to see if anyone lurked near, but couldn't discern another person. He turned to walk back to his room, but changed his mind. He leaned against the Buick for five minutes considering his next action. The note was scrawled on ordinary white notebook paper, a page ripped out of a spiral binder typically used by students to take notes for classes. Taking the threat to the Sheriff would be the thing to do. But he'd already smudged any trace of a fingerprint, the only likely means of identifying the prankster. He decided not to tell Joshua, but to talk to Jerry Preston about the note.

He wanted to characterize the note as a prank, but it was more. Someone had deliberately focused on his car and on him. Someone who knew about his activities related to the Jarvis case. And that knowledge was limited to a few people.

As he turned toward his room, he detoured into the motel office. The night clerk dozed behind the counter, but jerked awake when Fred asked, "Were you here all evening?"

Still dazed, the middle age man responded slowly, rubbing his eyes. "Came on at six. What's the problem?"

"Wondered if anyone asked about my registration —you know, room number, car license?"

"Don't recall such. Is something wrong?"

"No, it's okay. Sorry to disturb you."

Fred walked around the block, wary of noises and movement on the dimly lighted streets, the threat cascading through his thoughts. Ledbetter must be connected in some way, but why would a prominent attorney care one way or the other about a high school student charged with a crime.

Fred slept fitfully. Several times he suddenly woke to slight noises. Once he got up and peered through the window at his car, but nothing appeared unusual. Finally, he succumbed to weariness and passed out.

He came awake at seven-thirty. He worked through the groggy feeling, thinking about the note and the things he wanted to get done today.

After a quick breakfast of orange juice, a couple of muffins, and coffee in the motel cafe, he gave Jerry Preston a call and asked him to come by when he had a few minutes. Within thirty minutes, Jerry knocked on the door.

Fred showed him the note. "Found this on my car last night."

Jerry examined the paper. "Any idea who did this?"

"Only a few people know I'm interested. Comes down to Ledbetter, Earl Sloan and his parents who know I'm in town—Robert, Joshua, and you."

"Looks like a kid's writing."

"Or faked to appear such. Or by someone who seldom writes."

Jerry asked, "Are you going to show this to Sheriff Talbot?"

"I'm interested in his reaction. And maybe he has ideas of how to trace it."

Fred located Earl Sloan's home without difficulty by ten Saturday morning. The house was on the fringe of town, a decent looking brick and frame structure. The well-kept yard had a sprinkling of leaves from three large oaks. Immediately after he knocked on the front door, a tall man peered through the screen. "Dr. Ferriday, come in. Earl will be down in a moment."

Inside, Fred shook the man's hand. "I assume you're Earl's father."

"Yes. This is about Robert Jarvis, isn't it?"

"Yes, I hope Earl can help me better understand the relationship between Robert and Kathy Abrams. Perhaps tell us things to get started on a defense."

At that moment, a large teenager, dark brown as was the father, two hundred and thirty pounds plus, wearing a Pine County High sweat shirt and jeans, came through a door from another part of the house. "I overheard. I'll tell you what I know, but it's probably not much."

At the father's invitation, they found seats in comfortable chairs around a coffee table. Fred began, "Tell me about Robert and Kathy. Were they more than classmates?"

Earl didn't hesitate. "They were good friends. Robert wanted to date her, but he couldn't because of her parents objections."

"Did Robert tell you that directly or did you guess from their behavior?"

Earl grinned, placing a size sixteen foot across his other leg. "Actually, both. Robert's my best friend and we discuss a lot of things. We're drawn together in part because we're the only blacks on the football team. But it's more than that. We've played together since we were little boys. We always sit near each other in classes we have together. He's in some of the honors classes that are above my head."

"Were Kathy and Robert together often?"

Earl rubbed a huge hand across his face. "When the cheerleaders rode the team bus to out of town games, they always sat together." He stopped, and looked at his father who watched quietly from a corner chair. "They seemed to find each other and be together whenever there was an opportunity, such as a general school assembly, things like that."

"Did Robert ever talk to you about his feelings?"

Earl looked at the floor for several seconds. "I probably shouldn't tell you this, but I know you want to help him. I saw him at school yesterday. He said you'd been by." He continued to stare at his feet. "Maybe three weeks before the problem—you know, the murder—Robert and I were walking home from practice and got talking about the future. He planned to go to the University of Illinois because Kathy was going there. He asked me not to tell anyone what he'd said."

"So you guessed from that conversation the two were mutually attracted and the relationship was potentially a long one?"

"Yeah. Maybe as much from the tone than from the words."

"So, you believe they had an agreement to go to the same university next year?"

"Yeah. I'm sure of it. Robert has offers from several universities, but I believe the two of them had decided Illinois was the best place. And it would save her tuition money compared to an out-of-state school."

"Did you see Robert or Kathy together on the night of the murder?"

"Yeah. After the game, we left the dressing room together. Kathy was waiting near the gate to the stadium, but other kids were around, too. I started talking to some girls and saw Robert and Kathy walk away together. Like they did around school sometimes."

"You didn't see them again that evening?"

"Right, I didn't. I stood around until the group broke up, then came home."

"You have any idea where the two went?"

"I'd guess he walked her to her house. That's what they usually did, but I don't know for sure about that night."

"Did they ever go to a restaurant or pizza place together?"

"No. They wouldn't do that. Word would get back to her parents and get her in trouble."

"Would he visit her at home?"

"Not a chance. Her parents wouldn't let that happen."

Fred turned his head to include the father. "It's a strange world, isn't it, when two nice, bright young people can't have a normal relationship."

Sloan looked directly at Fred and responded. "Sometimes it's hard here." Earl nodded in agreement.

Fred asked, "Are you going to college next year?"

Earl grinned. "I hope to get a scholarship to Illinois. Robert and I want to play football together. Maybe room together in a campus dorm."

The father added quietly. "We hope he gets a scholarship too. It'll save me a lot of money."

Earl added with a smile, "That's why he and mom have me hitting the books night and day."

Fred stood and walked toward the door. "Earl, thanks for your help. If I can help you at the university, give me a call." As he got to the door, he turned. "Would anyone else know Robert well, such as a teacher, or coach? Someone he might confide in?"

After hesitating, Earl said, "Maybe Mr. Payne. He's the science teacher. Robert talked to him sometimes."

"Has Jerry Preston, the lawyer, talked to you?"

Earl shook his head. "Haven't seen him."

Fred shook hands with both Earl and the father. "Thanks, again. Probably see you around."

As he drove back toward the motel, Fred considered the conversation. No surprises, except Robert and Kathy planning to attend the same university next year and the strong possibility their relationship was more than just being classmates. Neither Robert nor Joshua had revealed that in earlier conversations. Maybe Joshua didn't know. Maybe Robert would shed some light on the matter when they met again. The meeting with Earl confirmed, in Fred's mind, Jerry's lackadaisical, detached approach to the case.

Fred chanced dropping in on the Sheriff and showing him the note just before noon on Saturday. Ross Talbot was in his office, but preparing to leave for the weekend when the dispatcher announced Fred's presence. Talbot, a short, stocky man with thinning gray hair and a ruddy complexion, came around his desk, piled high with papers and magazines, to greet Fred.

"I've been expecting you. Ledbetter, the lawyer, called to tell me you were asking questions about the Jarvis kid."

Fred replied, "Yes, I've become interested through Joshua Bull, the grandfather. He and I were friends as kids." He scratched his chin. "I'm surprised Ledbetter has made an issue of it."

Talbot changed the conversation. "Didn't you play football at Pine County High?"

"As a matter of fact, I did. I graduated in 1958."

"I remember now. You were a good player. I was two years behind you in school. I sort of followed your career at Illinois. You did well there, too." Talbot's round face exuded openness and sincerity.

"Thanks. You've been here since high school?"

"Most of the time. Spent eight years in the Army as an M.P. Then came back here as a deputy. Elected Sheriff five years ago."

Fred said, "The real reason I dropped in was to show you something." Fred explained how he'd found the note as he handed it to Talbot and added, "I wasn't thinking about fingerprints so if there were any, I've smudged them too badly to be identified."

Talbot turned it over a couple of times, read the scribble. His expression became placid, without hint of emotion, as he said, "Probably couldn't obtain prints from this anyway. I'd guess it was some youngster playing a prank."

"Don't think so. How would they know the car? Only one high school student, other than Robert Jarvis, knows I'm interested in the case or that I'm even in town."

Talbot stood and walked around the desk. "I wouldn't worry about it. Besides, we'd never be able to prove anything. Even if we were lucky enough to find out who did it. They'd concoct some story and walk away." He dropped the note in a box on top of the desk.

Fred said, "I understand. But I wanted you to know I've been threatened. It may not be serious, but it'll change the way I behave in Pineville. I have to treat this as more than a prank, knowing someone or some group doesn't like my questions about the Jarvis deal. I admit I don't understand the reason for any paranoia, but it seems to be present in someone."

Talbot grinned. "You could be right. Be careful." He returned to his chair.

Fred sat in one of the straight chairs across from the desk, barely able to see Talbot behind the mounds of papers. He said, "The other thing I'm interested in is obtaining for the defense of Robert Jarvis samples of tissue and semen from the crime scene. Jerry Preston hasn't pressed the matter, but has indicated that your office will not respond to his request."

"We turned him down, but it's not really my decision."

"The defense has a right to those samples. Findings might prove Robert's innocence."

"The County Attorney is still reviewing the situation about the samples and until he decides, it's out of my hands."

"I don't understand the delay. Are the county officials not interested in the truth here?"

Talbot's voice became harsher as though he'd been pushed beyond the limits of his patience. "We know the truth. There's no need to confuse the facts with a bunch of biology mumbo-jumbo and that kind of crap."

"It may be crap to you," Fred said, tamping down his anger, "but, believe me, I'll do whatever I have to do to obtain samples and use the findings in court." He turned to walk out, then turned back. "And if anything happens to those samples, I can guarantee this county will be in big trouble with the Justice Department." He wasn't sure he could deliver on his threat, but it didn't hurt to press.

Fred found Joshua on the front porch of his house, although the temperature was brisk. As he walked through the gate, Fred said, "How you doing? I've had an interesting day talking to people about Robert's situation."

"Learn anything new?"

"Not really. I came by to see if you'd like to get lunch. My treat."

"Can't turn down a free meal. Let me get real shoes." He disappeared through the door.

Fred and Joshua were the focal point of other diners in Sadie's, a small restaurant in the town square. The waitress was polite, but not friendly. Fred chalked up the tension to his being a stranger having lunch with a local black.

Deciding to ignore the situation, Fred said, "One thing I learned today is that Robert and Kathy left the game together on the night of the crime. Did you know?"

"He told me he walked with her to within a couple of blocks of her house. She lives on Nugent, a short street off Ninth that crosses Elm. Robert left her at the corner where the streets intersect."

"Isn't it strange he wouldn't stay with her to the front door? It would only be three more blocks."

"Fred, both of them were afraid. Kathy's parents had given Robert hell for being with her. They grounded her for a long time once when Robert walked to her house with her. The kids were trying to avoid that scene again. And you're right, it would be only three blocks from where they separated."

The waitress appeared with hamburgers and soft drinks, so they stopped talking. After she walked back to the counter and they had sampled the food, Fred continued. "Can Robert explain how strands of her hair were on his jacket? That seems to be the primary evidence, other than being seen together by other kids."

"He admitted they hugged and kissed before separating at the corner. But I don't think he'd tell anyone else. He won't do anything he thinks would hurt Kathy's reputation."

They both ate for a few minutes, each thinking about the two youngsters caught in the social climate of a community struggling to adapt to social changes as the larger world closed around it.

Fred broke the silence. "Any theories about what happened after they separated?"

Joshua thought as he drained the last of his Coke. "I've thought about it a lot. Only thing that makes sense to me is that someone or some group came along, grabbed her, and did those awful things." He ran gnarled fingers across his graying hair.

"How far from the corner where they parted, and where the body was found?"

Joshua thought. "Maybe two miles. Other side of town. Isolated park this time of year. If those youngsters hadn't been roaming around that day, it could have been days before her body was found."

"So a car was involved?"

"Had to be." Joshua drained the last of the soft drink as they both stood. "So that rules out Robert."

Fred picked up the bill, dropped a tip by his plate, and they eased through the tables to the exit, trying to ignore the looks from other diners.

In the car, Fred said, "I'm returning to Urbana this afternoon, but there are several things I intend to do this next week. First, I'm getting advice from a couple of lawyer friends at the university about the justice system in Pine County, and the handling of those samples. I'll go from there."

"When'll you be back?"

"I don't know. I've done all I know to do. But Preston needs to get on the ball or you need another lawyer. He isn't doing enough for Robert."

Joshua stared out the window as they neared his house. "Probably can't afford another. The Court appointed Preston."

"Do you know why Preston was selected?"

"No. I asked the Judge to appoint someone. I couldn't afford the prices of the regular lawyers."

"You know anything about the Ledbetter group?" He told Joshua about Ledbetter's call to Talbot.

"They've been around a long time. Never needed a lawyer before, so I don't know much about any of them."

"Haven't heard of any skullduggery or shady dealings by Ledbetter?"

"No. But I've heard he's got lots of power with the politicians."

"Does he have some kind of relationship with Sheriff Talbot? Have you heard anything that would connect the two?"

"No, don't know about those things."

Fred said, as they stopped in front of Joshua's house, "This visit has been revealing. Now I know Ledbetter won't push Preston to be more aggressive. In fact, he may be controlling Preston, holding him back Then Ledbetter's alerting of Talbot about my interest was strange."

As he waited in front of the gate for his friend to climb out, he continued. "Joshua, something is definitely not right here, but I haven't figured out how it all connects. Not yet, anyway."

CHAPTER FIVE

During his run early Sunday morning, Fred passed the house of a long time colleague, Bill Rinehart, a faculty member in the Law School, and remembered Bill could probably give him advice about the problems with Preston and Pine County.

He also spied Grace Bivens, still dressed in her robe and slippers, coming down her driveway to collect the paper. Grace called out to him as he neared, "Fred, I haven't seen you for several days. Have you been out of town?"

Fred slowed to a walk, stopped near her, and wiped his face across the sleeve of his sweat shirt. "Matter of fact, I've been away some. How've you been?"

"Fine. Want to come in for coffee?"

"Thanks, but I'd better keep moving. Lots to do today, plus I'm pretty sweaty." He eased away and ran again to avoid a long conversation. Since Martha's death, Grace had become overly friendly. She seemed to schedule her visit to the paper box when he passed on his morning jog. Fred thought she was seeking a relationship, but he wasn't attracted yet. She wasn't bad looking in a angular sort of way and he'd been tempted to take her up on her invitation. Strong images of Martha lingered, but had dimmed in the past couple of months. It had been a long time since he'd talked with an available female. And the notion of remarriage had not found a niche in his thinking. He recognized he'd become content with his single life, not bothered by anyone beyond the office and lab. He suspected some of his friends envied his freedom with no daily demands or expectations from a spouse.

After showering and eating a quick breakfast of orange juice, frozen waffles heated in the microwave, and coffee, he called Rinehart.

"Bill, Fred Ferriday here. I'd like to pick your brain if you have a few minutes today. I need advice about a legal issue."

"Sure, today's free." There was a brief pause, a voice in the background, then Bill added, "Hey, come over for lunch. The wife and I'll share a sandwich and a beer."

Fred spent the rest of the morning scanning the papers, doing two loads of wash, running the vacuum over the living area and the kitchen, and looking through the mail that always seemed to pile up on the desk in the den, his home office space. He seldom entered parts of the house and closed off the rooms he no longer used to save on the heating bill and avoid cleaning them. After Martha died, he'd given her clothes to Goodwill, but hadn't done anything else. For the most part, the residence remained as she had arranged it. At times he'd thought about selling and moving to a townhouse, but somehow he never got around to it. The place was much too large for one person and there were no children to visit home as Martha had never wanted the responsibility associated with kids.

He walked the three blocks to Rinehart's house and arrived just at noon. He and Bill had served on several faculty committees and governance panels during their time at the university and had become friends. On several occasions, they'd lunched together following a meeting of university panels to advise on some issue important to the faculty or students.

After the dishes were cleared and Stella Rinehart left the room, Bill and Fred remained at the table off the kitchen with their beers. Bill said, "So what's on your mind? I figured you never thought about anything except biology stuff."

Fred grinned and said, "I usually don't but I've been placed in an unusual situation." He explained the charges against Robert Jarvis, his concern about Jerry Preston and the Ledbetter firm, and the issue about samples from the crime scene. Throughout the five minute review, Bill sat quietly, sipping his beer infrequently.

As Fred stopped and looked at him, Bill said, "So you need to know potential options to pressure the system in Pine County?"

"That's part of it. In addition, I doubt the kid can get a fair trial in the community, so tell me about a change of venue."

Bill drank some of his beer, and rubbed his hands together, a habit Fred had seen several times. "The major problem is the lawyer. Your friend's son been assigned an naive youngster who's afraid to buck the system. Maybe he's inexperienced with major trials and doesn't know how to move forward. Maybe the firm has him on a short leash for some reason. But, a good attorney would take care of all the other issues. First thing, I'd work on either changing defense lawyers or somehow getting Preston on the ball." Bill stopped talking for a moment, then continued. "I don't know anything about the law firms in Pine County, but I could do some calling and find out some things. Maybe understand why Preston is failing to behave as a good defense counsel. That might give some clues about what to do next."

"I'd appreciate that."

"I'll work on it the next couple of days. I have better information at the office and can obtain other stuff in the library tomorrow, then make some calls to people I know around the region."

"I've begun to suspect some sort of hanky-panky."

"I'd doubt it. Who has anything to gain other than the guilty person or persons?"

"No one, as best I know." Fred pushed back his chair, preparing to leave. "Thanks a lot, Bill. I've been in a real quandary about how to proceed with this thing."

Bill stood. "You shouldn't have to. That's the lawyers job. And the court will expect a solid defense in what sounds like a high profile case. Connections between a star athlete and a beautiful young woman will generate interest in the media, not to mention the racial issue. Major media outlets will show up at the trial."

As they walked into the front yard, Bill said, "So you feel strongly about Joshua Bull. That's why you're so engrossed in this thing."

Fred kicked a twig off the walk. "It's really strange, you know. I hadn't seen him for thirty years or more when Preston called. But each time I've returned to Pine County I recall our times as kids. Somehow I feel I owe him support now. Bill, I had put all that behind me. I wanted to believe everything was better now, but things haven't changed much in Pineville. The race issues are maybe more subtle, but underneath, the hatred and suspicions are still strong."

"Fred, Pine County isn't the only place with those problems. The world is full of hate and mistrust. You've been in the biology lab too much. You should take a day and sit through the stuff the local courts routinely deal with. It's scary."

Fred grinned. "You're probably right about my isolation." In the past few days, he'd recognized how little attention he gave to events in the world. He scanned the local paper every day, still maintaining his interest in sports following the Illinois teams and the Bears, but he didn't delve into the other news other than scan the headlines and check weather forecasts. He lived in isolation, in his own world.

"Before you came today, Stella and I were talking about you. We think it's time you started looking for a female in your life. Martha's been gone over two years."

Fred laughed. "It's the lab again. But the truth is, I don't know if I'm ready for the social scene again. Probably couldn't have an intelligent conversation with a date, except tell her about DNA and biology."

"That'd be a start. Anyway, we'd like to invite you over sometime for dinner and to meet a friend of ours. We think you'd like her."

He reached to shake Rinehart's hand. "Thanks, Bill, for both considerations. I'll look forward to hearing from you about the Jarvis problem."

When Fred returned to his office from his graduate class on Tuesday morning, the voice mail contained a message from Rinehart. Bill suggested meeting for lunch at the Faculty Club. Fred called him back to confirm the time.

Fred waited a few minutes for Rinehart in the front lounge of the Club. Bill tugged off his light jacket when he came through the door. "Sorry to be late. Got into a major discussion with a group of senior students after class and lost track of the time."

"No problem. I've only been here a few minutes."

At a corner table, they ordered the daily soup and sandwich special. As soon as the waitress departed, Bill said, "I made a few calls yesterday." When Fred nodded, he continued, "Jerry Preston was an outstanding law student at Northwestern—good training, excellent instincts, a leader in his class, lots of promise for a fine career."

He waited until their food was placed and the waiter moved away. Then, Bill continued, "Pineville seems an unusual place for a Northwestern graduate. What's the catch?"

"I thought so, too. Evidently Preston comes from a rural background in downstate and wanted to practice in a small community. Apparently money is not a primary force in his life." Fred grinned. "And that's unique. I thought all lawyers were driven by money."

Bill laughed, his cackle attracting attention from adjacent tables. "For the most part, you're right. But once in a while, someone is different. Maybe Preston is one of those."

They gave attention to their food for a few minutes. Then Rinehart said, "So after that report, which encouraged me, I called a lawyer in the county next to Pine. Jim Calloway is one of our graduates who's done well and is respected in that part of the state. He regards Ledbetter as a shyster, but with tremendous influence in Pine County.

Calloway suspects there are tendencies in Ledbetter, and thus in the firm, to exert power and control over events in the county. When I told him about the case and the difficulties, he wasn't surprised. But he doesn't see a motive for Ledbetter's actions unless it's the race problem."

"So what can be done?"

"Bottom line, Calloway has the same opinion I have. Work on Preston. But it likely means he'll have to leave Ledbetter's firm and strike out on his own. If in fact, Ledbetter controls the judicial system in Pine County, Preston would be in a precarious position if he bucked him. And you can be certain Ledbetter controls those young attorneys in his firm."

Images of Ledbetter's face when they'd talked prompted him to say, "He can't. It'd be too hard. Bill, you don't know how mean these guys can be. Preston's career would be seriously jeopardized."

"Maybe not. It might actually enhance his reputation."

Fred was skeptical. "How do I cause things to start moving from here? I've told Jerry he wasn't doing his job already."

"Calloway and I discussed strategy a bit. You and the boy's father are the people to push Preston, since you know him and have a personal interest in the case. But Jim is willing to call or meet with him. Probably offer support if Preston is ready to take charge and do an adequate job of defending Jarvis. Having Calloway encourage him might be enough. At present he's alone and reluctant to buck the system Ledbetter has going."

"Any chance of Jerry moving to Calloway's firm if it comes to real conflict?"

"That possibility wasn't addressed, but I wouldn't be surprised. Calloway had nothing good to say about Ledbetter or the justice system in Pine County. And I know his firm is growing."

"What about the judge?"

"A guy named Peabody. Jim believes he's capable and probably not corrupted yet. He's been in Pine County less than a year."

Fred thought about his schedule and commitments. This Jarvis thing was taking too much of his time and worse, distracting him from his work. But he remembered the look on Joshua's face when he left him standing by the gate on Saturday. "I'll make another trip to Pineville and see Jerry over the weekend. Push him a bit and see how things go from there."

Fred reached for both checks. "I owe you more than lunch, but this is a down payment."

Bill responded, "I'm glad to help. Let me know how it goes. Get Preston to see Jim Calloway. That may be enough to get him moving."

Fred left the office around three on Friday. The drive to Pineville had become routine and the roads familiar again. His mind debated and reviewed the strategy he would employ to convince Preston to become fully engaged in the defense of Robert Jarvis, but at times his thoughts drifted to Bill Rinehart's suggestion that it was past time to become active in the social scene again. Maybe Bill had a point. The past months had included periods of loneliness he tried to ignore or shoved it aside and returned to the lab and his work. He missed Martha, although they had no longer been as close as when they were first married. She'd been a central part of his life, always there, doing all the small things to make his life comfortable. His response to her absence and the quiet house was to become more deeply engrossed in his job and avoid lengthy times at home. Maybe he'd take Bill up on the idea of dinner and meeting this woman friend. Maybe he'd give Grace a call since she seemed open to getting together.

Preston met Fred for breakfast at a downtown cafe, the Pineville Grill, on the west side of the square, on Saturday morning. The few other patrons in the place included Ross Talbot. The Sheriff acknowledged Fred's presence with a curt nod when their eyes met. Fred suspected Ledbetter would know he'd met with Preston before the morning sun attained its peak.

Jerry Preston's face paled when he recognized Talbot. From their table in the corner, he continued to glance around, quickly drinking coffee, setting the cup down, looking at the door. He didn't volunteer any information as they passed the time of day while eating. Fred attempted to direct the conversation by asking, "Any progress this week? Any news about the samples?"

Jerry peeked sideways at the table where Talbot and a deputy were sitting. Then in a tone just above a whisper, he said, "I'd rather not talk here, if you don't mind." He looked at his food, pushed it around a bit, sipped coffee, glanced at Fred. "I'll explain later."

As they left the cafe, Fred asked, "Where can we go to talk more openly?" He'd been amazed at Preston's reaction to the presence of the law enforcement officials.

"Come to my apartment. Just follow me. My car is the green Honda across the street."

At the apartment, Jerry offered coffee, but Fred declined. Jerry said, "My wife is visiting her parents this weekend, so we have a private place here." The living area of the apartment was furnished with a hodgepodge of mismatched chairs and a couch, probably things they'd been given by family or picked up at yard sales. Fred had read that young attorneys in small towns and rural communities struggled for years before making a decent salary. Jerry seemed to fit the mold.

"Back to my questions about the case."

Jerry gazed around the room. "Nothing has changed. We're where we were three weeks ago." He walked across the room to switch on a table lamp. "Not quite true. Robert is out on bail and going to school. Thanks to your support."

"I'm disappointed, but not surprised." Fred decided to push him. "I've done some checking on you. You graduated from Northwestern with high expectations and a bright future, but no one understands why you came to Pine County. There's real confusion about your handling of this case. No one quite understands why you're not doing the job a defense lawyer would typically do without prodding. Level with me, Jerry. What's going on?"

Jerry paced the room, touching objects, looking out the windows, turning to look at Fred. "Dr. Ferriday, I must admit I don't know how to handle this situation." He returned to the chair and leaned forward to stare at Fred, a deep frown on his face. "Each time I've pressed for the release of samples to the defense or raised questions about the flimsy evidence against Jarvis, I've been quashed by the Sheriff, the County Attorney, or Ledbetter. I've been told several times to let the case go forward and not rock the boat."

"Has Ledbetter threatened to fire you?"

"Not directly, but in oblique ways he's hinted I should do his bidding. I got the message. If I want to remain in Pine County and prosper, don't push this case."

"Give me an example?"

Jerry said, "The day after you were here the last time, I went to see Williams, the County Attorney, with a request as the defense lawyer for Jarvis to have blood and semen samples sent to the State Forensic Lab for analyses and matching with a sample of Robert's blood. After five minutes of stalling, he denied my request. So I said I'd get a court order and force the issue."

"What happened?"

"As soon as I returned to the office, Ledbetter called me in and told me straight out, I should forget those samples. That's all he would say when I tried to get him to tell me why or how he knew I talked to Williams, but you can figure out Williams had called him."

"What's their motive? Why do they care one way or another about Robert?"

"Can't answer that unless they are protecting someone. The real killer, maybe." He paused. "And they're willing to let Jarvis take the fall."

"Because he's black?" Fred stared into Jerry's eyes, the ramifications of Jerry's statement raising several potential possibilities, none acceptable.

He shook his head. "My opinion is that's only part of it. They've made it clear that he shouldn't have had a relationship of any kind with a white girl. That's the obvious one, but something else is involved. Maybe he's using the racial thing as a screen."

"But Abrams engaged freely. Robert didn't, probably couldn't have lured her into something she didn't want to do. She was an intelligent young woman with a mind of her own from what everyone says."

"I know. A couple of teachers I talked with said the two had been close friends since elementary school. But that's beside the point as far as Talbot and Ledbetter are concerned. They have their own ideas about what goes, and doesn't go, in Pine County."

"What are you going to do? It's obvious you're frustrated with the situation and you, or someone else needs to get moving on Robert's defense."

Preston leaned back and sipped coffee. "I've thought about it a lot. If I resign, the court will appoint another of Ledbetter's cronies and Robert will be no better off. I'll lose points with Judge Peabody and the larger justice system for backing out of a court responsibility. If I press the case, Ledbetter will fire me. Then I'm on my own with no resources or support, not to mention no income beyond the pittance the court will provide for this one case. I'd be forced to leave Pine County and start again but with a negative mark on my record."

Jerry's comment about other issues had passed Fred initially, but it got his attention as the conversation continued. He said, "Go back to what you said about something else being involved."

"It's a wild hunch. One day last week I surprised Ledbetter and Brown, another of the partners, in the men's room. They were talking about the Jarvis case, but when they realized I'd come in, they changed the topic. Both looked a bit chagrined, like kids caught with their hands in the cookie jar. I didn't really hear anything important or out of line, but the way their heads were together, and the way they reacted when I walked in, made you suspect there's something going on that's not on the up and up."

"What do they know that you don't know?"

"Maybe nothing, but the look and the quick change of conversation suggested they didn't want me to overhear what they'd been talking about."

"Can you press and get one of them to come square with you?"

"They'd balk. But I might talk with some of the kids around school." He paused, a slight grin. "That'll get me in trouble with Ned."

"Your idea of a cover up is interesting. It'd explain a lot of funny stuff, like Ledbetter's call to Talbot to warn him about my questions."

"It's a wild guess. But I can't think of any other reason for Ledbetter's actions. He's thrown around the race card, but usually he seems not to be racist. It's never in the open, anyway. And the firm has several clients who are black."

"Jerry, people are able to mask any racial tendencies until something happens to arouse the deep-seated feelings," Fred said, then asked, "I don't understand why you came here to start with. You could've done better."

"I've always wanted to practice in a small community. People in the smaller towns in this country aren't usually served well by courts, the medical doctors, or any other profession. They often get stuck with second-rate people."

"But why Pine County?"

"Ledbetter made me a good offer. The firm has a large case load and seemed attractive. They offered a much better salary than my classmates were getting in comparable situations. The firm generates quite a lot of business from St. Louis, so it's more than Pine County clients. The truth is they do most things very well. But the Jarvis episode is different. It wasn't until I was assigned this case that I began to understand the underlying forces within the community and I'd never been reprimanded by Ledbetter. In my sixteen months with the firm, all my cases were not controversial ones, civil suits that for the most part we settled out of court, divorces, minor clashes with the law. Until now."

"Tell me about the firm."

"As I understand the history, Ledbetter and Brown bought out Kline several years ago. Kline founded the firm thirty years ago and over the years established a solid reputation of honesty and reliability. It has always been a moderate size organization, but respected by everyone. When he wanted to retire or reduce his load, Ledbetter and Brown took over most of his cases or assigned them to a young attorney in the firm. They've grown the practice and brought in a half-dozen young attorneys, like myself."

"So Kline is only a name on the masthead?"

"A bit more than that. He comes in a couple of days each week to take care of a few clients he feels close to, but he hasn't taken on new cases for three or four years. This is according to Susan Newman, the head secretary with whom I talked about the history of the organization during my interview."

Fred walked around the space to get the cramp out of his legs and to think about the next step. "Do you know Jim Calloway in Dexter County?"

"No, why? That's the county east of here, right?"

Fred nodded. "Bill Rinehart, a friend on the law faculty at the university, called Calloway about this situation. Bill suggested you should talk to Calloway." Fred looked hard at Preston. "That is, if you are interested in pressing for a proper defense of Robert Jarvis. Just so you know, Calloway has no respect for Ledbetter and what goes on in this place."

"Fred, you understand if I press ahead, I'll have to leave this county."

"I understand, but can you live with yourself if you don't provide a solid defense for Jarvis? This case could determine the way your career will go."

Preston reddened slightly at the implications. "I've thought about that a lot. I've talked with Fran, my wife. I don't know how to proceed. I'm torn apart by this thing."

"Talk to Calloway before you decide."

Jerry glanced around the room and at Fred. "Okay, I'll do that."

Fred walked to the door. "Let me know by the middle of next week. If things continue as they have been, I intend to find a way to make changes. I don't know what they might be, but I'm determined to have Robert fairly represented." He touched Jerry on the shoulder. "I appreciate some of the pressure you feel. You'll do the right thing."

Jerry might not be able to withstand the pressures if he opposed Ledbetter and the Pine County system. The inexperienced youngster had been thrown into a situation he shouldn't have to confront. At the moment, it wasn't at all clear how he would respond to the conflicting forces. Doing the right thing versus risking his future could be scary stuff, no doubt more than Jerry had bargained for when Peabody appointed him to a seemingly straight forward case. Nevertheless, he had begun to like Jerry Preston and hoped he'd make the ethical choice.

Fred rang Grace Bivens' doorbell at five-thirty Sunday evening in response to her suggestion to come by for a drink. She'd ambushed him as he jogged past shortly after seven this morning and he'd responded positively, prompted by Rinehart's admonition and his own curiosity. Grace taught in the language department at the university and her husband, an engineer with the city, had died three years ago. She and Martha had been friends, but the couples had never interacted socially.

Grace offered her hand and led him into a formal living room filled with two lavender couches and matching chairs around a fireplace. She'd dressed for the occasion, a blue dress that revealed her shape, the neckline revealing a bit of cleavage, and nylons and heels that attracted his attention to her legs.

She said, "I have white wine," pointing to the decanter and glasses, "or I can offer other beverages if you prefer."

"Wine is fine," Fred responded, watching her sit on a chair and arrange her skirt over her knees. He took one end of the couch.

Grace handed him the wine glass, saying, "I'm glad you decided to come. You must be very busy as I seldom see you except when you dash past at dawn."

"My commitments at work seem to increase every year. You're right, it's been hectic. Lot of travel, new graduate students, grants to take care of ..... ." He shrugged as though the list could be endless and boring.

"You need to relax and get away from work at times. I try to do that, but it's hard as a single woman to do some things." She sipped the wine and crossed her legs, drawing Fred's attention to nylon covered knees and thigh.

"It's easy to get into a rut," Fred answered, "but I enjoy the things I do." He placed the glass on the table and sampled a snack from the tray.

Grace refilled the wine glasses, saying, "It's been strange since Jack passed on. We did everything together and I've floundered at times without him. Once in a while I attend some university event with a colleague in the department but I'm not close to anyone."

"I understand," Fred responded. "My friends worry about me, but the fact is I've been caught up in my teaching and research. They don't accept I'm doing okay."

To Fred's surprise and consternation, Grace moved from the chair to sit next to him on the couch, her perfume and closeness upending his reserve. When she crossed her legs and bumped his leg with her foot, he felt the urge to respond.

He put his arm around her shoulders, the warmth of her skin exploding through the sheer silk dress. He turned to find her mouth with his own. They kissed deeply, her arms pulling his head and neck as though releasing pent-up desires.

Aroused, Fred caressed her neck and brushed across her breast. But when he touched her knee, Grace pushed away, mumbling, "Let's stop before we go too far." She shifted away from him on the couch, straightening her skirt and brushing her hair in place.

They sat quietly for a moment, then Fred said, "Perhaps I should go, but maybe we can get together again sometime for dinner or some function at the university." He finished the wine in his glass.

"I'd like that," she replied, standing and smoothing her skirt across her thighs.

At the door, she leaned against him and they touched lips briefly.

Walking toward his house in the cool evening, Fred experienced relief the encounter had not ended up in bed. He acknowledged no deep feelings for Grace, but recognized she'd like to develop a relationship on her own terms. She'd like to control the situation. He'd been too aggressive for her.

But Rinehart had been right. It was time to connect again with people outside his work. Holding a female close had jarred him more than he could have imagined. Had Grace not backed away he would have taken her to bed. He accepted he needed someone to share his life again.

CHAPTER SIX

Remembering the threatening sound of Fred Ferriday's voice and his growing frustration in knowing he was not doing right by Robert Jarvis, Jerry Preston called Jim Calloway from his apartment on Monday morning following Fred's visit. He started, "I'm Jerry Preston. I'm working on a case in Pineville . . . ."

Calloway interrupted. "Yes, Bill Rinehart from the University thought you'd call. He told me the circumstances and I volunteered to listen if you're interested."

"I'd like to visit soon if we can find a time. I'd prefer an evening."

Calloway guessed Jerry didn't want Ledbetter checking on him during regular office hours. "Why don't we meet for dinner at the Holiday Inn in Du Quoin? It has a reasonably good restaurant. Seven on Tuesday okay?"

"Thanks, Mr. Calloway. I'll be there."

Jerry drove the forty miles, leaving his office after everyone had left for the day. The familiar sign of the Inn jumped into sight as he entered the town from the west. He found Calloway waiting in the lobby. Five-ten, light brown hair, brown eyes, round face, Calloway came forward to shake Jerry's hand. His tailored suit, matching silk tie, and polished loafers suggested he was doing well.

Jim said, "Let's get a drink in the dining room. Sometimes the service is slow, but the food is always good."

Jerry felt nervous, although he had thought about how much he should tell Calloway. The gin and tonics arrived by the time they had talked about hometowns, law schools, and weather. After a sip, Jerry said, "I appreciate your meeting me. As you've probably figured out from what Dr. Rinehart told you, I'm struggling with how to proceed with the Jarvis case because of resistance from everyone who should be interested in justice, including the head of my firm."

Calloway, a middle aged man, slightly balding, pleasant demeanor, nodded. "Rinehart told me about your background and something about the case. He suggested I advise you about options you might have going forward."

"You understand the situation?"

Calloway placed his drink down. "I think so. Pine County has a reputation of a closed system, maybe closed minds, about certain issues. Mixing of races is one which seems to persist. Sometimes justice can be trampled by the hatred and desire to control."

"Even if the facts are unclear?"

"Apparently in the Jarvis case, the County Attorney and the Sheriff have certain evidence that points to the young man. If they can convict, anything else becomes irrelevant in their minds." Calloway sipped from his glass.

"Fred Ferriday, a professor at the university who grew up in Pine County and knows the family of the accused, is pressing me to force the release of samples collected at the crime scene and held by the Medical Examiner and to aggressively seek additional evidence. Thus far, I've hit a brick wall."

"Go directly to the presiding judge. As the counsel for the defense, you have a right, even an obligation, to all the samples and to the results of the evaluations. Nobody can stop that process."

"Give me advice about dealing with Ledbetter. He wants me to take a passive stance. Ignore the samples, refrain from talking with people who might have ideas about the crime or who know the accused."

Calloway's tone became stern. "Regardless of those who seem to have an interest in the case, it's your responsibility. The Court appointed you and expects you to fulfill your obligations to the defendant. Ledbetter can't interfere or the Illinois Bar will become involved." He sipped from his drink, then continued. "If you don't fulfill your responsibilities for the defendant, there'll be grounds for an appeal, things judges don't like."

"The other thing is I'm concerned Ledbetter will fire me if I do as you suggest." Jerry hoped he didn't sound as though he was whining.

"You'll have to take your chances. You can cause trouble for the firm if it's clear there have been blocking tactics or meddling with the evidence. He can make your life miserable in the county and probably damage your career if you remain there. But if you win the case or present a credible defense, there'll be other opportunities. Plus, if the Bar becomes involved because of suspected illegal or unethical practices, Ledbetter could lose his license. That's something you should remember. Maybe even remind Ledbetter about the possibility."

The waiter brought the food. They paused while he placed the plates and both began to eat. As the waiter moved out of range, Calloway asked, "You're not necessarily committed to a lifelong practice in Pine County, are you?"

"No, I could move at any time. Fran, my wife, teaches school, so moving on short notice would be a problem for her. She wouldn't want to leave in the middle of the school year."

"Most of these rural counties have substantial turnover. They don't pay well enough. They hire graduates fresh out of school, keep them for two, three years, then lose them to urban schools, or the teacher is so burned out they leave the profession." Calloway cut a chunk of roast beef. "She shouldn't have difficulty finding a slot next year."

Jerry wiped his mouth with the cloth napkin. "This will sound bizarre, but I've a hunch that Ledbetter and another partner know something about the Jarvis case that I don't." He related the conversation he'd briefly overheard in the rest room.

"Talk to Ledbetter or the other guy about it. You may have guessed wrong. It may have been some issue quite removed from the Jarvis thing."

"Don't think so. I heard Jarvis mentioned and they were embarrassed at getting caught."

"Maybe, but you won't know until you press. Threaten to call one of them as a witness."

Jerry chewed a bite of roast beef for a moment, then looked at Calloway. "I've come to the conclusion I must represent Jarvis better. I hate to admit it, but I've been intimidated by Ledbetter and Ross Talbot."

"Talbot is the Sheriff?"

"Right."

Calloway shoved his plate away. "Bottom line, Jerry, you have to do what's right." He paused, then said, "Interested in dessert and coffee?" He signaled the waiter lounging against the far wall.

When the pumpkin pie and coffee were brought, Calloway asked, "Have you seen Robert Jarvis play football? Sports reporters say he's one of the best from this part of the state in several years. I've heard most of the big time football powers are recruiting him."

"I've read about him in the paper, but haven't been to any games."

Calloway insisted on paying the bill. As they walked to their cars in the almost empty lot in front of the motel, Calloway said, "You have to go all out to defend Jarvis. You'll get resistance, but you hold several solid cards yourself. If it gets too bad, too personal, let me know. I won't hesitate about calling the State Attorney General to become involved."

"Thanks for everything. I'll keep in touch." Jerry was impressed with Calloway. No doubt a solid lawyer who knew his way around. Easy to talk with, even on this tricky issue. Working with Calloway would be a pleasure. If he could win this Jarvis case, he might approach Calloway for a position. Winning the case would seal his fate with Ledbetter and he'd spend the rest of his career doing menial tasks.

Jerry called Fred at seven-thirty Wednesday morning. "Hoped I'd catch you before you went to work."

"I'm on my way out. Another two minutes and you would have missed me. How're things?"

"I had dinner with Jim Calloway last night. He encouraged me to do several things, all of which will irritate Ledbetter. But I feel better about this case. I'll accomplish something today."

"I'm pleased. Let me know how it goes."

Jerry laughed softly. "I'll likely be seeking another job as soon as the trial is over, if not before."

"That may not be too bad. You can't do your best when your boss is threatening every move you make."

"When are you coming down again?"

"I'm trying to arrange to get there by late Friday afternoon. Joshua wants me to meet his sister and see Robert's game. I'll stay over until Sunday morning."

"One thing I intend to do," Jerry said, "is to visit with some of the youngsters from school."

"Good, and you may want to meet with a teacher named Payne. He's a science instructor at the high school and Earl Sloan says he was close to Robert." Fred liked the sound of confidence in Jerry's voice. It hadn't been evident previously.

After putting the finishing touches on a property settlement case between a husband and wife, Jerry called the school and requested that Payne call him when he had a free period. When Payne returned the call an hour later, Jerry communicated his interest in meeting about Jarvis. They arranged to meet after school.

At the small restaurant near the school, each ordered coffee. Donald Payne was dressed in tan slacks and a blue dress shirt with a button-down collar, but no tie. He tossed a khaki colored windbreaker into the corner of the vinyl covered booth.

Jerry said, "I appreciate your seeing me. Maybe a starting point is understanding the relationship between those two kids. So tell me what you can about Robert Jarvis and Kathy Abrams. Friends?"

Payne ran his hand across his head, moving a lock of brown hair into place. "I'd say they were close, more than classmates. In Pine County High, everybody's on a first name basis and you get to know the students reasonably well. I taught the two of them in general science and two years later in chemistry. They always sat next to each other. I'd see them walking together around school a lot. As far as I know, they were not in any clubs or activities together. Kathy was into everything. Robert focused on athletics and his class work."

"One of his friends says he confides in you, maybe seeks your advice about school work, other things."

Payne sipped his coffee. "I'm his academic advisor, but we've talked about things other than classes. For example, he's asked about colleges. We've discussed potential majors. From my perspective he's a fine young man with a bright future if he survives this charge against him."

"Did he ever talk to you about Kathy Abrams?"

Payne drank the last of his coffee, and straightened his hair again. "Once they both came to see me about an incident involving the two of them. I think they were sophomores then. He'd walked her home after school and her parents gave them hell. They were seeking advice about how to maintain their relationship and avoid such incidents.

I wasn't much help given the concerns of her parents. I couldn't in good conscience recommend outright rebellion, although I suspected she'd not go that far anyway."

Jerry waited, thinking he would continue. When Payne stopped and looked around the place, he asked, "Would you think Robert could kill her?"

Payne twisted the coffee mug. "It's difficult to believe he would. He seemed quite fond of her. You could tell by the way he looked at her and the way he treated her, respectful, protective, supportive, all the right motives." He paused. "Now if someone were to have abused her, he would have reacted with considerable vigor. He's a strong young man. My guess is he would have defended her with all his being."

"How would you characterize Robert, high strung, laid back?"

"He's fairly low key, bright, alert, responsible, reserved, doesn't talk much, never heard of him losing his cool and blowing up."

"Have you talked to him since the murder?"

"No. Should have, but haven't gotten around to it. He's back in school, so he'll come by soon."

"Were they having a sexual relationship?"

Payne shook his head, the lock of hair falling out of place. "I doubt that very much. There wasn't the opportunity. From what they told me, they never had real dates. They were never alone, except when they were walking together and others were around then." He looked up and grinned. "But you never know. These youngsters can be quite ingenious when their hormones start boiling."

"Does Robert have any enemies, other students who obviously dislike him?"

"No one I'd classify as an enemy. He's a role model to many, especially the younger kids who are able to see past the race differences. But some of the older boys may be jealous. That may be exacerbated by skin color. But I've never heard of fights or conflicts with others. No one regards him as a trouble maker or bully."

"What does he do after athletics?"

Payne considered his response. "He doesn't have much free time. He plays all the sports, runs track, basketball, baseball. He has a weekend job, so his time is fully occupied." Payne called the waitress for a refill. "I'm sure he studies diligently. Makes excellent grades, unusual for an athlete of his caliber." Payne paused, seeming to think about Robert, then added, "In many respects, he's a loner and he's never known what it is to have supporting parents. His grandfather has done his best and there's great affection between the two of them, but still different than most families."

"Did Kathy date other boys?"

"Yeah, she did at times. I've chaperoned some of the school dances. She was usually there with a classmate."

"A steady?"

"Don't think so. Seems it was always with different boys, but I couldn't keep track. Never had any reason to until this incident. The kids would know better than I."

"Did she have enemies? Maybe boys she refused dates?"

"Not aware of any." He stopped, drained the coffee again, rubbed a hand across his forehead. "Now that you raise the question, I remember passing Kathy and a boy in the hall between classes and they seemed to be arguing. He was red in the face and she was standing with her hands on her hips, but I don't know what had happened. When I came near, he walked away with a scowl on his face."

"Remember a name?"

After fifteen seconds, he said, "Scott Little."

"You recall when?"

Payne turned over the small napkin on the table. "Reasonably sure it was just after school started this fall." He grinned. "It had to be, because I wouldn't remember things like that from last year."

They talked for a while longer. Payne had been in Pineville for ten years after graduating from Southern Illinois. His wife taught in the elementary school, so Jerry discovered a common bond and compared stories relayed by their wives. Payne liked the people in the community and the students were bright enough he could obtain satisfaction from their development.

Jerry returned to his office and worked on the request to have samples from the crime scene released to the defense. He almost forgot he was to pick up Fran after a late school activity. She was waiting in the front hall when he pulled into the drive.

"Almost forgot, didn't you?" She smiled at the running joke between them.

He leaned over to kiss her quickly. "Guilty. I've been talking to Donald Payne, the science teacher at the high school, about Robert Jarvis and Kathy Abrams."

"Any progress?"

"Probably not, but interesting. How would I get to some of the students who know both Robert and Kathy Abrams?" He stopped at one of the four traffic lights in the town. Looking at her, he said, "Without making a fuss of it. You know, avoid attention as much as possible."

"That's hard, unless you know one of them." The light turned green and he started driving. Fran said, "Get that buddy of Robert's to get some of them together for pizza after school. That might work. He'd know the ones to invite."

"It'd be a start. Good idea."

He called Earl Sloan as soon as he thought the boy was home from football practice. Earl answered the ring.

"Earl, I'm Jerry Preston, the defense attorney for Robert Jarvis. Wondered if you could do a favor for me. And it could help Robert."

Earl remained silent for several seconds. "Might. What is it?"

Jerry explained his idea of getting together several students who had interacted with Kathy and Robert. "I thought you'd know the ones they were close to."

Earl seemed reluctant, suspecting some trap. "Don't know if I can."

Jerry pressed through Earl's hesitancy. "I know this seems like a strange request, but I'm trying to understand better the relationship between Kathy and Robert. I need to know if either had serious enemies. Maybe there were other students who didn't like them or were jealous of them. Classmates will know better than anyone else." He paused, thinking about a clincher. "I'd be willing to spring for pizza"

89

"Well, they'd go for the pizza." A soft laugh.

Jerry pressed the opening. "When's a good time?"

Earl thought out loud. "Maybe Thursday. Practice is shorter because we play on Friday and coach doesn't want us worn out."

"Try to get six or eight who knew them. And Earl, I'd like Scott Little to be there."

A quick response. "He's not a friend of Robert's."

"I know. But in his case, I have a different reason." Jerry hoped Earl would not tip his hand. It was likely a blind alley anyway, just a kid frustrated because this pretty girl wouldn't date him..

They arranged to meet at the Pizza Hut at four-thirty on Thursday. As he replaced the telephone, Jerry felt good about this case for the first time. He called Pizza Hut and reserved a small room off the main dining area.

By the appointed time on Thursday, Earl and the other students were gathering. They were quiet and wary, glancing at Jerry and each other, not sure what was coming. Earl hadn't told them much, other than Robert's lawyer wanted to talk about Kathy and Robert and free pizza would be available.

As the last girl arrived and slid into a chair, Earl said, "This is the group I asked."

Jerry looked at each of them, five boys and three girls. He decided not to make an issue of names. Jerry assumed the large white boy wearing a football letter sweater had to be Scott. If he wanted to confirm later, Earl would help. Maybe anonymity, along with the pizza, would cause the kids to be more open. As he waited a few seconds, the waiters brought in the food and soft drinks.

Jerry started, "I'm Jerry Preston. I'm sure Earl told you I'm the defense lawyer for Robert Jarvis. I appreciate your coming and I won't keep you long. As Earl likely told you, I'd like to talk about Robert and Kathy, but before we start, help yourself to pizza. I know you're always hungry."

They giggled or smiled, reaching for slices of the pizza and cups of drink. Jerry let them eat for five minutes. They seemed more relaxed now, quiet conversations beginning with the person next to them around the table.

Jerry smiled and glanced around the group again. "As I've worked on Robert's defense, I've realized it's important for me to understand the connections between Kathy and Robert. And maybe with others in the school or community. You know more than anyone else, including teachers or parents. So tell me about them."

As expected, no one wanted to start. Jerry looked at Earl without asking directly. Earl responded, "I've told a Dr. Ferriday, who knows Robert's grandfather, what I know. They were good friends. They were together a lot, especially in the past year."

One of the girls said, "I'm Jane. Kathy was my best friend." Her voice choked. Tears filled her eyes. She put the slice of pizza on her plate, and wiped her eyes with a tissue from the pocket of her jeans. "I'm sorry, but it's still hard to talk about her. We all miss her so much." Then in a steady tone, she said, "Kathy and Robert were close. She was frustrated they couldn't be more open with their feelings. We talked some about it. I promised not to tell, but it doesn't matter now."

Jane stopped, apparently uncomfortable with what she intended to say. She looked at Jerry. "Parents and teachers believe high school kids don't know about love, but Kathy loved Robert. I'm certain he loved her, but I've never talked to him. The way he treated her tells a lot."

Earl said, "He did. He would have done anything for her. Nobody knows this, but they planned to go to the U. of I. next year. They looked forward to being more open about their feelings at a large university and being able to do things together in the public."

Jane nodded. "That's true. She told me the same thing."

"I understand she dated others. Did Robert get upset about that?"

Jane said, "She went to school events with other boys because she couldn't go with Robert, but it was just friendly. She wasn't serious with anyone else."

"Was Robert jealous?"

Earl said, "He understood the deal. He wouldn't have liked it much, but he never talked about it with me."

Jerry waited for the others, then asked, "Could he have killed her?"

Earl responded, after looking around at his classmates. "No way. He wouldn't have hurt her." After a pause, he added, "He would have protected her though. No one could've messed with her without dealing with Robert." The others nodded agreement. Most of them had heard about Robert roughing up some boy who'd given Kathy a hard time on the team bus.

Jerry asked, "Were there students who didn't like them?"

It was a hard question. Even if they knew, they would be reluctant to tattle. Jane, the most outspoken of the group, said, "None I knew about. Everybody liked them."

"Anybody resent their being together?" He knew they would understand the race issue.

One of the boys at the end of the table said, "I'm Reggie. I've heard some talk about that. I know guys who tried to date her got mad when they saw her with Robert, but they wouldn't hurt her." Jerry had been giving as much attention to Scott's reactions as possible without obviously staring at him. Now he saw him shift in his seat and pale slightly as Reggie talked.

Jerry went the next step. "Would you give me names of those who said things?"

Reggie said, "I'd rather not. They wouldn't have done anything to hurt her and I don't want to get them in any trouble."

"I understand." Jerry smiled. "Anything else you can add?"

When no one responded, he said, "Finish the pizza. And thanks for coming. This has been helpful."

At nine that evening, Earl Sloan telephoned. When Jerry answered, he said, "I did something I probably shouldn't have done. I called Reggie and sort of forced him into telling me those names."

Jerry didn't ask about the force, but he could imagine. Earl was probably four inches taller and seventy pounds heavier than Reggie. "I assume you're calling to tell me."

"They were Bill Talley and Scott Little."

"What do you think? Would either have been involved with the crime?"

"I'd be surprised. Talley's a little guy who talks a lot and thinks he's some Romeo, but he wouldn't have the guts to do anything like that."

"What about Little?"

"He's mean. Likes to boss around kids smaller than him. But I'd doubt he'd do anything like kill someone."

"Thanks, Earl. No one will ever know you told me."

Returning to school after being released on bail had been a strange experience for Robert. He became engaged in his normal activities, but he acknowledged different treatment from his classmates. They were more distant, less friendly. Eyes were averted when they passed him. Members of the football team were more open, welcoming him back, telling him everything would be okay. It felt good to practice again after being cooped up in a jail cell. He'd run the ball with his usual power and speed during the game on Friday. Pine County had won because of him.

After a few days, he dropped in on Mr. Payne, the one teacher in whom he confided. Payne was grading class projects when Robert knocked on his door.

Payne waved him to have a seat. "Robert, how're you doing? Glad you're back."

"I'm okay. It's good to go to class again."

They talked about the victory on Friday and the biology projects. Then Robert said, almost gushing the words. "Mr. Payne, I didn't do those things to Kathy."

"I know you didn't. You cared for her, didn't you?"

"I miss her so much. It's really hard." He rubbed his hand across his face.

"It'll be tough for a while, but time will help. You have most of your life ahead of you." He walked to Robert and put his hand on his shoulder.

Robert's eyes were slightly glazed as he looked at Payne. "I don't know why anyone would kill her."

"I can't imagine it either, but some things in life are not easily explained or understood."

Robert walked to the windows of the classroom, touching objects as he moved around. "I'm going to spend a long time in prison for something I didn't do."

"Probably not. Usually the guilty person is found."

"My grandfather says they're not looking. It's been decided I'm guilty."

"I've talked to your lawyer, Jerry Preston. He's asking a lot of questions. Don't give up yet."

Robert returned to the chair adjacent to the desk. "That's what Dr. Ferriday says too."

Payne asked, "Robert, who might have done this thing?"

"Can't think of anyone who didn't like her."

"What about boys she turned down for dates or dances, things like school activities?"

"She never told me those things."

"The two of you were together a lot. What'd you talk about?"

Robert hesitated several seconds, looking at Payne. "School things, mostly. Sometimes about next year. How to deal with her parents' reactions to our being together."

Payne suspected they discussed more intimate feelings than Robert would admit. He asked, "They didn't like your being with her?"

"No." His response was strong, almost defiant. "If they found out, Kathy got punished. She didn't like to go against them."

"But her feelings for you were strong?"

"We wanted to do things together openly, have real dates, go to a restaurant together. We didn't like sneaking around, trying to hide from everybody."

"What about next year? You mentioned you'd talked about it."

"We'd planned to go to university together. We thought things would be easier some other place. You know, a new start."

"I hope you won't abandon your plans about more education."

"I won't. My grandfather won't let me." For the first time, a semblance of a smile creased his face.

Payne walked from behind the desk. "I have to go to class now, but come back. We'll talk some more."

Robert stood, three inches taller than Payne. "Thanks for hearing me, Mr. Payne. I don't know if I'll ever forget all of this." He walked toward the door, then he turned back. "I'll never forget Kathy." His soft brown eyes flooded with tears. He swiped his shirt sleeve across his cheeks.

Jerry Preston located the homes of the two youngsters who had discovered Kathy's body. Enlisting the assistance of the mothers, he met the boys in the park near the site where they'd found the body. He sat at a park table, the kids on the opposite bench of the weathered furnishing.

Jerry told them his responsibility of defending Robert. "How'd you happen to find her?"

The two exchanged looks, unsure of this stranger, although their mothers had said it would be okay to talk to him. The taller, Jimmy, said, "We sorta stumbled on the body. We'd been fishing in the creek and riding our bikes along the paths." He turned to point at the small stream. "We'd started home when we saw her. We thought at first she was taking a nap or just resting in the sun."

Ted took up the story. "We crept up close, thinking we'd yell, wake her up, then run away before she knew who we were." He looked at Jimmy. "But when we saw blood and the way her head was all crooked, we jumped on our bikes and raced home. We told Jimmy's mother who called the police."

"You didn't touch anything, did you?"

Jimmy said, "No. We just wanted to leave."

Ted agreed. "It was scary, the way she was so still."

"Has the Sheriff talked to you?"

"The day they came to get her he asked about how we found her and what we did."

"Could you guess how long she'd been there?"

Jimmy nodded. "It must have been overnight. She still had on her cheerleaders uniform. I've seen her at the games when I go with my parents.

Ted added. "So have I. She must have been the prettiest girl in the high school."

CHAPTER SEVEN

When Fred arrived in Pineville at three on Friday afternoon, he called Jerry Preston at his office as soon as he'd stored his gear in the motel room. Jerry answered the first ring.

"Jerry, it's Fred. How're things?"

"Moving along. I filed a request with the court this morning to have samples released." He told about the discussions with the students and with Payne, sounding more upbeat than on previous occasions.

"Any flak from Ledbetter?"

"Not yet, but he probably doesn't know about the filing yet. My guess is he will by the close of the day."

"How'll he find out?"

"I suspect the clerk or someone called him by the time I was out of the building, but Ned's been out of the office. I've come to suspect he has spies in every county office."

Fred laughed. "Maybe we're both paranoid about him." He continued, "I'm planning on meeting Joshua Bull. We're going to the football game tonight. This may be my only chance to see Robert play."

Jerry said, "How'd you like to have dinner tomorrow night? There's a restaurant in Du Quoin that's quite nice. Fran and I've been a couple of times and she'd like to meet you."

"You mind if I invite Joshua and his sister? They may have other plans, but I'd like to ask them. I suspect Joshua never gets out except for work, to shop for groceries, gas up his car, things he must do."

"That'd be nice. Fran wants to meet Joshua, too. And I've never met the sister either."

"Sounds good. I'll come to your place at six." He continued, "I haven't seen the sister since we were small kids, but she teaches at a college in St. Louis and is close to Robert. I vaguely remember her, but Joshua reminded me she's five years younger than we."

"Married?"

"Don't think so. Apparently she visits often to check on Joshua and Robert."

Joshua drove his ten-year old Ford into the motel lot forty-five minutes prior to game time. Fred climbed in the back seat. Joshua turned slightly, smiling. "This is Louise, my sister. You last saw her when she was a child."

Louise twisted in the front seat to see him. She smiled and nodded. "I don't remember you, but Joshua has told me about the good times you two had."

Fred laughed. "Those times have gotten more dangerous and much funnier now when we reminisce about them."

Joshua eased out of the parking lot and toward the stadium, only a few blocks away. The bright lights for the field served as a beacon for anyone needing direction. In Pine County, as in other small communities, high school football received considerable attention, often serving as a rallying point for the entire population. The traffic was heavy, suggesting a large crowd, although the late October night was cold. Joshua parked in a grassy lot next to the school, two hundred yards from the stadium.

Fred remembered playing on this same field. He told Joshua and Louise of the excitement of those times as they found their seats on the forty yard line half way up the stands. The stadium had been upgraded, now with solid wooden tiers of numbered seats rather than the rusty metal stands he recalled.

Fred leaned across Louise to ask Joshua, "You come to all the games?"

"Nah, maybe half." He leaned forward to see Fred better. "Robert doesn't mind if I don't come."

Turning to Louise, he asked, "You come to the games often?"

She smiled, dazzling teeth in light brown face, nose slightly upturned. "I've seen Robert play three or four times. I'd like to come more often but it's difficult with travel and work commitments."

After the first few offensive plays of the first quarter, Fred understood the raves about Robert's ability. Strong and quick, he consistently faked or ran through would be tacklers and gained yardage each time he carried the ball. Midway through the first quarter, Robert broke a tackle, dodged a line backer and outran the secondary for a sixty yard touchdown. Pine County High never looked back and won by thirty-five points.

Fred observed to both. "He's a wonderful running back. I understand why so many colleges are interested."

Louise said, looking into Fred's face, "Josh reminded me you'd been a star at Pine County."

"I had fun. We had a good team my last year." Fred wanted to look at her more closely, her eyes and features like a magnet, but didn't want to stare. He added. "Of course, the best thing about it all was I got a scholarship to Illinois that paid for my education."

"I hope it works out for Robert to do the same thing," said Louise, "but with this trial hanging over his head, who knows what will happen." She shrugged and turned back to the watch the field of play.

Nearing the car after the game, Joshua said, "Want to come to the house for a drink? You and Louise may want to talk more. It's hard in the crowd. But I need to wait for Robert to change."

"Tell you what. I'll walk back to the motel, then drive my car to your place. That'll save you going out again."

At Joshua's, Robert met Fred at the door. Louise and Joshua brought in drinks and chips. Robert sipped at a soft drink while he paced, working off the residual excitement of the game. The aroma of brewing coffee wafted in the air.

Fred said, "Great game, Robert! I can see now why Illinois and others are after you."

"Thanks for saying that. Since you were here before, I've read about you in he yearbooks and articles in the school library about past teams. All the writers say you were the best quarterback ever to play at this school. I don't know if you realize it, but you still hold all the passing records." Robert's face was sad, even in the adrenaline rush of a big victory and an outstanding personal performance. Fred started to ask him a question about Kathy Abrams, but thought it would only accentuate his depressed mood.

"It's a different game these days," said Fred. "Better equipment. We got beat up more because we had no face masks and less padding. Most of us lost some teeth. But the players then were much smaller. Guess it evened out."

While he talked, he glanced around, able to see Louise without her heavy coat and cap. She was almost as tall as Joshua, maybe five-seven, slim build but definitely female curves, light coffee colored skin, pretty smile, delicate facial features, short black hair. A nice looking woman, most observers would describe as beautiful.

Fred turned to her, "Joshua tells me you're an English teacher."

She nodded. "I do English and American literature at Fontbonne in St. Louis."

"I've heard of the school. You enjoy teaching and the students?"

Louise looked at her hands, glanced at Fred with a slight smile. "Actually, I'm trying to be a writer. Three years ago I took leave and obtained a Masters degree in the writing program at Iowa. Teaching supports me and gives me some freedom to write. But yes, I like the school. We have small classes and know the students better than faculty at the larger universities." She looked at Joshua, then back to Fred, asking, "Tell me about yourself, after you escaped from Pine County."

Joshua and Fred laughed. Fred talked about his scholarship to Illinois, graduate school at the University of Wisconsin, then returning to Champaign-Urbana after a stint on the faculty at Missouri.

Robert excused himself. "I need to get some sleep. Have to work early tomorrow." He walked over to touch Louise on the shoulder and smiled at her. She reached to hold his hand for a brief moment.

Fred stood and shook Robert's hand. "Good luck. Things are going to be okay."

Robert shrugged. "Hope so." His face and posture suggested he didn't believe it as he walked away to another part of the house.

Louise said to Fred, "So you've done well. Joshua said you've recently won a major award for your research. Congratulations."

He grinned in response. "Fortune smiled. I continue to enjoy the work with the continuous challenges. What you saw in the St. Louis paper and sent to Joshua represented the outcome of a lot of work by me and many others to determine how to use cell components as identifying markers of individuals. The information can be useful for many reasons, only one of which is in crime detection."

"That was the part that caused me to read it more carefully and send it to Joshua because of the possibility it might hold for Robert. But, explain it a bit more, if you don't mind." She laughed, crossing her legs and straightening her slacks. "In everyday language."

Fred paused to think about what he might say. He did this each time anyone asked about the complicated subject and wanted a brief explanation. "Well, each person has cellular structures slightly different from anyone else. Or different enough so the probability of being exactly like someone else is quite unlikely. For example, the basic genetic material, DNA, is different in some of the minute components for you and Joshua, even though you have the same parents and grandparents. With appropriate analyses and comparisons, we can identify the individual involved in a crime. All we need is a small amount of biological material, such as blood, hair, skin, semen, muscle tissue, so on." Fred told them about the mass testing in England that resulted in identifying a rapist and murderer. He concluded, "That was the first major breakthrough as far as any application in forensics and there's been further progress since then."

"You need matching samples, of course." She uncrossed her legs and leaned forward to clasp her knees. Fred noticed slim fingers with a topaz ring on her right hand.

He nodded, looking into her eyes. "Indeed you do. The forensic people take samples from the crime scene and attempt to match DNA with suspects. It's possible to eliminate certain suspects because of a non-match. That's what we hope to do in Robert's case. If it works out okay, we can demonstrate conclusively he wasn't involved."

Louise thought ten seconds before asking, "What if there is a match?"

"Then we've gone a long way toward proving he's guilty, but none of us believe that'll happen."

She frowned. "Well, I certainly don't believe he's guilty, but it sounds like you're taking a chance. He could lose everything if by some quirk his DNA matches."

Fred shook his head. "Only if he's the actual perpetrator. There's essentially no chance of a match of his genetic material with another person's."

"Do you do the analysis?"

Fred said, "I could do it in my lab, but the Court will use the State Crime Lab or a commercial lab which has been certified for this kind of work. And in this situation, I'd be suspect of rigging the data."

"Interesting. Let's hope and pray it proves him innocent." The frown on her face revealed her concern about her nephew's fate hinging on this new biological technique in the unpredictable justice system.

"It will, but first we have to get samples." He turned to Joshua. "By the way, Jerry Preston has filed a motion with the court to have samples from the crime scene released. He thinks the judge will respond quickly."

"Good. That'll be progress."

After a pause in the conversation, Fred glanced at his watch, and stood. "Better be going. It's been a long day for all of us."

Louise walked to the door with him, and put her hand on his arm. "Thanks for what you're doing for Robert."

Hoping she hadn't noticed the flush he felt at her touch, he mumbled, "I'm glad to help and believe it'll all work out."

Holding the door ajar, he turned back. "I almost forgot. Jerry Preston and his wife are having dinner at a restaurant in Du Quoin tomorrow night. They'd like all of us to go with them. I promised to ask you."

Louise glanced quickly at Joshua, then said, "We'd like that. Thanks."

Fred thought about his reaction to Louise's touch, her presence, as he was driving back to the motel. He hadn't had such a feeling in years. Maybe not since Martha and he were first married. He attempted to pass it off as not having been so close to such an attractive female in a long time, but deep down, a different sensation stirring around inside warned him this could be different. He looked forward to seeing her again tomorrow night.

When they arrived at Jerry's Saturday evening, Fred explained why only Louise and he were there. "Joshua had some duty at his church. Or so he said. Louise thinks he wanted to watch television and not be bothered with getting dressed to go out."

Louise added, "He no longer likes to go to unfamiliar places. This issue with Robert seems to have made his insecurity even worse."

Shaking her hand, Jerry responded, "Well, we're glad you could come."

Turning to Fred, he asked, "You driving?" He and Fran pulled on coats. Fran was small, five-one, bright face and smile, blond hair cut short and slightly tousled.

During the forty-five minute trip, Louise and Fran shared experiences about teaching. Neither Jerry nor Fred talked about the case. The light conversation led to an immediate ease among the four, erasing Fred's worries about a strained evening.

Their table was ready when they arrived. As Fred assisted Louise with her coat, his hand brushed her hair and he was intrigued by her light perfume. He didn't know what it meant, but the scent and her closeness jarred him, more than last evening. She was a striking woman. The black dress and simple jewelry were elegant. Surprised and disconcerted when she took his arm as they moved through the room, he noticed several males turning to stare at her.

Dinner flowed nicely. The steaks were tender; the *Cabernet Sauvignon* proved an excellent choice. Jerry talked about his and Fran's courtship, making it more humorous than it likely had been, but everyone laughed.

Louise seemed to be enjoying herself. Fred watched her as much as possible.

As they waited for the check, Fred became aware of someone standing to his right rear. He looked up to see Ned Ledbetter, smiling and looking at each member of the group.

Ledbetter put his hand on Fred's shoulder. "Nice to see you again."

Fred stood, almost bumping into Ledbetter. "Surprised to see you here." He recovered his wits. "I'd like you to meet Louise, Joshua Bull's sister. Of course, you know Fran and Jerry."

Ledbetter bowed slightly. "Good to see you." His mood and facial expression became stern as he focused to Jerry. "Let's talk first thing Monday. I'm disturbed by rumors floating around about your case." With that, he lumbered toward the exit. Jerry's face paled as he watched Ledbetter's retreat, then looked back to Fred.

Jerry became very quiet on the return trip. As he and Fran got out of the car, he leaned forward to Fred, "Sounds like a big showdown coming. I'll let you know."

Fred was glad Louise hadn't pressed for information about the exchange between Ledbetter and Jerry during the drive back. He hadn't volunteered, thinking she would only be upset if she knew. At the house, she said, "Come in for a nightcap? Joshua must have something around other than coffee and soft drinks."

"That'd be nice." He opened the door for her and offered a hand as she swung out of the seat.

Louise rummaged through the cabinets in the kitchen and discovered a half bottle of Scotch. "This will have to do. Josh doesn't keep much liquor around. In fact, I think this is something I brought six months ago." She found glasses and brought the drinks to the living area.

Sitting across from her, Fred raised his glass. "To a very nice evening." His eyes were drawn to her legs when she crossed them and smoothed the dress to reveal less of her thighs.

"I enjoyed it. Thanks for inviting us." She frowned slightly. "But I didn't understand the change in everyone when that man Ledbetter stopped by."

"May I explain later? It's complicated."

Neither said anything for a while, sipping the drinks, the silence awkward. They smiled at each other, waiting for the other to continue the conversation.

Fred asked, "May I ask a personal question?"

When she nodded, he continued, "I intended to quiz Joshua, but it seems okay to ask directly. Are you married or seriously involved in a relationship?"

Louise laughed. "Josh calls me his old maid sister. I've never been married and am not seeing anyone on a regular basis."

"I'm surprised. So I'd guess you've been pursued by lots of suitors."

"Suitors sounds old-fashioned." She laughed softly, then her expression became serious. "Truth is I've been on lots of so-called dates, even had a couple of semi-serious relationships, but things never worked out. Josh thinks I'm too picky. He often reminds me he'd like nieces and nephews before I get too old."

"Some time I'd like to tell you more about Martha, my wife. Right now I'll tell you that she died more than two years ago after we'd been married for over twenty years."

"So you're single again?" Her face remained expressionless.

"I am. I've not dated, but my friends tell me it's time to start. Guess that's old fashioned too."

Louise smiled slightly, but said nothing, her eyes regarding her foot snuggled in a black pump.

Fred said, "This will come across as strange, but I'd like to be honest and straight forward with you. When I'm with you, I have a feeling I've not had in years. Maybe it's nothing more than a lonely middle-aged man getting excited in the presence of an attractive woman." He paused, expecting her to interrupt. When she remained silent, but staring at him, he continued. "The truth is I'd like to see you again. I'd like for us to know each other better."

Louise frowned. "It can't go anywhere, Fred. You're Josh's friend and you seem to be a fine man, but it'd never work "

Fred broke in when she paused for a second. "Why do you say it can't go anywhere?"

Louise walked over to sit by him on the couch. She placed her hand on his arm. "Did you see the way people in the restaurant looked at us, as though we were different?"

"I noticed people looking, but to be honest, I didn't think it unusual. They were captivated by a beautiful woman. That's all."

She smiled. "You're kind, but naive. They were thinking how unusual for a white man to be escorting a black female."

"Maybe, but I couldn't imagine the race difference would be a significant problem for us."

"You say that, but the looks and whispers wear you down. You become resentful." Louise shifted her position, crossing her legs and inadvertently nudging into Fred. His eyes were drawn to her knees, then back to the serious expression on her face.

"Perhaps overly suspicious." He didn't like the trend of the conversation.

"I don't think so. After you've lived with this all your life, it's expected as the norm. But still hurtful."

Fred looked into her eyes, wanting to touch her. "I can be quite persistent when I need to be. I'd like to see you again. Let's see where it leads."

She pressed his arm. "I'll think about it. I just don't want either of us to become frustrated. Fred, this race business is powerful and insidious. Some people can't accept mixed couples even today, after all these years of our society trying to sort out equality. It's devastating when family and friends turn against you, when they ignore you, leave you out of occasions to which you were previously invited." He tried to interrupt, but she ignored him. "Consider what you think when you see blacks married to whites."

"I don't doubt I'm naive. The truth is I've not given attention or thought about this issue in years. Coming back to Pineville has reminded me. But I'd guess society generally is not like here."

"You'll be surprised again. In Pine County, it's visible, and people know and accept the deep feelings. In other places, it's more sophisticated and less open, but just as powerful. It can be even more damaging because you've thought everything was going to be okay. When the viciousness appears, you're almost destroyed."

Fred glanced around the room. "No, I don't comprehend such a level of hatred. But as some of my friends remind me, perhaps I've been in the biology lab too long. Or, maybe around a large university with a wide diversity of cultural backgrounds, the issue becomes more common and people accept it more easily."

"Maybe you understand superficially why I'm reluctant to see you again, except as Josh's friend on occasions like tonight."

"I take it you've experienced tremendous disappointments in your life."

Louise looked at her hands, and leaned forward to clasp her knees. "Yes, there have been unhappy relationships. Maybe I'm afraid to expose myself again."

Fred stood, then reached to take her hands and pull her up. "You ask me to think about this. I want you to do likewise. Let's not give up before we know." He grinned. "When you know me better, you'll probably not be interested anyway. I'm a pretty dull character, but let's give it a chance."

As they walked to the door, he put his arm lightly around her waist. "I'll call you soon. Joshua will give me the number."

At the door, he turned to face her, taking one of her hands. She said, "I'll do what you ask. I'll think about us. And I did enjoy this evening." But her eyes revealed her doubts.

Thinking about the conversation with Louise, Fred pulled onto the street from the driveway, but didn't become aware he was being followed until a vehicle, driving without lights, bumped solidly into the rear of his Buick. After he recovered his balance and regained his position in the seat, he slowed, braking slightly, thinking it was an accident or the driver behind was having difficulty. Then the vehicle rammed him again, this time harder. He almost lost control. He knew the second time was no accident. He was being attacked. His entire attitude changed immediately. The advice of an old coach flashed through his mind—when the opponent becomes aggressive, you have to respond by being even more forceful. But this was different than a game.

Fred accelerated and moved away momentarily from the attacker, but the other car responded and slammed into his car again. He began to watch carefully the movement of the car trailing, alternately accelerating and braking to change the rhythm. He couldn't tell with certainty, but he believed the aggressor was in a pickup truck. Neither could he discern if the truck had one or more occupants.

He deliberately headed for the middle of town, intending to drive directly to the Sheriff's office. He gunned the Buick, increasing the speed to seventy, dangerous in an increasingly dense residential area. The aggressor remained close behind until he apparently realized Fred's goal. Suddenly lights switched on, and the truck, now confirmed, began to move to the left lane, intending to pass or run Fred off the road. Fred wouldn't let him pass and edged into the middle of the street, zig-zagging to confuse the other driver, who began to blow his horn, alternately dimming and brightening the headlights, and again slammed into the rear of Fred's car.

As they neared the main square, the truck followed closely. Fred, watching for other cars, waited until the truck got very close again, then braced himself and jammed hard on the brakes. The truck crashed into the rear of the heavy sedan. Fred maintained the sharp braking, tires of both vehicles screeching on the paved street, until both vehicles came to a stop in the middle of the street, twenty-five yards from the Sheriff's office. Fred cut the motor, scrambled quickly to the passenger side of his car, and jumped out. The driver of the truck was caught by surprise as he charged the driver's side of the car. Then a second man emerged, unsteady on his feet, leaning against the truck for support, apparently having banged his head in the collision.

Fred dashed to the second man, still wobbly. Still thinking he should be overly aggressive, Fred slammed his right fist into the man's stomach, then chopped him under the chin with a solid left. The man dropped to his back, not moving.

The truck driver, frustrated by Fred's disappearance, raced around the front of the car, saw Fred hit his partner, and rushed to his aid. He jumped on Fred's back and they both went down on the asphalt. Fred realized the opponent was huge when he grasped Fred firmly around the waist, trying to pin his arms to his side, growling and muttering. Somehow, they struggled and stood.

Recognizing the man intended to squeeze the breath out of him, and beginning to experience pressure on his ribs, Fred raked his shoe down one shin, a tactic he remembered about dealing with assaults from the rear. At the same time, he butted his head backward into his attacker's face. The man grunted in pain and the hold relaxed some. Fred slammed his foot against the instep, hearing a cracking sound. The grasp loosened and the man stumbled against the truck in pain. Fred cracked him in the neck with a left hook. The man collapsed to his knees.

By then, several other people, attracted by the crash and the scuffling, approached. Fred yelled at a teenager, "Get the Sheriff!"

The boy scurried away. In thirty seconds, a Deputy appeared on the scene, demanding in an official voice to know what was going on.

Fred told him as quickly as possible. The first man from the truck struggled to stand up, grabbing onto Fred's car for support.

The Deputy took charge, his hand on the gun in the holster. "Everybody into the station. Let's get clear what's happened here." He turned to a second deputy who'd arrived in a patrol car. "See what the damage is to both vehicles. Maybe we'll need a wrecker to clear the street."

As they walked the short distance to the station, the deputy said to Fred, "I'm Jack Barnes. I'll want you to write out a statement describing what happened. From what you've said, it sounds like you were deliberately rammed. Any idea why?"

"Nothing I could prove, but I have a suspicion."

By then, Fred and Barnes were in the station, seated around a table. The attackers were being held in another room, waiting their turn to record their story.

115

Barnes said, "While I talk to the others, write down the details of what happened." He handed Fred a pad of yellow paper and two pencils.

Thirty minutes later, Barnes came back. He scanned Fred's statement. "I'll have this typed early tomorrow. If you'll come by around nine, you can make any corrections and sign it. I'll have the others do the same." He gave no hint of how he viewed the situation.

As Fred stood, Barnes said, "By the way, your car is damaged, one tail light is out and several dents, but still driveable. We've parked it in front. The dispatcher at the front desk has the keys."

Fred asked, "Are you charging those guys with anything?"

Barnes scratched his chin, feeling the stubble of hair growth. "Don't know at this point. Sheriff Talbot will decide in the morning. But I'll hold them overnight."

Unwilling to leave it there, Fred said, "The attack was deliberate and sustained. It was more than an accident."

Barnes said, "It sounds that way, but the Sheriff will decide."

Fred returned to the station at nine the following morning. The dispatcher called Barnes from a side office.

Fred said, "You must have been here all night."

"Pretty late. We have your statement." He handed Fred the typed copy.

Fred sat in a straight chair against the wall and read the statement. "It's okay. I don't wish to change anything."

Barnes handed him a pen. "Sign in the lower right below the last line and put the date on it."

Fred signed. Barnes said, "I'll get a copy for you." He walked into the main room.

When Barnes returned, Fred asked, "Any decision about charges yet?"

Barnes looked at the floor. "Sheriff Talbot decided it was an accident."

"You mean he decided before talking to anyone about what happened?"

"He talked to the others earlier this morning then released them. Said there'd be no charges."

Fred gritted his teeth and leaned close to the deputy. "Deputy Barnes, you know something isn't right about this thing. Those goons deliberately set out to wreck me, maybe do personal harm. Not only did they ram my car several times, they intended to knock me around after we stopped."

Barnes turned away. "I'm sorry. I can't do anything more."

Fred turned to walk away in disgust, but then said, "I'd like to see Talbot."

Barnes said, "I'll see if he's available."

Fred waited fifteen minutes before Talbot came out and motioned to Fred. In the Sheriff's office, Fred said, "I don't understand your decision to release those guys who banged me around last night."

Talbot sat down behind his desk, the ever present high stack of papers. "Insufficient evidence is the way I see it. Their word against yours." His tone was stern, unyielding, official.

"But you didn't talk to me."

"Saw your statement. They said their lights went out and they accidentally bumped into your car."

"My statement said the truck hit my car five or six times, the lights were being turned on and off. Then as soon as we stopped, they intended to beat up on me."

Talbot smiled. "Not the way they remember it."

Fred stood, leaned over the desk, resisted the temptation to rake the stacks of papers onto the floor. "Sheriff, something is very wrong with your operation. Or maybe the problem is you. This is the second time I've been threatened or attacked and you've sat there with a smug grin. I don't know what's going on, but I'm considering asking the Attorney General's office to investigate."

Talbot blanched. "Nothing would happen."

"Don't bet on it!" He turned and walked out, slamming Talbot's door.

CHAPTER EIGHT

When Jerry arrived at his office on Monday morning, shortly after eight, a message on his answering machine summoned him to see Ledbetter as soon as possible. Jerry had expected the call, but the rush of apprehension flowed through his system. He had worried all Sunday how to react after Ledbetter's not-so-veiled threat at the restaurant on Saturday evening. The easy thing would be to just cave in and follow Ledbetter's demands. But, remembering the advice of Jim Calloway and Fred's not-so-subtle admonitions, he'd decided, after long deliberation and soul searching, to take a firm stand. He'd told Fran he'd likely lose his job, but he thought there was no other way. He went down the flight of stairs and walked into the main office. He waited five minutes while Ledbetter completed a call.

When he entered the private office, Ledbetter, leaning forward in his chair, immediately yelled, "What the hell are you up to with this Jarvis business? I warned you about those goddam samples from the crime scene. Now I learn you've filed a motion for their release. Plus, I run into you Saturday night with Ferriday who's been meddling around, and some black woman. You've done everything I warned you against." He banged the desk with a large hand. Several pencils went flying, a couple spinning off the desk and onto the thick gray carpet.

Jerry, still standing in front of the immense desk, said, "I intend to give Jarvis the best defense I am capable of and need those samples as an important piece. I suspect Jarvis is not guilty. Results of those samples along with other evidence may prove it."

"You went against my orders." Ledbetter shifted around in the huge leather chair, clenching and releasing his hands, his face contorted with rage. Jerry thought he was headed for a heart attack.

"The court appointed me to defend Jarvis. I intend to do it as best I can." Jerry looked straight at Ledbetter as he talked, but it was hard to maintain eye contact in the glare of the man who'd hired him and who controlled his destiny.

"The court appointed you on my recommendation."

"Nevertheless, I'm the lawyer of record and the judge will hold me responsible, not this firm nor you."

Ledbetter, now calmer but still red-faced, scowled, "You are to withdraw your request for the samples."

Jerry hesitated, knowing his future hinged on the response. "I can't do that. It may be crucial evidence to the defense."

"I don't give a good goddam about the defense. Let things ride along. I've told you from the outset not to rock the boat."

Jerry walked closer to the desk, leaned forward with his hands on the corner. "Mr. Ledbetter, I can't believe you said that. I didn't believe it before. You're insisting I'm not to mount a proper defense. That goes against everything I know about this profession."

"It's a different world than law school. Sonny, this is real."

When Jerry didn't respond, Ledbetter continued. "Another thing. I've heard you've talked to some of the high school kids."

"It's true. I met with eight of them last week to discuss several things. Mostly about the relationship between Robert Jarvis and Kathy Abrams. Those kids know a lot more than the adults about what goes on among the students."

"That was unnecessary. As far as this community is concerned, they couldn't have any kind of relationship."

"But they did. Apparently, a very special one."

"Now she's dead because of it."

Jerry remembered the conversation he'd interrupted between Ledbetter and Brown. He had nothing more to lose by pushing Ledbetter a bit. "Mr. Ledbetter, I've thought about this situation a lot. Frankly, I don't understand your interest in the outcome. What do you know that you've not told me about the case?"

Ledbetter paled slightly, then bluffed. "Nothing. I know the people in this county. They won't tolerate what was happening between Jarvis and Abrams."

"So someone decided to stop it and Kathy got killed."

Ledbetter leaped up, slamming the chair against the credenza. "Goddam it, don't jump to that conclusion. That's not what I meant."

"Then what are you insinuating?"

"Nothing." For the first time Ledbetter averted his eyes and looked down.

"Anything else?" Jerry asked, when Ledbetter did not continue.

"I'm telling you for the last time to let this thing ride along. Just do as I tell you. Go withdraw your request."

"Mr. Ledbetter, I can't do that. I believed you hired me because I had some promise as a lawyer. Now you're demanding I not do what's expected in the most important case I've had with the firm."

"This firm brought you on because you had a good record and we believed you'd fit in Pine County. We seem to have been wrong." Ledbetter paced around, gripping the back of the chair, his knuckles white. "You have until five today to reconsider. If you haven't complied with my recommendation, I'll ask the court to replace you."

Jerry hadn't anticipated this outright interference in the case. He remembered the conversation with Calloway. "If you do, I'll ask the Illinois bar to look into the matter. If I understand the process, only the defendant can ask for my release, unless there is a major illness or cause for a long delay. Then the court may replace me to expedite the case. Otherwise, I suspect interference is a basis for disbarment."

Ledbetter walked around the desk to stand close to Jerry, towering over him by five inches. "Think about it, boy. You could lose your job real quick." He walked into the reception area, leaving Jerry standing in the private office. Jerry turned and followed him. Neither said anything, but the clerical staff, having heard the outbursts from the inner office, watched wide-eyed.

Jerry called Monday night as Fred loaded the dishwasher. He replayed the confrontation with Ledbetter and Ledbetter's threat to intervene with the court. "I think he's bluffing on that point, but someone had told him about my request for the samples. Just as I expected."

"So what're you going to do?"

"Nothing until he does something. I didn't withdraw my request, but Judge Peabody would have had me on the carpet had I done so. I'm sure Ledbetter will fire me within the next few days. For the moment, he's waiting for me to cave in. He'll know soon, if he doesn't already, that I didn't withdraw the request today."

"Can you stick by your guns?"

A slight pause. "I intend to. Tomorrow may be the key. After that, I may go see Calloway again for advice."

"You may want to call Bill Rinehart in the law school here. He's the one who recommended Calloway. And he will know what could happen if Judge Peabody is threatened by Ledbetter." Fred was thinking he'd gotten Preston into this mess by pressuring him. Maybe there was an alternative. "Jerry, I feel some responsibility for this situation. I pushed you to challenge Ledbetter."

"Don't. I should've been stronger from the outset. You made me see what I could have become, a patsy with no integrity or self-respect."

Fred told Jerry about the incident on Saturday night and Talbot's refusal to charge the attackers. He added. "Jerry, I wouldn't be surprised if Talbot and Ledbetter organized the thing. Somehow Talbot's connected. He's such a smug little bastard."

Jerry responded, "You may be right about his organizing the incident. But I'd bet Ledbetter called him after seeing us in the restaurant with Louise. The more I uncover, the more it seems like a major conspiracy, but the motive isn't obvious."

Fred told Jerry about Ledbetter's call to Talbot when he'd first appeared in Pineville. "There's something between the two. It doesn't make sense, but you might ask around."

"It would be interesting, but I don't know where to begin. Everything gets back to Ledbetter and fast."

Tuesday morning brought Jerry another summons to Ledbetter's office. He knew this was a final showdown, a test of his courage.

Ledbetter stood when Jerry was shown in by the secretary. Immediately he said, "You didn't do as I ordered. I'm disappointed." His voice was calm and even. Ledbetter seemed to be playing the role of a senior advisor and had obviously rehearsed what he intended to communicate.

Jerry looked at him. "I really couldn't, Mr. Ledbetter. I have to live with myself. If I don't provide a proper defense for Jarvis, I've abandoned my profession and my integrity."

Ledbetter ignored Jerry's effort to insert professional ethics into the debate. His face clouded, eyes glaring from thin slits. "You have until noon today to clear your personal things out of the office. We'll pay you until the end of the month, but as of this moment, you're no longer associated with this firm."

Stunned by the suddenness of the decree, Jerry didn't move for several seconds, then turned and walked out. He had roughly three hours to remove his books and reference materials from the premises.

In his office, he called Calloway and arranged to meet with him for dinner. He decided to wait until tonight to tell Fran. No reason to upset her further during the school day. By then, he'd have a working space in the spare bedroom of the apartment. He flipped on his computer and began to print out records and documents important to the Jarvis case. He pulled a few folders from the file cabinets and sorted through the papers, then went into the work room to make copies. He'd leave the originals with the firm, but he'd have access to the information for the Jarvis trial if and when he needed it. He left intact the files of other pending cases. He transferred his personal items from the desk drawers to cardboard boxes he'd retrieved from the storage closet. At eleven-thirty he flipped off the lights, closed the door, and walked out, dropping his keys on Susan's desk.

Fran came home shortly after four. She'd been crying and appeared forlorn, more than Jerry had ever seen in her usual bright and happy face.

"So you've heard." Jerry said as he brushed her cheek with his lips.

She seemed not to hear, fresh tears running down her face. "I've been fired."

"When? Why?"

She waited for several seconds, wiped her eyes again. "The principal called me in after the last class today. Said I'd been negligent in my work, kids were unhappy, parents were complaining. I've been suspended until the principal meets with the school board and reviews the situation." She wiped tears away.

Jerry banged his fist on the door frame. "It's not your performance. It's Ledbetter. He fired me today, but that wasn't enough. He had to throw his weight around and force you out too. What a vindictive bastard!"

"You don't know for sure, do you?"

"No, but I'd bet on it. He was mad as hell when I wouldn't cave in on the Jarvis case. He's mean enough to take out his frustrations on everybody connected to me."

"But what would suspending me accomplish?"

"Nothing, except to show everybody how powerful he is. Maybe exact a bit of revenge because I refused to fold. He doesn't like to be crossed."

"What're we going to do?" A tinge of fear emerged in her eyes.

"Don't know yet. I'm supposed to see Jim Calloway in Du Quoin tonight about my situation. Maybe you should go with me."

"I will. I don't want to stay here alone." She sat on Jerry's lap, her arms around his shoulders, and wiped her tears away. He held her close, wanting to protect her from the forces unleashed by Ledbetter and his cronies.

Calloway paled and his mouth gaped open as Jerry told him about Fran's suspension. "I've heard Ledbetter wielded power in Pineville, but I never expected this level of retribution." Calloway drank several sips of his gin and tonic before he placed it on the table. Then he asked, "Have you heard from your request about samples?"

"Not yet." Jerry sipped from his drink. "I expect Ledbetter will attempt to stop it."

Calloway sputtered a bit of drink. "He can't do that. But if he can, the Pine County judicial system is more corrupt than I'd ever imagined. Our only option will be to call in the state Attorney General."

"I never dreamed he'd jump on Fran though." He reached to take her hand.

"He's a real son-of-a-bitch when his dander is elevated." Calloway closed the menu he'd been scanning.

Jerry said, "From the very outset of this Jarvis thing, Ledbetter has been on edge. I'm not around him much, but he's usually jolly and telling jokes, even when there's a serious discussion going. Lately he's been almost morose, withdrawn. I thought it was just around me, but the secretary mentioned his behavior to another of the junior lawyers who told me."

"What're you suggesting?"

"He's covering something or somebody. It's more than Jarvis and Abrams, but it's connected in some way. He's using race as a distraction, but there's something else . . . ."

"Any hard facts or just a guess?" Calloway's tone suggested doubt.

"A hunch which started with the conversation I partially overheard between Ledbetter and Brown. They were whispering in the rest room and Jarvis was mentioned as I walked in. They saw me, looked chagrined, and stopped talking."

Arrival of the food gave them time to pause, sample a few morsels, and think about the situation. Jerry continued, "Also, Fred Ferriday got a threatening note on his car during an earlier visit and was attacked by two hoodlums in a pickup truck last weekend. Sheriff Talbot dismissed both events as a joke. Fred thinks Talbot is in cahoots with Ledbetter. Somehow the County Attorney is going along with them or is directly involved. That's why they've resisted analyzing those samples. My suspicion is the results will indicate that Jarvis is not guilty, but may point to someone else, someone they're shielding."

Calloway sipped water, while looking at Jerry. "Sounds like a long reach. Be hard to connect all those coincidences."

"But you've got to admit, it makes sense. If not, why all the resistance? To the point of threating to get me removed from the case. And why harass and attack Fred? Each time someone tries to dig around about the Jarvis case, they are assaulted or threatened. It can't all be happenstance."

Calloway shoved his plate away. "Maybe you have something, but where do you start."

Jerry put his fork down. "With those biological samples. If I'm right, Jarvis will be exonerated. Then there'll have to be further investigations to determine the real killer."

Calloway shrugged, then turned to ask the waiter for more coffee. "You may be correct. Keep pressing. Visit the Judge Peabody tomorrow and find out if he's reviewed your request. Get him moving if possible."

When Jerry didn't respond, Calloway continued. "Could you get one of the secretaries in the firm to talk to you about Ledbetter's mood. Maybe she'd reveal more."

Jerry stirred his food, wondering which one to approach, or if it was a reasonable idea. "Don't know. It could get her fired, though."

"You'd have to do it on the hush-hush. Secretaries know a lot more about what's going on than anybody realizes or gives them credit for."

Fran had been quiet throughout the discussion, and had eaten only small amounts of her food. "I'm worried about how we'll survive," she said. "Neither of us has any money coming in."

"I'd suspected Jerry would get fired as soon as he crossed Ned," said Calloway, "but I'd no idea you'd get the axe too. I'm prepared to offer Jerry a position with my firm starting immediately. Or to assist him in locating with another organization if he prefers."

Jerry said, "That's more than generous on your part. Of course, I'd be interested in talking about a slot with you."

Calloway nodded. "We've talked about adding another junior person for three or four months because of our increasing client base. You'll be a good fit and we'll work you hard."

"If I survive the Jarvis case."

Again Calloway picked up the bill. As they walked out into the crisp evening, he said, "Fran, I'll make some calls tomorrow about you. There's always a need for substitute teachers. Send me a resume and I'll circulate it to a couple of superintendents."

Jerry asked, "Should we just let Fran's firing go without a whimper. The more I think about it, the more I believe we should challenge the way it was done. I'm sure Ledbetter was behind it."

"I plan on talking to the representative of the teacher's union," Fran said, "but I don't know much about how they operate or if they have any influence."

Calloway said, "That'd be a reasonable thing to do. From what I know, the organization will not let your suspension go unchallenged."

"I'd like to challenge the school officials quickly and directly," Jerry said. "If you think it won't do more damage to Fran's situation."

Calloway dug out the keys for his car and opened the door. "Go by and talk to the principal. Tell them you're representing my firm on behalf of Fran. Shake them up a bit. Threaten a suit, whatever. See what their reaction is." He grinned. "When you get going, you're ready to challenge everyone, aren't you?"

"Nothing more to lose." He took Fran's hand. "Plus, I get irritated when these guys pick on my wife who was an innocent bystander."

On Wednesday morning, Jerry made an appointment with the judge and with the principal for later in the day. Working out of the apartment evoked a different feeling than having an office, almost like he had returned to school and had no professional identification.

Judge Charles Peabody had been appointed County Court Judge a year ago after being recommended by the Pine County Bar Association, although he had been in the county only slightly longer. A slight man in his fifties, he stood to shake Jerry's hand when he entered. His suit jacket hung across the back of his chair; shirt sleeves rolled up a couple of turns.

"I assume you're here to find out about your motion related to the Jarvis case."

"Yes. I need to move forward. The trial is scheduled to begin on December 9th."

Peabody pulled out a legal pad from a desk drawer. "I've reviewed your request. I consider it a routine matter and I'm granting it. In fact, this is the draft of my order. Should be processed by the end of work tomorrow."

"That's good news."

Peabody walked around the desk and closed the door to the outer office. He said, "Mr. Preston, strange events are connected with this case. Harold Brown, one of the partners of the Ledbetter firm, called late yesterday demanding your removal as the defense attorney. Nothing solid in his rationale, but trying to convince me they'd made a mistake by recommending your appointment in the first place. I told him I'd like to talk to you before doing anything. The fact is, I'd asked my clerk to set up an appointment when we discovered you were coming by."

Jerry was uncomfortable with revealing his confrontations with Ledbetter. He wasn't sure of Peabody's loyalty. Everyone else seemed to jump when Ledbetter asked. He said mildly, "I thought they'd do that."

"Why?"

"Mr. Ledbetter hasn't been pleased with my handling of the Jarvis case. Actually, he fired me yesterday for submitting the request about samples."

Peabody frowned. "That's most unusual. I can't understand why he'd do that." He shrugged his shoulders. "To tell you the truth, Mr. Preston, I've contemplated talking to you. I'd about concluded you weren't preparing to defend Jarvis appropriately and I'd end up with appeals based on an improper representation. I'm sure the ACLU and the NAACP will be interested in this trial, so I want it done right."

Jerry smiled for the first time in three days. "You don't know how relieved I am to hear you say that. Ledbetter had indicated he'd have me removed if I pressed ahead."

"He tried, but I refused." From hints dropped by Ledbetter, Jerry was reasonably certain Peabody had been courted by Ledbetter during the consideration by the Bar Association. No doubt Ledbetter had dropped veiled suggestions he could take care of lots of things and open doors for Peabody after he was appointed.

"I'm glad. Judge Peabody, I'll work hard to defend Jarvis. I believe he's innocent. Results of those samples will likely prove it. And there are other questions about the prosecutor's case."

Peabody smiled. "We'll see. Thanks for coming in. By the way, I'm ordering the Medical Examiner to send all specimens you asked for to the State Crime Laboratories with a request to expedite the analyses. I expect we'll have the data in ten days or two weeks."

Peabody looked thoughtful. "You have any idea about what's going on with the Ledbetter firm? They've been deeply interested in this case from the very outset."

"Is that how I was appointed for the defense?"

"Yes, I thought you knew. Ledbetter recommended you for the job, even brought a resume over himself. I didn't think it unusual at the time, but the recent calls and demands have made me think more carefully about the entire situation." Peabody wiped a hand across his eyes. "What's going on?"

Jerry said, "I have an idea, but nothing solid yet. I'd rather not speculate unless you insist."

"It'll likely be obvious before the trial is completed." Jerry wondered if Peabody was beginning to think Ledbetter and friends were close to obstruction of justice, but he wanted to withhold judgment for the time being. Even in his limited experience Jerry knew firing the defense attorney from the firm, then demanding the court remove him from the case represented interference at the least.

Jerry met with Donald Evans, the principal of West Side Elementary School, after the last class period on Wednesday afternoon. As Jerry entered the building, Evans met him in the hall and escorted him to a private office behind the school office. Two secretaries seemed not to notice as they passed through the outer room, a large square filled with desks and file cabinets,

Jerry began, "Mr. Evans, thanks for seeing me on such short notice. I'm here because of two interests. First, as the husband of Fran Preston who was fired without notice yesterday. Secondly, I'm representing the firm of Calloway and Givens for the same reason. If the facts are as we deem them to be, we're planning to file a suit in County Court on behalf of Mrs. Preston. I'm here to get your side of the story. We want to be sure there aren't reasons for the suspension which weren't made clear to her."

Evans seemed taken aback by the aggressive posture of the lawyer. In this office, he was usually the one asking the questions and making the demands. He stammered a bit, shuffling through several papers on the desk, not looking at

Jerry. Finally he mumbled, "We let Mrs. Preston go because of poor performance. I told her when we talked."

"It seems unusual to fire a teacher in mid year without prior warning."

Evans, still looking at the desk top, said, "She'd been doing well. Then for no explanation, kids complained, parents called to demand she be relieved. I don't know what happened. She had become a different person in the past three weeks."

"Did you ever discuss the problems with her? Maybe she required help." Jerry had difficulty maintaining the charade. Fran was the same person he'd known for seven years Each morning she was eager to get to the school. She loved the kids and felt rewarded when they learned.

"The Assistant Principal talked to her, but things didn't improve."

"That's interesting. She never told me about the discussion or any concern about her performance. She usually tells me those kind of things."

Evans glanced up at Jerry, then looked back to the papers on the desk top.

"Mr. Evans, we've reviewed all of her performance evaluations since she was employed here. All were highly complimentary, actually exemplary marks for almost two years. Those were completed by you personally."

Evans didn't respond, rubbed a hand across his forehead. Jerry changed tactics. "Our firm believes pressure was applied by someone outside the school system resulting in your action. Am I correct?"

Evans became flustered. His face reddened; sweat appeared on his upper lip. "That's not true. I don't know where you'd get such an idea."

"I'll tell you where. I was fired on the same day by the Ledbetter firm. Our suspicion is someone from that firm pressured you or someone in the school system to do likewise to her."

Jerry thought he'd pushed it as far as he could. Evans was probably the pawn in the middle. Jerry had mixed emotions as he looked at Evans' discomfort. The man had sacrificed his integrity. Jerry knew he'd almost done the same thing.

He stood. "Mr. Evans, the personnel records of Mrs. Preston may become a key document in this situation. I must warn you that any tampering of those papers will be regarded as a serious matter by the Court. In addition, I'd like the names and addresses of all the students in Mrs. Preston's classes. We'll talk to some of the parents, maybe some of the kids, to make an independent assessment of their feelings about Mrs. Preston. I'll come by in the morning to pick up the list.

"I'm certain the teacher's association will be interested in reviewing the action on her behalf," Jerry added, when Evans remained silent. He stood. "But our firm is interested because of the potential interference in an upcoming criminal trial." Jerry hoped he hadn't gone too far.

At the door, he turned back. Evans had slumped in his chair, his head in his hands.

Fred called Louise on Wednesday evening. When she answered on the second ring, he said, "I hope you're still thinking about our talk of last Saturday."

She laughed, "Fred, how're you?"

"Good. I called to suggest something for your consideration. I've got to be in Dallas next week. I've thought about coming back to St. Louis on Thursday night rather than returning here. I'd hoped we could spend some time together on Friday and Saturday."

She didn't respond for several seconds, so he said, "The silence is rather clear. You're not interested in my proposal."

A soft laugh. "Not necessarily. I've thought a lot since Saturday. I want you to realize clearly the implications of a relationship, even a friendly one. I don't want either of us to regret later what we've done."

"Then it's not an absolute no."

"I'd like to see you again. But Fred, I'm cautious."

"Let's see how the weekend goes. I'll make a reservation at a place near you and call you when I get in, unless it's very late."

"When's your flight scheduled to arrive?"

"Let's see." He fumbled through his travel file and dug out the ticket. "Seven-fifteen on American flight 318 from Dallas."

"I'll meet you at the airport and I'll make a reservation for you since I'm familiar with the area." Her tone more upbeat now.

"That's kind. You don't have to, but it would help."

"Then, I'll arrange for a motel room and see you at the airport. Have you talked with Joshua this week?"

"No, but I've heard from Jerry Preston twice. He was fired by Ledbetter, but things are progressing otherwise."

"That's the kind of reactions I'm scared of."

"Our situation is different."

"It's all springs from the small minds of people." She laughed. "Enough, I'll see you Thursday night next week."

To Jerry's surprise, Donald Evans had the names and addresses of children in Fran's class when he returned to the school on Friday morning. He'd anticipated some foot dragging, but the secretary at the first desk clearly expected him. As soon as he walked in, she reached for a manila envelope on a table next to her desk. "Mr. Evans said you were coming by for this." Her blank face revealed no hint of her feelings.

Jerry said, as he pulled a paper from his briefcase, "Please give this to Mr. Evans. It's his copy of a court order regarding telephone records."

At that moment, Evans entered from the hall. When the secretary passed the document to him, he stopped, and scanned the paper. "I don't understand."

Jerry said, "We're interested in any calls from upset parents. Those records will provide some idea of the volume. And we can trace the numbers to help locate the problems quickly." He didn't add it might reveal calls from the Ledbetter firm.

Evans turned white; small beads of sweat broke out on his forehead. "Mr. Preston, you're making a big deal out of this."

"No, we're not, but someone did. When an innocent woman, a good teacher, is fired because her husband doesn't go along with some big-wig attorney, there's reason to be concerned." Jerry could feel his face redden with anger. "There's something wrong with this system to let such a thing happen."

Evans edged toward his private office. At the door, he turned to Jerry. "You won't be able to prove anything."

"Maybe not, but we can turn over a lot of rocks. Make people think about firing good employees in the future." Jerry shrugged. "Who knows what we'll find." He walked out, Evans still staring at him, the secretaries looking at each other. On the sidewalk, Jerry remembered Ledbetter's spies and decided he'd know soon about his threats to the school official.

As he had time, Jerry called parents on the list. The first four were not even aware Fran had been released, the children believing she was away sick. He'd begun to consider the telephoning a fruitless exercise, but the fifth call yielded promise.

"Yes, this is Mildred Gartenberg."

Jerry said, "I'm a representative of Calloway and Givens, the law firm in Du Quoin. We're investigating a complaint initiated by Mrs. Fran Preston. She's been suspended by West Side Elementary School. The principal told her several parents complained about her work and relations with the youngsters. Since there'd been no record of unacceptable performance, I'm trying to find out what parents really thought about her and the nature of their complaints."

A brief delay. "My son, Jeffrey, is in her class. He likes her. We've been impressed with her. As far as I know, all the parents and kids thought she was doing well."

"Are you aware of complaints?"

"No." A quick, firm response.

"Have any other parents talked to you about Mrs. Preston?"

"No one has griped to my knowledge. Everybody seemed pleased with her."

"Were you aware she'd been released?"

Brief pause. "Jeffrey brought home a note from Mr. Evans indicating Mrs. Preston would no longer be the teacher. The implication was she'd left the community."

Jerry said, "I've a list of parents, but I don't know any of them. You could help me by identifying two or three who are leaders in PTA."

"I'm as active as most. But call Eleanor Stone. She's the President of the school PTA. Her daughter is in the same class with Jeffrey."

Mrs. Stone worked at the Farmers and Merchants Bank. When Jerry called there, she suggested immediately she'd call Jerry at his home number after work hours and asked for his number.

She explained when she called around seven, "Mr. Preston, so you understand my cutting you off this afternoon, I don't take personal calls at work. The manager doesn't like it, so I always return personal calls from my home."

Jerry explained his mission. Eleanor Stone replied, "No, no one complained to the PTA officers." She paused, then asked, "What's this really about?"

139

Jerry said, "We believe Mrs. Preston has been wrongly treated by the Pine County Schools and fired without cause. She plans to take her case to the Illinois Teacher's Association, but there are other implications about the event which concern us."

"Have you talked with Donald Evans, the principal?"

"Of course. His position is that parents and kids complained. Truth is Mrs. Stone, he was quite defensive about the decision."

"Doesn't sound like his usual behavior. But I'll ask about. No one asked the PTA to do anything and that's usually the first place people gripe about a teacher." She laughed. "Or anything else."

Jerry decided she should understand a bit more about the situation. "Mrs. Stone, I don't know anything about you or your family, but be careful who you discuss this with. Our belief is Mrs. Preston was fired because her husband crossed a powerful individual who was able to vent his wrath on her as well by pressuring the school officials. If our contention is true, I don't want you to be caught in the crossfire."

The line was quiet for several seconds. "I've heard of such things. I'll be discreet, but I expect you're wrong in your assumption."

"Maybe, but I don't think so." The idea he was becoming paranoid crossed his mind.

Eleanor Stone called back in two days. "Mr. Preston, I've not discovered anyone who was unhappy with Fran. To the contrary, many parents are upset she's no longer in the classroom. Almost everyone I talked with would be willing to testify or provide a deposition revealing their opinions. I'll be glad to send you those names so you won't have to go back through the list again."

"Thanks, Mrs. Stone. I'll begin to collect statements soon." He wanted to charge out and begin immediately, but he reminded himself he had a lot to do for the Jarvis trial. He thought he'd better scan through some of his law books about jury trials. Then, maybe some experienced person in Calloway's firm could review his strategy when he had it worked out to his own satisfaction. And he needed to meet with Jim Calloway and confirm his potential appointment to that firm

CHAPTER NINE

Jerry called Earl Sloan. He'd been thinking about their telephone conversation involving Scott Little and the teenager's reaction during the meeting at Pizza Hut. Something kept nagging him about the kid's demeanor, as a ache requiring attention. Jerry decided he should push him a bit more, but needed an opening and hoped Earl could help.

"Earl, it's Jerry Preston. I'd like to ask you more about Scott Little."

"Okay, I'll try to help."

"Who're his friends? You know, who does he hang out with?"

Silent several seconds, then Earl said, "I've seen him around school and after games with Gil Brown and some other kid." A bit of hesitation, then he said, "I think Joe Dobbs, but I'm not sure. I don't know him at all."

One name struck a sharp note. "Is Gil related to Brown, the lawyer?"

Earl stopped. "Don't know. Let me ask Mom. Hold on a second."

Jerry heard the receiver being placed down and footsteps, then talking in the background. Earl came back. "She's pretty sure the lawyer is his father. They're the only Browns around here she knows about."

"Thanks, that helps. By the way, how's Robert doing?"

"He's into his usual stuff, but he's sad and worried."

"I'll try to see him in the next couple of days. Tell him things are getting better. We're making progress on his defense."

Deciding he had to be direct if he were to fill the void in his thinking, Jerry called the Little residence and asked to speak to Scott without identifying himself. When Scott came on the line, he said, 'Scott, you'll remember me from the meeting at the Pizza Hut. I'm the lawyer, Jerry Preston. I'd like to talk to you again, just the two of us. Could we meet somewhere after school tomorrow?"

"Not sure I want to do that."

Jerry wasn't certain how to entice him to a meeting. He didn't want to scare him away by being overly aggressive, but he didn't wish to let Scott wiggle out of it either. "I remembered you were very quiet at the meeting. I thought you wanted to say something. I'd like to let you do it privately. How about we split a pizza at four tomorrow afternoon?"

Scott's voice was filled with reluctance. "I might."

"You don't have to answer any question you're uncomfortable with. I just thought from your reactions to some of the comments, you'd seen a side of Robert Jarvis the other kids hadn't seen. All of them view him as a hero, someone to be modeled after, but I have the feeling you don't. Maybe there's a part of his personality, maybe a mean streak his friends don't know or won't talk about. Maybe you've seen something in him others haven't experienced. I'd like you to share your opinions with me if you will."

Jerry hoped he'd not overdone it, but that Scott would see this as a different angle and an opportunity to tell things about Jarvis which were not flattering. He was rewarded when Scott said, "Okay, I'll meet you. Same place as before."

Jerry arrived ten minutes early, found a booth in the back corner, and ordered a medium pepperoni pizza. He'd let Scott eat most of it. Jerry had begun to think Scott had backed out, but at ten after four, he came in, looked around and saw Jerry.

As he slid into the other side of the booth, he said, "Coach kept us late today. We couldn't get one play right. Must have run it twenty times." He pushed long brown hair back in place.

"Thanks for coming. I didn't mind waiting." Jerry offered Scott pizza, which he took eagerly, taking a huge bite out of a slice as soon as he could.

"As I said on the telephone, I'd like your honest opinion of Robert Jarvis. I suspect you don't agree with the other kids. You didn't say anything at the first meeting, so I thought you might be holding back rather than disagree with the others."

Scott finished a slice of pizza, wiped his big hands on a napkin, tossed it aside, reached for another piece. "I've never been his friend. We've had tussles during football practice, but never actual fights. The coaches always got between us too fast."

"What caused those?"

Scott frowned, again raking a heavy wisp of hair back across his head. "Jarvis thinks he's a big star. Once he got mad when I tackled him too hard."

"You liked to hit him pretty hard, I take it."

Scott had finished another slice, and took a slurp of coke. He grinned. "Yeah, but hitting people is what I like about football."

"Does he have a lot of friends?"

"Earl Sloan's his best buddy. They're together most of the time. Only blacks on the team. He used to be with Kathy Abrams a lot around school. Now it's only Earl but I see Jarvis by himself a lot of times."

"Did you know Kathy Abrams?"

"Yeah, everybody at school did."

"Did you ever date her? Take her to school dances, things like that?"

Scott reddened slightly. He said gruffly, "Nah, she'd never go with me."

"So you had invited her for dates?"

"Few times. I gave up." He shifted in the seat. The entire booth rocked a bit.

"What about at school dances? You dance with her?"

"Only once. She refused every other time."

"Did she say why? That seems unusual."

"Said I was too rough. Didn't like the way I held her."

"How'd you hold her? From what everybody says, she was a very beautiful girl."

Scott grinned, apparently remembering the dance. "I pulled her really tight against me. I liked to feel her boobs next to me."

Jerry grinned in return, trying to establish a bond with this rogue. "She didn't like it."

Scott frowned more deeply. "She liked being with Jarvis though."

"Everyone says they had a special relationship. Do you think they were having sex?"

"I bet they did. I've seen them kissing. Joe Dobbs lives next door to her. He says they were never alone except when walking along the streets, but I don't believe him. Jarvis would've found a way to get into her pants."

"When did you see them kissing? More than one occasion?"

"We saw them on the night she was killed. They were on Elm street. That's the only time." Jerry hoped his face didn't reveal the tingle of his nerves.

"Who was with you that night?" Jerry hesitated to push here, close to something not known previously. A break through.

"Joe Dobbs and Gil Brown. We were riding around in Gil's car and passed them."

Jerry tried to imagine what would make Scott keep talking. "So they were really into it when you saw them?"

"Oh yeah. I thought they were going to do it right on the street."

"You mean have sex?"

"Yeah. They were rubbing their hands all over each other, kissing so long."

"Were you upset, mad, when you saw them?"

"Yeah. I didn't like her making out with Jarvis."

"But you didn't do anything."

Scott hesitated, his face paled, his eyes diverted from Jerry's. "No, we kept driving."

"You didn't see them again that night?"

No hesitation in Scott's response. A quick "No."

"Do you think Jarvis killed her?"

Scott looked around the room. "Maybe, but don't really know." There was an element of hesitation, of guarded reflection.

"So Gil Brown is your best friend?"

"We do things together. He can always get his dad's car."

"And the other boy, Joe Dobbs?"

"Sometimes he comes with us. He and Gil are good friends from the church they go to."

"Would either of them know things about Robert and Kathy you've not told me?"

"No." The response came too quickly and too forcefully, the emergence of a scowl across his face. "They won't tell anything." Jerry made a mental note to follow up.

Scott began to push out of the booth. "I gotta go. My mother worries when I'm late getting home."

"I understand. Thanks for talking with me and good luck with the games."

Jerry watched Scott lumber through the tables and out the door. Something had not been said. Something important. Maybe revealing about the crime. Clearly, Scott didn't want Jerry talking to the other boys who had observed Kathy and Robert on the fateful night. Those three boys probably had been the last to see Kathy Abrams alive—except the killer.

The implications of Scott's responses nagged Jerry. He reviewed the conversation with Fran, then made some notes. Had he detected a threatening tone in Scott's answer to his question about the other two boys he'd been with on the night of the murder? Or was it stretching his imagination? He decided he'd try to talk with Joe Dobbs, thinking Gil Brown would be more protected by his lawyer father who'd seemed interested in the case when Jerry surprised him and Ledbetter discussing the situation. And Brown had contacted Judge Peabody asking that Jerry be dropped as the defense attorney.

When Jerry called the Dobbs home, Joe's mother answered and arranged for Jerry to come to the house when he told her he wanted to talk about Kathy Abrams. She told Jerry she couldn't get past her sadness about the death of Kathy, a next door child she'd watched grow into a beautiful young woman, and wanted to help in any way possible. But she was not prepared for Joe's reaction when she told him Preston was coming. She'd never seen him turn so pale. She thought for a moment he would faint. He'd turned before she could react, and retreated to his room.

Two hours later, Joe came into the kitchen. He'd tried to find a way out of the meeting, but he couldn't without lying. Somehow he had to alert his mother. He said, "I'll meet with this lawyer, but you have to promise not to tell anyone. Okay?"

She couldn't imagine what was bothering Joe. Whatever, it affected his speech and brought on a desperate look. For several days, she'd noticed how his eyes were sunken with dark circles. She tried to console him. "I promise. It's just between you and me."

Jerry arrived at the Nugent street address at nine-thirty on Saturday morning to be met at the door by Joe and his mother. She offered coffee and muffins which he readily accepted.

"Joe, as I told your mother over the phone, I'm trying to talk to several students who knew Kathy Abrams, about her relationship with Robert Jarvis. Not necessarily their good friends, but others who might have a different version of things. Since you live next door, I thought you might have a perspective no one else has about them. Understand?"

"Think so." A slight boy, Joe probably didn't weigh a hundred and twenty pounds, and shorter than any of the others Jerry had met. Mrs. Dobbs brought in coffee and muffins, then to Jerry's relief, retreated to another room.

Jerry bit into a muffin. "Good. I like blueberry." He continued. "Give me your opinion about Jarvis and Kathy." He thought this was a good, safe, non-threatening starting place with a youngster obviously on edge.

Joe seemed to relax. He took a muffin off the plate. "I saw them together a lot. She lived next door to us. Often Robert walked part way home with her from school, but he didn't go all the way to her house."

"So he'd leave her before they got close?"

"Usually they separated at the corner of Elm and Ninth." Joe finished the muffin and wiped his hands on a paper napkin. "Once he came to the front door with her, but I heard that her parents didn't like that. They grounded her for a week"

"How'd you know?"

"Her mother told mine. They didn't like Kathy seeing Robert."

"Because he's black?"

"Think so, but they were really protective of her." Joe put one foot across the opposite knee and tugged a white sock.

"Do you know Robert well?"

Joe stared at the muffins on the table. "Everybody knows him. He's by far the best athlete at the school. But I'm not a friend. He probably doesn't know who I am."

"You ever talk to Kathy?"

He smiled thinly. "Sometimes we walked to school together. She was nice. You know, spoke to everybody."

"Did she ever talk to you about Robert?"

"No. She never did. But she liked him a lot. Even after she got grounded that time, she kept seeing him."

"You ever see them smooching, kissing, things like that?"

"I'd see them holding hands when they walked together. Saw them kissing once."

Jerry skipped forward to a critical point. "Was that on the night she was killed?"

Joe blanched, shifted on the sofa, looked down at the floor. "How'd you know that?"

"Scott Little told me three of you had seen them."

Joe stared through glazed eyes at the wall, his face bleached of color. Jerry prodded softly. "What else happened that night?"

Joe almost wailed. "Nothing." Beads of sweat popped onto his forehead.

"After you saw them at the corner, you didn't see them again?"

Very softly, Joe said, "No." His eyes clouded with tears. He wiped his face with the napkin. His hands trembled so he almost dropped the napkin.

"Did you see anyone else lurking around or another car following them?"

"No."

Jerry waited for several seconds, then he asked, "What about Scott Little? Would he hurt Robert or Kathy?"

The response was so soft, Jerry could barely hear. "He's a mean guy."

"Are you afraid of him?"

"Sometimes he threatens me. He picks on people smaller than him."

Jerry said, "I suspect he doesn't like Robert. Also, he was mad because Kathy was seeing Robert. Is that true?"

"Yes. He'd never take on Robert though. He complained Robert ran over him and hit him too hard during football practice."

"But he didn't challenge Robert directly. You know, try to fight him?"

Shaking his head, Joe said, "He's scared Robert would really hurt him. Scott only hits people who aren't as big or as strong as he is."

Jerry said, "Joe, you've answered my questions. But the defense may call the three of you who saw Kathy and Robert the night of the crime. Until I talked to you and Scott, no one admitted seeing them after they left the stadium together. That information may be important."

Joe didn't say anything, but he blanched even whiter by the possibility he'd be called into court and asked questions under oath. Jerry guessed he knew more than he'd revealed, but he didn't want to push him too hard at this time. The kid was really scared. Maybe only of Scott Little, but it might be more.

Jerry stood. "Joe, thanks for talking with me. And thank your mother for the muffins and coffee. I'll see you around." He found his way out the front door. Joe was still standing in the door when he drove away.

Fred answered Jerry's call on the third ring. "Jerry Preston, things okay with you?"

Fred had come in from raking leaves, an annual job he didn't look forward to doing. "I just finished a little yard work. Busy week at the office. And I'm trying to get ready for a big meeting next week. What's up?"

"I wanted to update you about Robert's case." Jerry summarized his meetings with Scott and Joe. "Those kids know something they're not telling. Joe Dobbs is scared out of his skin. Scott's belligerent and defensive."

"Could they have been involved in the crime? Maybe they saw something they're afraid to tell anyone, like a person or two grabbing Kathy and pulling her into a car."

"It's hard to tell. I'd like to meet with the other boy, Gil Brown, but it'll be tricky. His father will shield him if he knows I'm seeing him." Fred recalled Jerry's conviction Brown and Ledbetter had more interest in this case than usual circumstances would dictate.

"You'll figure out something. I assume the Medical Examiner has sent those samples to the State Crime Laboratory in Springfield?"

"Day after the Judge issued the order."

"You know what he sent?"

"My understanding is the clothing with blood and semen. Bits of skin fragments found under the victim's nails. And I believe hair found at the scene."

"We'll need to get blood from Robert to compare to the sample at the scene. I can get the State Lab to run those also. That'll remove any doubt of poor analyses or hanky-panky handling of the information. Get an M.D. to take the blood and send it directly to the State Lab. I'll call my contact on Monday so they'll understand the need to push it through."

"I'll do it Monday or Tuesday."

Fred said, "You know, Jerry, it'd be interesting to have blood samples from those three kids who saw Kathy and Robert."

Jerry almost gasped. "Oh, wow. I'd not thought of the possibility. But they'd never agree to do it."

"If you can convince Peabody about your suspicions, he'd probably issue a court order forcing them to submit."

"It's worth a try. They know something they're not telling me."

Fred added, "And if there were hairs found, add that to your request. It can't hurt."

Fred switched gears. "Fran doing okay?"

"Think so. She's recovered from the shock, but we've not heard from Calloway about a slot for her. Probably too soon. And the teacher's organization is looking into her suspension."

"How's Robert? You talk to him recently?"

"I'm meeting him after school tomorrow."

Jerry picked Robert up after football practice. On the short drive to the apartment, Robert sat quietly watching the street ahead, and Jerry considered the appropriate questions to discover important information, and at the same time demonstrate support for the young man.

In the apartment, Jerry found some root beer and snack crackers. They sat at the small table in the kitchen.

Jerry, seeking a transition from the mundane to the necessary, said, "Robert, you seem to be doing well, back in school, on the team again, but you must think about this situation a lot. I'm sure you worry about the outcome of the trial and how it'll impact your future."

Robert was quiet, seemingly unsure where to begin in response to Jerry's discourse. "It's in my head all the time. Even when I'm busy with school work or football, it's in the back of my mind."

"Let me ask several questions to help me understand your relationship with Kathy and how others may have been involved, directly or otherwise. Okay?"

"Sure, it's okay." His arms rested on the table as he leaned forward.

"I understand that you and Kathy had a close relationship. Some have guessed you were lovers."

Robert rubbed a hand across his brow, looking at the table top. "Mr. Preston, we loved each other. But I don't want people to know because of what they'll think about her." He started, stopped, and said, "We tried to be together as much as possible when the situation seemed natural. We wanted to prevent others talking and it getting back to her parents."

Jerry pushed the snacks closer to Robert. "You knew she dated other boys. Did it bother you?"

"Yeah, it did. But we'd talked about it. We'd agreed she would date others for things at the school. She wanted to go, but she couldn't go with me."

"So did you go to the dances and parties?"

"No. I never went. I thought it would cause trouble for her."

"Did she tell you about those dates? How they went, whether she had a good time, things like that?"

"Sometimes she did. I tried not to ask." He frowned. "I suppose I didn't want to know too much."

"Tell me how your relationship started and how you became such close friends."

Robert said, "I'll have to think about this." He drank some Coke, then walked across the room, and leaned against the refrigerator. "We were in classes together since first grade. Sometimes we got paired together for school activities. We both made good grades so we were in the same track for some subjects. We talked sometimes, you know how little kids are. I guess I had a crush on her since fourth or fifth grade."

Jerry asked, "So your feelings toward her developed over a long time?"

Robert smiled slightly. "Right. When we got to high school, we didn't see much of each other for the first year. Then I made the team and she became a cheerleader. We were together on the bus and other times when the two groups traveled together for away games."

"When did you realize you cared deeply?"

Robert frowned, ate a cracker. "That's hard to pin down. It just sorta grew on me." He paused again, then returned to the chair, crossing his legs. "Once we were waiting for the bus in Haynesville to come back from a game. Couple of the guys started messing around with Kathy, you know, trying to put their arms around her, tickling her in the ribs, pinching her butt. She kept asking them to stop, but they wouldn't. I got mad and stepped in. One of the guys swung at me. I hit him pretty hard, knocked him down. Later, she asked me why I had done it. I told her I didn't like other boys touching her. On the bus, we held hands for the first time. Maybe that was the start of our being serious, but I can't be sure. It happened over a long period."

"Maybe it marked the first time others realized how you felt."

"Probably. Nobody messed with her again, not when I was around." His tone was matter-of-fact, not threatening. He leaned forward in the chair.

"You miss her, don't you?"

Robert's face clouded, his hands clasped together on the top of the table. "So much. I realize now how much she meant to me."

Jerry said, "Time will help you forget."

Robert rubbed his eyes. "I don't know. Maybe. I'll always remember her. Even when I'm as old as Grandfather."

"Let me ask you if Kathy ever talked about boys she refused to date?"

"Couple of times. I guess the one she disliked most was Scott Little. He asked her out several times, but she always refused. He got mad at her, yelled at her in the hall."

157

"What'd you do, anything?"

"I told her I'd talk to him, but she didn't want me to do that. I let it go by."

"Have you had trouble with Scott or others guys at school?"

"Not much. Scott's a bully." Robert uncrossed his legs, and rubbed an ankle. "Scott likes to smash into other players when it's just a drill. He did it to me once. I ran into him and busted his nose on the next play." He shrugged. "He doesn't like me, I know."

Jerry said, "To change the direction some, let me ask if you understand about DNA testing?"

"Not really. But I've read about it in the papers. We had a couple of lessons about genetic materials in biology class, but I know very little."

"We think such evidence is crucial to proving your innocence, so we have to get a small amount of your blood for matching with specimens from the scene of the crime."

"I'll do it. Anything to help." Jerry was relieved there'd been no hesitation on Robert's part.

Jerry said, "You must understand, if your blood matches with anything at the scene, it'll be a setback for us." Jerry knew setback was too mild a description, but he didn't want to alarm Robert.

Robert smiled, perfect white teeth. "It won't."

"Go to Dr. Morton's tomorrow after school. He'll take blood and send it to the State Lab. Dr. Ferriday is going to call them with instructions."

"I'll go right after practice or maybe during the lunch break."

"One more thing," Jerry said, "on the night Kathy disappeared, you walked with her to the corner of Ninth and Elm. Did you see cars near that corner or cars driving slowly past, maybe one passed you more than once."

"I've tried to remember, but nothing seemed unusual. Several cars passed us on Elm, it's a busy street. Cars were parked in front of houses on Ninth, but that's just people who live there. Nothing different that caught my attention."

Jerry looked at his watch. "I think we've covered most things. Now I should get you home, but if there's something important I've not asked, you call me. I don't want to miss anything that might prove useful to your defense."

Robert asked, as they climbed into the car. "About the trial. Will I have to testify?"

"I haven't decided yet how I'll present our case. But a few days ahead of the trial date, I'll go over everything with you, including any questions I'd ask, if I think your testimony is appropriate. And I'll try to get you ready for the prosecutor's questions."

"I'll do whatever you decide is best. I'll tell what I know."

Jerry arrived two minutes early for his appointment with Judge Peabody. When Jerry had called, Peabody had insisted the County Attorney be present, so he wasn't surprised to find Jim Williams waiting in the outer office.

Peabody invited them in at precisely three-thirty. Without any mundane conversation, he asked Jerry to review his request.

Jerry tried to be succinct. "I've been meeting with several individuals who knew about Kathy Abrams and Robert Jarvis, and who might have seen them after they left the stadium area on the night she was killed. I started down that line because I was struggling to find any clue about what had really happened. Since the prosecution seemed content with the evidence at hand, I felt as though I was thrashing through a large field searching for the proverbial needle.

"I stumbled onto something. Three high school boys who observed from a car on Ninth Street the separation of Abrams and Jarvis, just as he says. That's about all I can get from them. But I believe they know more. I'm convinced they were the last to see Abrams alive. I'd go so far as to suspect they were the ones who assaulted and killed her, but I have no evidence to corroborate my suspicion. Judge, that's the reason I'm requesting a court order to obtain blood and strands of hair from those three boys for the purpose of comparing with samples from the scene."

Williams broke in. "Seems pretty shaky. You're operating on a hunch and a wild one. There's no solid evidence they were involved."

Peabody asked, "Jim has a point. It's not very solid." He turned to Williams. "But I'm both interested and concerned since the prosecution, especially the Sheriff's office, didn't reveal this information. To my knowledge, you haven't even looked for such things."

Jerry jumped at Peabody's frustration with the law enforcement officials. "On the surface, my request may appear to be unfounded, but when I talked to two of the boys, it's clear from their reactions they know more than they're willing to tell me. In addition, Judge, several incidences have suggested there's more at work here than the assault and murder charge. I could recount those, but I believe you know what I mean."

Peabody nodded, remembering Jerry's firing and the attack on Ferriday. He said, "Do you really suspect those three kids of having done the crime?"

Jerry didn't want to reveal all his suspicions with Williams present, but neither did he want to miss out on the opportunity to obtain samples. He hesitated for several seconds, looking into Peabody's face. Then he said, "Judge, I harbor several ideas and a theory about what really occurred, but I'd like the opportunity to write out a brief for your review, prior to your decision about this request to obtain samples."

Williams said, "I'd like to review your statement and have an opportunity to object. In fact, I disagree with this entire procedure. It places three innocent kids at the whims of some fancy blood analyses that nobody believe has merit."

Peabody said, "But you must acknowledge it would do no harm. No one has to know beyond the boys and this group. No one's reputation should be damaged. If anything, it could clear them of any further suspicion." Jerry remained still, silently thanking Peabody for his position.

Williams disagreed. "Just suppose one of those samples matches with one from the scene. We're exposing an innocent kid."

Jerry responded, "If you believe the experts on DNA patterns, there's almost no chance of a random match. Jim, if one of those kid's blood matches the evidence picked up at the scene, we've discovered the real killer. Not an innocent lad. And the hair matching could be another important piece."

Suddenly Peabody stood. "Mr. Preston, I've heard enough. I'll issue a court order for the Medical Examiner to bring in the boys individually and without anyone knowing. Samples will be sent to the State Crime Lab for appropriate analyses."

Williams, red-faced, muttered an objection. "I don't like this, Judge. It's infringing on the rights of those kids."

Peabody looked at Williams. "Your objection is noted, but the order will be forthcoming."

Jerry pushed a bit. "So, will it be necessary for me to bring in my theory?"

Peabody glanced at Williams, then back to Jerry. "I think not. Let's see how things play out."

Jerry hoped he could hold his yell until he was out of the court house.

Scott Little worried. He'd been tricked twice into the meeting with the lawyer. Trying to put Robert Jarvis in a bad light, he'd inadvertently revealed that he, Joe and Gil had seen Robert and Kathy on the night she was killed. He decided to talk to the others in case they'd been caught in some trap by this lawyer for Jarvis.

Gil picked up Scott and Joe in front of the drugstore and they drove to the parking lot by the stadium. Scott, sitting in the front seat, turned so he could see both. "That lawyer, you know the one defending Jarvis, talked me into a meeting."

Gil said, "Why'd you do it? Remember what we agreed on. Don't talk to anybody."

Scott responded gruffly, "I know, but Earl Sloan got some of the kids to meet once with Preston. I went along to see what'd happen and get free pizza. Didn't say a word myself."

Joe, from the back seat, his voice shaking, asked, "So what'd they say?"

"Nothing much. He asked a lot of questions about Kathy and Robert. How they got along, did they have enemies, kids who didn't like them, stuff like that."

Trying to be analytical about the situation, Gil asked, "So why'd Preston call you again, if you didn't say anything?"

From the back seat, Joe said, "He suspected something when you were so quiet."

Scott responded. "That's bullshit!" He turned to glare at Joe.

Gil chimed in. "I'm not so sure. Strange he'd pick on you."

"For all I know, he's called everyone. I'll try to find out."

Gil said, "Preston knows something. But how?"

Irritated by the suspicions of his conspirators, Scott lashed out. "Hell, he's guessing. How could he know what happened?"

Gil retorted, "Maybe he's guessing, but he's putting clues together. I don't understand why he picked you if he's just stabbing in the dark. There's something we don't know."

Joe asked, "How'd you get invited to the first meeting?"

Scott thought about the circumstances. "Earl Sloan set it up. He said Preston wanted to talk to some of the students about Robert, and wanted some who were not his close friend. Preston offered free pizza, so I went."

Gil said, "Maybe no damage has been done. But none of us should get into the same situation again."

"That's why I wanted to see you," Scott said, "to warn you to watch out for Preston. He can't make us say anything."

Gil had lived in a lawyer dominated household all his life. "He might if he hauls us into court. I'll ask my father."

Scott growled. "Let's go. We shouldn't be seen together anymore until after the trial. But I'm warning you about Preston. If anybody talks, I'll deal with you myself." He slammed his fist into the top of the seat causing dust and lint to fly.

Gil warned, "Sounds like you're the one he's after. Don't threaten us."

Joe Dobbs remained silent as they returned to the drugstore. By nature a worrier, he'd become desperate. Almost every night now he jerked awake in the midst of a recurring nightmare. Visions of Kathy Abrams, the newspaper pictures of her so still and quiet on the ground, blood on her, remembering her smile and enthusiasm for everything, always friendly, even to nerds like himself. He didn't dare tell the others Preston had talked to him at his home. He prayed Preston didn't come around asking more questions.

CHAPTER TEN

The meetings in Dallas were hectic and contentious. Prolonged sessions with collaborators from across the U.S., coupled with deliberations with representatives of several federal agencies about funding priorities related to the continued development of genetic fingerprinting and its application in forensics, had resulted in disagreements and haggling. Fred had been tired when he boarded the plane but pleased to arrive in St Louis on time. On the two hour flight, he'd dozed a few minutes after the meal had been served. He had eaten sparingly, not sure of Louise's plans.

As soon as he came through the entrance from the ramp, he saw her standing to one side of the primary flow of traffic, leaning lightly against a column. She looked elegant in black slacks, gray blouse, holding her coat across her right arm. As he started toward her, she recognized him, smiled and took several steps, then waited for him. His hands were full, holding a briefcase and a garment bag, preventing him from hugging her without dropping all the gear.

She touched his arm. "Right on time. I didn't have to wait long."

"Thanks for coming." They were separated momentarily in the throng moving through the long terminal, people weaving across the flow of traffic to reach a gate or digress to the newsstand or rest room.

He smiled at her when she put her arm through his. "We won't get separated this way. You have other luggage?"

"This is it." Her closeness, the scent of her perfume, and the pressure of her arm brought back the feelings he'd experienced previously.

Talking became difficult until they were in her gray Chevrolet coupe parked on the third level of the garage adjacent to the terminal building.

As they cleared the toll booth, she said, "I reserved a room for you about three blocks from where I live, but I'd like for you to come to my place, then I'll take you to the motel. You must be hungry."

"Snacked a bit on the plane." He glanced at her profile several times and once caught her eyes. Both smiled. He realized this was the first time they'd really been alone.

After a thirty minute drive with numerous stops at traffic signals, she pulled into an underground parking garage of a huge apartment building several miles from the airport. "This is it. I'm on the tenth floor."

In the apartment, Fred removed his coat and Louise hung it in the entry closet, along with her own. She said, "Would you like a drink, something to eat?"

"Whatever you planned will be fine."

"I have wine and light snacks. Have a seat while I get things organized." She disappeared through a door. Fred scanned the room, a large, comfortable couch and matching chairs, modern art on the wall, pictures, including one of Joshua and Robert, on the end tables. Neat, no clutter. None of the excess cushions and pillows important to many women.

Louise returned quickly with glasses of white wine, a tray of small sandwiches, and cakes. They sat near each other on the couch, the tray on the glass coffee table.

He said, "This looks good." Raising his glass, he continued, "Here's to a couple of good days."

Louise touched her glass against his. "Agreed."

She said, "Tell me about your trip."

"It was a meeting about the use of biological materials in forensics. Each participant presented a summary of their recent work." He sipped wine, took a bite of a sandwich, then continued. "Then to meet the goals of the organizing agency, we tried to organize a set of priorities for future research to receive funding. That was the more difficult part. We all have our own agenda and it's hard to find compromises and agree on the most promising endeavors." The first time he'd been involved in such discussions had opened Fred's eyes to the combative nature of scientists as they attempted to protect their turf by persuading agencies to give priority for future funding. One guy had blown his stack and walked out when the group refused to include his area of research, one in which the knowledge base had been firmly established with decreasing attention of front line investigators and the likelihood of any significant new findings remote.

"How'd you get interested in those issues?" She reached to take another sandwich.

Fred turned on the couch to face her directly. "I've become interested in the last three or four years about the application of biological science in criminal cases because it seemed to offer a practical application of basic science. The first case to be solved happened to be in England after the police had been unable to pinpoint a killer using traditional means. I'd done some work on DNA and protein synthesis, so it was an easy switch to examine some of the methods being tried in the crime labs. And it generated support from a different group of funding sources."

"What was your paper about?" She refilled the wine glasses from a decanter, rivulets of condensation seeping along the sides.

"I've been focused on the effects of contaminants on DNA analysis. Samples from a typical crime scene aren't usually clean. For example, the police take clothing which has blood on it, the labs extract the blood and go from there. But the clothing is usually dirty. Same is true for hair samples. Often there's oil or grease from the street, sometimes soap, hair sprays. Everything imaginable can show up. So the validity of DNA data becomes questionable when the body fluid has been exposed to all those other materials. In some cases, the evidence has been thrown out because of concerns about purity."

"And?"

"Under most conditions, the DNA remains stable. Once you clean away all the other gunk, the analyses and the results are quite reliable."

"So it's a good source of information?"

"Usually. Maybe sunlight is most destructive. But in most cases, the analysis provides solid data." Fred paused. "But, there's a lot yet to be done."

"Sounds like your work might fit directly into Robert's trial."

"It could. I'm sure the question of contamination will be raised." He reached to touch her hand. "You worry about him, don't you?"

"Sure. He's my only nephew and one with great promise." She didn't move her hand away.

"Jerry Preston seems to be making progress on his defense. I'm confident Robert will be cleared."

She stood and moved in front of the couch and table. "Would you like coffee?"

"That'd be nice." He followed her to the kitchen and watched while she started the Braun coffee maker. He moved out of her way as she retrieved the cream from the refrigerator. She brushed against him and smiled.

They were silent for several seconds as they sipped coffee. She placed the cup and saucer on the table and said, "I'm glad you came." She laughed, her eyes lighting. "In spite of my reservations."

"We're both finding our way."

"I'm always cautious. It goes back to our conversation last weekend."

He reached to take her hand. "Let's not push things. Just proceed slowly. See how it develops." He grinned. "After these couple of days, you may decide against further contact."

She squeezed his hand in return. "Come on, I'll take you to the motel. I have classes tomorrow, but I'll be free by four."

"Would you like to have dinner at a nice place?"

She laughed softly. "In fact, I've made reservations."

In front of the motel office, she asked, "What'll you do tomorrow?"

"I always have work with me. I want to prepare for Monday's class, and edit a manuscript." As he closed the car door, he said, "See you tomorrow."

Fred remained awake a long time. Maybe this would play out okay. Louise seemed pleased he'd come and more at ease tonight than she'd been in Pineville. Conversing with her tonight had confirmed her sensible nature. She looked more beautiful than he remembered from Joshua's house and the restaurant. She'd not been as reserved as he thought she might be, touching his hand and sitting closer than he'd expected. Tomorrow could be the crucial test of how the relationship would go. He wanted to impress her.

Louise felt good about their time together. She'd thought about Fred a lot during the past week, especially since he'd called and suggested the visit. In a way, she'd been surprised he'd followed up so soon after her efforts to persuade him of the potential difficulties. Most males she'd known would have been discouraged to the point of giving up any future contact.

His call had relieved her apprehension she'd been too convincing and had diverted any interest on his part. She admitted she'd been pleased when he hadn't given up so readily. During her analyses, she realized she viewed him as an attractive man, maybe fifty, five years older than she, slim, but a solid six-feet plus, obviously took care of himself, no excess flab like most middle aged guys she knew, smiled easily, brownish hair clipped short and receding a bit. Probably more lonely than he admitted or even recognized, since his career seemed such a major component of his life. And he clearly enjoyed his work at the university, another sign of a stable life style.

But she intended their relationship to progress cautiously. She couldn't tolerate another major disappointment. She must be secure with her intuitions. As she pulled on her nightgown, she smiled to herself when in a brief moment of fantasy, she wondered how Fred would be as a lover but pleased he'd not made an attempt to get her into bed at the first opportunity.

At the motel Fred awakened at seven, an hour later than usual with no alarm to signal another day. He dug out his running gear and after splashing warm water on his face and doing five minutes of stretching exercises, he tucked the room key into a pocket of the shorts and set out on a jog. The morning was clear and crisp, typical early November day. He realized immediately the street ran through a heavy business district, something he'd not noticed in the darkness of last night. To get away from the traffic, he cut away on a side street and loped along in a residential neighborhood of middle class homes, large trees and shrubs nestled in well-kept lawns. Approximately thirty minutes later, he returned to the motel, energized but soaking from his exertions.

He found breakfast at a Waffle House in the next block. By now, the heavy traffic on the main street moved continuously, an occasional horn from an impatient driver, the air dense with exhaust fumes. He scanned a St. Louis paper as he consumed the waffle and sipped black coffee. News as usual focused on tragedies and the presidential contest between Bush and Dukakis. He must remember to vote next Tuesday.

The morning passed quickly. For a while he lost himself in the manuscript he'd brought along. The draft, prepared by a second year graduate student, required a lot of editing and revising, although the essential thrust was adequate. Around twelve-thirty, he walked out to find a sandwich at the small restaurant near the motel. Throughout the afternoon, his concentration on the lecture materials was interrupted frequently by thoughts of Louise and his mounting anxieties about tonight. And he took the unusual opportunity to nap for thirty minutes.

Louise called at four-fifteen. Fred laid aside the lecture notes. "How're you doing? Out of class?"

"Good, survived another week." She paused. "I'm still at the office, but ready to leave. Can you come to my place at six-thirty? I made reservations for seven."

"Sure. I assume this is a dress-up place."

"It's a nice place near the Arch and the river."

Fred walked the three blocks to her apartment building. With the sun fading, the air had become brisk. The topcoat felt good. For the first time in years, he'd worried about the match of tie and suit, feeling like a high school sophomore on a first date. He'd brought his best navy blue suit and dusted off his shoes with his running shorts.

Louise opened the door immediately after the bell chimed. Fred tried not to gawk as he looked at her. "You look wonderful." The dark maroon dress clung to her figure, decidedly female, top of the knee length. The light make-up, barely noticeable, highlighted her eyes and mouth. Her black hair framing her face and a single strand of pearls with matching earrings added to her sophistication.

Louise, abashed by his reaction, reacted by twirling around. High heels and sheer nylons emphasized long and shapely legs. She said, "I wanted to impress you."

"You most certainly have."

Louise collected her coat from the closest chair. "Mind if we take a cab? I'd rather not drive since it's so hard to find parking close."

At the front entrance of the apartment building, the attendant had a Yellow Cab waiting. "Have a good evening, Ms. Bull." Fred realized the burly man was more than a bell hop. He served a security role as well, likely knew everyone in the building.

Fred asked, as the cab moved into the midst of steady traffic, "Is security a problem? Your attendant made me identify myself when I came in."

"It used to be before we employed an agency. Now someone's on duty round the clock. The outer doors to the building are locked at six. After that, security opens the door for you. There's a card used to enter the parking garage." Fred recalled a brief stop at a gate when they'd entered the previous evening.

"You feel safe there?"

"Reasonably so." She placed her hand on his arm as they sat close in the back seat, their shoulders touching as the vehicle swerved around corners. "As safe as I've ever felt."

The Warehouse, the name no doubt derived from a previous use, was clearly an upscale restaurant, the name misleading, located on the street bordering the huge river. A section of the Gateway To The West Arch and large barges moving along the Mississippi caught their immediate attention from their table next to a window.

As they scanned the menu, Fred said, "This is nice. I've never been here, but I've been to places farther down the river." He looked at her, sitting to his right, continuing to be engrossed by her appearance. "Any recommendations?"

"I've only been here once before. You probably can't go wrong with seafood. That's their advertised specialty."

Both ordered broiled trout with wild rice and salad. At the waiter's recommendation, Fred asked for a carafe of the *Blanc fume.* Both abstained from cocktails, waiting for the wine.

The salads were placed within three minutes. After a couple of bites, Louise asked, "You travel a lot? Joshua said you'd been to London recently."

Fred nodded, his mouth partially full. "I interact with people in my discipline all over the world. Since the publications about DNA in forensic work, I've been asked to consult a lot with lawyers and their clients. Even gave seminars to several groups of law enforcement types. This DNA stuff is so new everyone in the legal system is interested in learning about the possibilities."

With a slight chuckle, she said. "So you've become famous."

Fred shook his head. "I wouldn't say that, but I'm better known now than when I started in this business. At first I spent all my time writing grants and doing experiments in the lab. Now I depend on graduate students to do the routine work. And I'm looking for another post-doctoral fellow for next year to help with the supervision of less experienced students."

Louise asked, "You teach undergraduates at all?"

"I have a large section of beginning biology each spring semester. Maybe three hundred freshmen and sophomores. As you'd guess, I don't get to know those students at all. But I like to do the course. It keeps me in touch with changes taking place in the basics of the science because those texts are continually updated." He'd discovered early that research scientists could easily become experts in a small segment of a field and lose out on the broad discipline.

"So mostly graduate classes?"

"Usually one each term. Those require a lot of background searching if you give them the most recent information. I have fifteen graduate students in my lab. Working on projects, doing their own research as part of grants."

"Traveling must be exciting."

"Earlier in my career it was great, but now it's a drag. Really tiring. But the worst part of it is, all my work stacks up while I'm away."

"It must interfere with teaching."

He nodded and smiled. "I have to schedule carefully, but it does get in the way at times. I'm forced to get substitutes or let post-docs and graduate assistants give lectures."

"Compared to your schedule, mine seems tame and unexciting."

Fred laughed. "Mine is never boring, but I'd trade sometimes." He continued. "What about your writing? You mentioned you were using your free time to write."

"I've published several short stories and I'm working on a novel now." She smiled, and reached to touch his hand. "That's where the money is assuming you can find a publisher interested enough to advertise and push the book."

"You find it difficult freeing up time?"

"Sure. The main problem is continuity. I write on weekends, and sometimes in the evenings, but the teaching takes most of my time and energy."

"I guess the loads are heavy."

She nodded. "During most semesters, I have four classes and they're all different." She shifted in the chair. "But I enjoy the students and it's satisfying to watch their skills and confidence develop and improve. And I don't have to upgrade my lectures very often since the material is quite basic."

After a brief lull in their conversation, Fred asked, "When'd you leave Pineville?"

"When I started high school, thirteen years old. Our parents thought I'd be better off in St. Louis and my aunt and uncle were willing to open their home to a teenager. I'm sure I got a better education."

"It seemed to have worked out well."

"Guess so. One never knows how it would have gone had I remained at home."

"Joshua believes he was short changed by the schools in Pine County."

"Maybe. But Josh lost interest in school. He wanted to make money, leave home, get married."

"But those separate schools weren't good. He wasn't challenged." Fred wasn't sure why he was defending Joshua.

"That's what he says now. As a teenager, you don't know except you're not interested and bored. You suspect the teachers aren't very good. Support is poor. It's easy to give up or find excuses."

Fred grinned, remembering his visit to Joshua and the home place. "Joshua and I had great fun when we were kids. But the social system separated us. I didn't see him much after I entered high school."

She laughed. "He's told me. I'm surprised I don't remember you."

Fred shrugged. "Mostly we met in this place we'd made in the woods." He grinned. "And you were too young." He touched her forearm.

They were finishing coffee and dessert before they realized there hadn't been a drag in their dialogue. After he'd signed his credit card receipt, Fred asked, "Ready?"

Cabs cruised continuously. One stopped at Fred's signal. In the car, Louise said, "It's cold." She moved closer to Fred and put an arm through his.

They were silent until the cab pulled up at her apartment building and Fred paid the fare. On the curb, she said, "Come up for a while?"

"I'd like that."

The security attendant opened the heavy glass door. He said, "Cold night, huh?" He nodded to Fred, his face a blank, but his eyes shifted between the two.

She smiled, "It's winter out for sure."

In the apartment they removed coats, and Louise invited him to sit on the couch. "Want anything, coffee, brandy?"

"I'm okay. The meal was more than I usually eat. We had a lot of wine, too."

She sat next to him, and crossed her legs. Several inches of thigh revealed by the shortness of the maroon dress grabbed his attention. Aroused but remembering her wish to proceed slowly, he wasn't certain what he should do. Follow your instincts was his thought as she turned slightly toward him.

Taking her movements as a signal, Fred turned her face gently and caressed her cheeks and upper neck with his fingers. He leaned closer and kissed her gently on the lips, then pulled back. Both were quiet as his arm tightened around her shoulders, nudging her closer. He could feel her leg and hip pressing against him.

He kissed her again with more intensity this time. Louise responded by slightly opening her lips and pressing against him. After several seconds, she pulled back, straightened her skirt, recrossed her legs, the nylon hose whispering.

Fred continued to hold her around the shoulders, but his hand moved across her back, gently caressing. She turned and they kissed again. Her mouth parted and her tongue pressed into his mouth. He responded and they held each other firmly. Fred moved his hand down her back to her waist. Holding her close, he touched her knee, resisting the temptation to go farther. Louise continued to kiss him with mounting passion, her arms cradling his neck.

They broke apart. Louise's eyes were partially closed. Fred was aware of his erection and the deeper breathing of both, her skin hot against his fingers. Their eyes fixed on each other, Louise stood and pulled Fred's hand. She led him into the bedroom.

Between kissing and touching sensitive places, they undressed each other and moved to the bed, hands caressing and exploring, their desire mounting.

Fred came awake later. He had no idea of time. Louise faced him, her eyes open. She smiled and touched his face.

Fred asked, "What time is it?"

She rolled over to find the clock on the table. "Two-thirty."

"Should I go?"

"Please stay. I'd like to wake up with you here in the morning."

"You're assuming we ever go back to sleep," he said as he pulled her close and kissed her. She responded, pulling him on top of her.

They woke with bright sun streaming through the blinds, their arms around each other. Fred kissed her on the forehead, then her eyes and lips.

She laughed. "We'd better get up."

After coffee and strawberry muffins, Fred returned to the motel, checked out, and brought his bags to Louise's apartment. The security guard eyed him somewhat suspiciously, but didn't say anything.

In the apartment, he said to Louise, "I've ruined your reputation as a shy, retiring school teacher."

She chuckled. "No doubt your coming back here will raise eyebrows among the security people, but they're quite close mouthed about the residents."

"So, what'd you like to do? I assume you're free to participate in sinful or recreational things today."

She laughed and came to stand next to him, looking up into his face. He kissed her on the cheek. "I didn't plan anything. Didn't know what would happen yesterday."

Fred said, trying to look serious. "We know what'll happen if we stay here. How about we take a bus down to the river and walk around the park near the Arch, have lunch, then see what hits our fancy?"

"I'd like that. How cold is it?"

"Dress warmly. It's cold and windy out."

They walked for about an hour in the park and along the streets, through a historic church near the park, and then had coffee in a small cafe by the river. Without thought, they held hands whenever possible, relishing the touch of the other like teenagers who'd discovered the mysteries of the opposite sex.

In early afternoon, they stopped for soup and coffee at a restaurant near Busch stadium. As they sipped the second cup of coffee, Fred asked, "You want to go out to dinner again? We probably should make a reservation."

Louise looked at him. "I'd rather stay in tonight, if you don't mind. I'd like to buy some fish at the market and cook you a dinner." She led him to a market near the river. Louise discussed options with the older man behind the counter, settling on salmon.

After a dinner of broiled salmon, rice, salad, and wine, they moved to the couch to finish coffee.

Fred said, "You look seductive. I may not be strong enough to resist making a serious pass." The black skirt and green blouse intensified her sexuality.

"I'd hoped you'd notice," she said, as she turned on the couch to face him, swinging her legs up under her. She reached to kiss him.

On Sunday morning, she drove Fred to the airport for the eleven-thirty flight to Champaign-Urbana. She didn't park, but dropped him at the terminal door. As she pulled the car to the curb, Fred leaned across to kiss her.

Fred said, "Louise, I'm going to miss you. I'll call tonight."

She laughed. "We promised to progress slowly and see what happens. I'm not sure we understood slow." Her expression changed. "I'll miss you, too."

Fred watched her car disappear in the traffic, accepting that his life had changed dramatically in the past few hours.

Jerry called Susan Newman, the head secretary in Ledbetter's firm, at her home number on Saturday morning. When she answered, he said, "Susan, it's Jerry Preston. How're you doing?"

She responded quietly. "Okay." Not her usual enthusiasm. A clear note of caution.

He said, "I know this is unusual, but I'd like to talk to you." Jerry understood he was taking advantage of her good nature and desire to assist people she knew.

"About what?"

"Couple of things, the Jarvis case for one. Ledbetter's mood."

"Mr. Preston, you're asking me to do something that's sure to get me in trouble with the firm. I can't afford to lose my job."

"I understand the potential predicament I'm putting you in, but your opinion might be helpful in the Jarvis case. I really need your help."

He could almost hear her brain spinning during a brief silence. "I'll do it under two conditions. First, you come here tonight so we're not seen in public. Second, I want your promise I'll not be called to testify under any circumstances. You must understand, neither Ledbetter or Brown must ever know I talked to you. Nobody must know."

"Sounds like a fair deal. It'll be between you and me. I'll come at eight tonight if that will be okay."

Jerry parked a block away from the address Susan had given him and waited five minutes in case anyone had followed him before he walked to her apartment building. He avoided the elevator and went up the service stairs, peeking into the hall before leaving the stairwell and knocking gently on her apartment door. Susan responded immediately and led him into a small living area and offered coffee.

"Susan, I understand this is difficult for you and I appreciate it. First, talk to me about Ledbetter's mood since the Jarvis thing happened."

She pulled her legs under her on the couch, reached to straighten the twist in the leg of her jeans. "It's hard to say, but he's sometimes more defensive. He's distracted often. Doesn't trust us like he did previously. You could call it suspicious, like he's certain someone in the office is doing something underhanded and he hopes to discover them in the act."

"How about strange or unusual telephone calls?"

She laughed, a nervous response. "We've always have those. You probably don't know, but Ledbetter has deals going that no one else knows about."

"Except you?"

Her voice firmer, she said, "I mean no one. No records, no files, no names recorded, nothing. Some calls go past my desk on his private line." She walked over to refill Jerry's coffee cup, then returned to her position on the couch. "But he tapes some conversations."

"Any unusual or different set of visitors since Jarvis?"

She said, "Two observations. I've thought about this since you called and maybe neither is meaningful. But Brown and Ledbetter have spent more time closeted together in the past couple of months than I ever recall. I've noticed because they seldom got together previously. Also, Sheriff Talbot has been in four or five times. Never before had he darkened the door."

"You aware of any special litigation that would cause the two partners to confer so often?"

"No, but that doesn't mean there isn't. I don't pretend to understand all the implications of the cases we're dealing with."

"Has he talked to you or others about Robert Jarvis and the charges against him?"

"No, but he says openly that Jarvis is guilty. Everybody around the office knows his position."

Jerry reviewed notes on a small pad he carried in his coat. "Susan, would you characterize Ledbetter a racist?"

She stood to rearrange her position, shuffled a cushion on the couch. "It's hard to say. He uses derogatory language about Blacks at times, but other times, he's sympathetic and supportive of their causes." She raked a hand through thick black hair. "He's difficult to categorize."

"Maybe it's the specific person or time or whatever that brings it out?"

She looked serious. "That's one way to put it."

Jerry asked. "Has he been more difficult to work for recently?"

"Not really. He's always been demanding. He expects everybody to jump when he wants something done."

"He treats you fair though? You've been with the firm several years."

"I've learned to deal with him. When I first joined the staff, he made several passes. Made it clear he expected me to have sex with him. He even suggested one day we do it on the desk in his office in the middle of the day. I refused, telling him I'd leave if he persisted. It's never been a subject since but I recognize he stares when I walk near."

When Jerry looked back at his notes, Susan asked, "Jerry, what're you grasping for?"

He laughed softly. "It's obvious then I'm reaching for something. I'll recognize it when it's in the open, but I'm not sure how to tell anyone." He scratched his chin as though considering his next comment. He looked at her. "To be flat honest, I believe Ledbetter and Brown, maybe Talbot are covering for someone in the Jarvis case, probably the guilty person, and they're willing to use Robert Jarvis as the pigeon. Let him take the rap and allow events to return to normal. But I can't prove it, and it's been difficult to get a handle on a solid clue."

Susan's eyes widened as he talked. "That's why you were fired."

"Yes, because I began to ask questions and seek evidence essential to defend Jarvis. In doing so, I potentially exposed the real criminal. Ledbetter became furious when I refused to stop my probing, so he fired me. Obviously, his reactions and warnings made me even more suspicious because I can't figure out why he'd care one way or another about the outcome of the Jarvis case."

She shook her head. "It's hard to believe. He liked you and thought you were doing well."

Jerry continued. "Not only did he fire me, but I suspect he pressured people in the school system to fire my wife from her teaching position."

Susan turned somber, a deep frown on her usual smiling face. "Jerry, he called the school superintendent ten minutes after you walked out that last day. I shouldn't tell you this, but I can't believe he'd be so mean and vindictive."

"How did you know about the call?"

"I went in to put some papers on his desk. Overheard him asking for the superintendent on his private line, but I didn't give it further thought until you told me about Fran."

Both sat quietly, thinking. After a substantial pause, during which they stared at each other, Jerry said, "I'd guessed such. You've confirmed one suspicion."

She said, "He can't ever know I told you about the call."

"I promise he won't. Susan, it could be more than your job. They've played rough with a couple of people. Be careful until this thing passes. Don't do anything to raise his suspicion or even let him know you've thought about the Jarvis episode."

"Are you looking for another position?"

Jerry grinned. "I've lucked out and have been offered a place with the Calloway firm in Du Quoin. I'm working from there now, but we still have an apartment here."

Jerry stood and walked toward the door. Still thinking about the last comment, Susan followed. "If things get too bad for you with Ledbetter, let me know. I suspect Calloway would be pleased to have you."

"I might come begging if things don't change soon. It's too oppressive now with everyone on edge."

He reached to shake her hand, but she placed her arms around his neck and hugged him tightly. He held her for a moment, then walked out.

CHAPTER ELEVEN

The eighteen-seat commuter plane from St. Louis bounced around in the gusty winds of November. The fasten seat belt sign remained on and the usual offer of soft drinks was canceled. Three passengers utilized the plastic bags provided for air sickness. But they arrived at the Champaign airport only five minutes behind schedule. Fred passed on the snack, still sated from the brunch with Louise.

Following his ritual after being away, Fred went by his office to scan through the stack of mail. Nothing unusual, an acceptance letter for a manuscript from the *Journal of Biochemistry*, and an invitation to give a seminar at the University of Iowa in the summer. For later reading he stacked aside the usual flood of memos from university officials. He chatted for ten minutes with two graduate students working in the lab adjacent to the office. They seemed to be doing okay, trying to make progress on their research projects with the building almost empty on a holiday Sunday.

On the route home, he stopped to pick up a beef and broccoli dish from the Chinese take-out. After consuming the food and a glass of wine, he dialed Louise. She answered on the second ring. "How're you doing?" he asked.

"Good, but I miss you already." She laughed lightly. "I've been thinking about the weekend. You said we'd go slowly. You broke your promise."

"Sometimes things get carried away. I thought about us, too." He paused, thinking ahead. "What're your plans for Thanksgiving?"

"Classes are over at noon Wednesday. I haven't made firm plans, but I usually spend the holiday with Joshua and Robert. Typically I go there Wednesday night and return here on Friday morning or sometimes I stay for the weekend."

Fred said, "I'm to call Jerry Preston tomorrow. He'll probably want me to come to Pineville and check on things during the break. Maybe we could stay in Du Quoin, go over to Joshua's on Thanksgiving, and I could visit with Jerry. What do you think?"

"I'd like that."

"I'll call you tomorrow after I've checked with Jerry."

Fred stuffed his travel clothes in the washer, checked on his food supply for the next couple of days, then with no specific plan, he wandered through the house for several minutes, looking into spaces he'd not touched in months, thinking about Louise fitting into this place and changing his life. Then he laughed to himself acknowledging she might have different ideas, even assuming their relationship became a permanent one.

Fred called Jerry at noon on Monday, thinking he'd catch him at home. Jerry responded immediately. "Hoping you'd call. Can you come down on the weekend after Thanksgiving? Results of the samples should be available, and I'd like you to go with me to talk with the Medical Examiner. I don't know the right questions about this biological stuff."

"How'd your session with Peabody turn out?"

"Great. He agreed to order those boys to give blood for DNA analyses."

"I suppose Williams objected."

"Violently. But Peabody went along with my request because the prosecution has been so lax. He was irritated they hadn't discovered the boys observing Robert and Kathy on the night she was killed."

"You have to look to discover anything." Fred didn't reveal his plans with Louise, but added, "I'll meet you at your house on Friday morning. Go ahead and set up times with the M.E. mid-morning or later."

Jerry said, "I'll wait till you're here to update you, but I've made progress with some other pieces of the puzzle. I'm convinced there's a cover up, but it'll be difficult to prove it." He didn't tell Fred about the conversation with Susan. He hadn't even told Fran.

Fred liked Jerry's aggressiveness. "Okay, take care."

Fred rushed through the day in meetings and classes, but his thoughts returned to Louise and the Jarvis case whenever a slight break occurred. He reminded himself to get on with his own agenda and put Pineville behind him. He smiled, remembering he'd said it to himself before.

He called Louise around eight Monday night. As soon as she answered, he said, "How about a rendezvous with an old man next weekend?"

Her deep throated laugh reminded him of how she looked smiling. "Might be enticed, if you promise to control your urges."

"No fun doing that." He continued, "I'll need to see Jerry for a lot of time on Friday, but the rest of the time can be ours. By the way, I've made a reservation at the Holiday Inn for Wednesday night through Sunday morning. It's under your name."

"Pretty sure of my response, weren't you?"

"I risked taking a chance."

She laughed again. "I'll see you Wednesday. Probably be six or later before I can get there."

As he prepared to leave the office at noon on Wednesday, a graduate student stuck her head in and wanted to talk about data, suspecting something was incorrect. Fred asked her several questions, and received appropriate responses suggesting she was doing the right things.

He asked, "Your internal standards come out okay?"

She shoved a summary to Fred. "From ninety-eight to one hundred percent recovery each time I've run the procedure."

"Then the method and your analyses seem okay. Could be we're onto something which doesn't quite fit the norm."

She shrugged her shoulders. "Maybe, but I'm not certain yet. Should I keep going with the analyses?"

"Sure. Don't stop. But let's call around next week and find out if anyone else is finding the same kind of thing." He rearranged some papers on his credenza. "I'll call Brubaker at Purdue. You met him at the New York meeting after your presentation. He might have ideas or suggest another lab when we talk to him. And, if you have time, you might scour the recent publications for hints of any new trends."

As Fred headed south on U.S. 45, light snow had begun to fall, a solid indicator a messy drive and weekend were in store. He hoped Louise would get an earlier start to avoid accumulating slush on the highways.

At Mattoon, the snow descended more heavily, forcing him to reduce speed and set the wipers at the fastest speed. He was relieved when he arrived in Du Quoin at six-thirty without incident and more relieved when he saw Louise's car in the parking lot.

When Fred indicated his reservation, the desk clerk, a smirk on his face, volunteered, "The other party arrived earlier." Fred let the slight note of sarcasm pass without response, but wondered if this type reaction represented the things Louise worried about.

He knocked on the door before inserting his key and walking in. He heard the shower. While he waited, he hung his clothes on the rack near the door and shoved his socks and underwear in one of the drawers.

Louise came out in a long chenille robe, still drying her hair on a huge towel. She seemed not surprised by his being there. "Thought I heard the door. I'll have to hook the security chain from now on." She walked to him, circled her arms around his neck and kissed him firmly. Fred pulled her closer, then he reached inside the loosely tied robe to fondle her back and stroke her buttocks.

She responded, "I can see how this is going to go." But she increased the pressure of her lips on his.

Around eight, he said, "Should we find dinner?" He rolled from under the covers, pulled on a robe and peeped out through the drapes. "Snow still coming. We'll have to stay here or walk to a place nearby."

"Maybe there's room service." She pulled out the information packet for the motel and found a menu.

"Here, look. There are possibilities."

After scanning the menu, Fred said, "Would you order while I have a shower? Whatever you get will be okay."

They felt secure in the warmth of the room with the pizza and a bottle of wine. They talked about their work, compared travel woes caused by the snow, and planned for the remainder of the weekend. By eleven, they were dead asleep, holding each other.

When Fred peeked through the drapes at seven on Thanksgiving morning, snow covered everything. He called the desk and asked about travel conditions.

The clerk said, "Local TV weather indicates roads are mostly closed. The highway people are recommending people stay off unless absolutely necessary. There've been several reports of minor wrecks and a pile up involving at least a dozen vehicles on the highway near the town limits."

When he relayed the news, Louise said, "Maybe we shouldn't go to Joshua's. I'll call and see what he thinks."

"He'll be shocked to find out we're together."

"Maybe I won't tell him. Keep him guessing."

Fred shaved while she telephoned. She called through the partially closed door. "Josh says we should stay here. Ten inches of snow and the roads are icy. He and Robert will walk to a neighbor's who invited them when the weather turned bad."

"So we're stuck. Let's see if this place has any breakfast type food."

"You're always hungry, aren't you?"

He grinned and chuckled, "Yep, if not food, other things." He leaned to nibble her bare shoulder. "What'd Joshua say about us?"

"Nothing. Big silence for several seconds when he realized we were together." She punched his arm. "But I don't know if he understands how together."

In the hotel coffee shop they sat at a table next to a window. As they ate a bran muffin and sipped coffee, they watched a car slipping and sliding as the driver attempted to find sufficient traction to exit the parking lot.

Passing the desk on the return to their room they discovered the Holiday Inn had scheduled Thanksgiving buffet starting at eleven and lasting until early evening. They made reservations for one-thirty.

After the gigantic feast in a less than crowded dining area because of the storm, they decided to try walking out. By then, almost four, the snow had ceased, the roads had been plowed and sidewalks were partially cleared. They digressed into a residential neighborhood, walking around drifts on the walks and streets. Traffic was almost non-existent, only a couple of cars and a snow plow passing them during the hour they wandered around.

Returning to the warmth of the room, they both fell asleep on the bed, fully clothed. After six, Louise stirred and found Fred looking at her.

"How long have you been awake?"

"Twenty minutes, watching you, so peaceful and quiet. I thought about us."

"What specifically?"

He touched her cheek with his fingers. "How close we've become in such a brief while. How good I feel when you're with me."

Louise took his hand. "I've been surprised too. I didn't know it would be like this." She turned his hand over in hers, and looked at him, "But so far, we've not had to deal with other people."

"It'll be okay." For a while they remained quiet, thinking about their future.

Later, he said, "What'll you do tomorrow while I'm with Preston?"

"If the streets are clear, I'm going to the shopping center about five miles back. Just walk around, kill time, something I seldom get to do in the rush of work."

By Friday morning, the main streets and highways had been cleared. Huge mounds of snow and slush bordered the highway, but other than reducing his speed, Fred had no difficulty driving to Pineville and found Jerry Preston waiting for him inside the entrance to the apartment building.

As Jerry climbed into the car, he said, "We're scheduled to see the Medical Examiner at ten. Your timing is perfect."

Henry Neal, a pleasant man in his middle fifties, had been the Pine County Medical Examiner for fifteen years and had observed every kind of case and evidence possible. After Jerry introduced Fred, Neal said, "I've read about you in the medical forensics journals and your work in developing better techniques for DNA analyses. I've also heard you were a football star at Pine County and later at Illinois."

Fred said, grinning, "I'm not sure about star, but I had a good time. Even got a solid education out of an athletic scholarship." Fred rubbed his face, realizing this had become his standard reply to comments about his athletic career.

Henry gazed up and down Fred's long frame. "You're still in pretty good shape."

"Not bad, for a lab worker and pencil pusher."

Neal pulled out a file from his desk. "This is what you're interested in. Use the table in the conference room. We'll make copies of anything you'd like to have."

Fred and Jerry pulled chairs close together at the table and spread the photographs of DNA patterns of the several samples. Fred showed Jerry the comparisons of bands representing fragments of the substance. After several minutes, Fred said, "There's no match between samples from the scene and Robert's blood. It's obvious he didn't commit the crime."

Jerry said, "That does it then. The charges will be dropped."

Fred grimaced. "You're right, but it's not so straight forward. There's still the problem of admissibility. The prosecution will object and try to get this thrown out. It'll be up to the Judge. We must convince him this evidence is both reliable and applicable."

Jerry thought a minute. "I'm going to see Judge Peabody on Monday, if possible, and request a pre-trial hearing about this data. Maybe I can keep Robert out of the trial."

"Good idea."

Jerry requested copies of the entire file. Neal promised to have the materials by Monday afternoon. "I'd do it now, but our office is really hurting. Most of the staff couldn't get in because of the snow and the holiday break."

Fred, taking advantage of his reputation in Neal's mind, asked, "Do you know if Judge Peabody has experience with DNA type evidence?"

"He does. We had a trial fourteen months ago in which the prosecution tried to use DNA."

"You mean Peabody wouldn't allow the stuff to be admitted?"

Neal nodded. "That's right. Something about improper handling of the samples by the police. I wasn't that close to it, but Peabody believed the information wasn't accurate."

Fred turned to Jerry. "That's not exactly a plus for us. But we won't have to start at ground zero with him. He's been exposed, plus there are many more court cases now in which DNA has been utilized."

Jerry said to Neal, "I guess you haven't heard from the samples for the three other kids?"

"No, those only went in on Tuesday. Probably be three weeks before we get results."

Looking back at Neal, Fred said, "I understand skin samples were found under the fingernails of the victim. What happened to those analyses?"

Neal was flustered momentarily. "Still have them. You didn't ask for their release. The County Attorney told me to hold everything not specifically listed in the court order."

Fred scowled, his frustration evident. "I'd advise you to protect those very carefully. Those samples will become very important after Robert Jarvis is cleared and the search for the real killer begins. In addition, if the Judge refuses to allow the DNA data, we'll be back to ask about skin samples."

Neal didn't respond for a moment. He accepted Fred knew what he was talking about, and in spite of the local law enforcement people, he could be in big trouble if something went wrong with potential evidence in a murder trial.

Then Neal muttered, "No one has asked, but there were hair samples recovered from the scene, actually from the fingers of the deceased. The shading doesn't match the victim. You'd guess they were from her killer, wouldn't you? Or from an accomplice."

Fred touched Jerry's arm. "Then we must attempt matching with those three boys you've talked to."

As they turned toward the outer door, Jerry stopped and went back to where Neal was returning the materials to the file. He asked, "Did the Sheriff know about the hair found at the scene?"

Neal nodded. "I told him the day after the crime when we discussed the evidence from the scene."

When Jerry relayed the information to Fred in the car, Fred shook his head, then said, "Sounds to me like obstruction."

"I might put Talbot on the stand and let him explain."

Back at the apartment Jerry spent until noon bringing Fred up to date on his discussions with the high school students. "The trial is set to begin in less than a month." Jerry reminded Fred.

Fred said softly, "Your task is to defend Robert. If he's found not guilty, you'll be out of this."

"I know, but the tarnish on his character won't disappear until the guilty person is identified."

"That's the job of the county officials. Be careful of becoming an amateur detective and vigilante."

Jerry laughed. "You're correct, but I've been treated so shabbily by these guys, I'd take pleasure in turning the tables on them." He stopped, and rubbed a hand across his face. "You know, Fred, my hunch is the county officials responsible won't press forward to determine the guilty party if Jarvis is released. They'd likely let the matter drop and do nothing more."

"Let's see what happens. It's hard to believe they wouldn't follow through."

Jerry frowned. "Oh, I'm sure they'd go through the motions of searching for evidence, but I'd bet nothing would ever be discovered. The case would disappear after a while, then be shelved in the inactive file."

As Fred walked toward his car, Jerry called from the front door. "I'll call you about the pre-trial. You'll need to come, remember."

Jerry met with the Abrams on Friday afternoon, an appointment he'd tried to schedule several times previously. When Jack Abrams opened the door, Jerry said, "After I requested we meet, I remembered this might be a day you spend with relatives. I could do it another time."

"No, this is okay. In fact, I'd rather meet when both Janet and I can be present."

After they were seated in the comfortable living room, Jerry said, "Well, you know I'm representing Robert Jarvis. I'm talking to as many people as possible who can tell me about interactions between Kathy and Robert or between either of them and others. To be candid, I'm looking for someone who may have had a motive for committing the crime."

As Jerry spoke, the Abrams looked at each other, then at him. Jack took Janet's hand. "Mr. Preston, you're wasting your time. Everybody's convinced Jarvis did it."

Jerry didn't wish a debate on the issue. Gently, he said, "Maybe they're correct. But my task is to defend him as best I can. Let me ask about their relationship from your perspective."

Frowning, Janet said, "They liked each other or that's what Kathy told us on several occasions. But we didn't want them to be together. They were too young to understand the implications of a steady relationship, especially one involving racial mixing. We didn't want Kathy hurt by all of the negative feelings in this community or in society generally." Her hands trembled as she talked.

"So you discouraged them?"

She said, "We tried our best to stop any contact beyond the usual school activities." Her face was grim, a deeper frown. She looked at Jack who nodded.

"Did you ever talk directly to Robert?"

Jack said, "No. Kathy wanted us to meet him. She tried to persuade us we'd like him, would accept him, if we knew him on a personal level."

"You disagreed?"

Janet said, "Actually we met him briefly after a football game last year. We were waiting for Kathy. She brought him over, still in his game uniform. But we didn't talk to him, only said hi."

"Everyone raves about his athletic ability."

Jack responded. "He's a fine player no doubt, and his teachers say he's quite intelligent. But that's beside the point as far as a relationship with our daughter was concerned."

"He has a bright future."

The Abrams looked at each other and shrugged. Jack said, "Kathy told us he was a good person, but there were more important considerations."

"You have any thoughts or ideas about what happened the night of the crime?'

Jack said, "We've talked about it some, when our emotions don't take over. We're convinced Robert did it. Ross Talbot and "Red" Williams say they have sufficient evidence to convict." His hands became fists. "Sooner, the better. We need to get this behind us and try to move on with our lives."

Jerry waited for a moment, then said, "Of course, one of the obvious flaws in the case against Robert is the fact that a car was involved, but Robert doesn't have access to a vehicle. Haven't you considered that might implicate someone else?" Jerry didn't want to reveal the outcome of the DNA tests, concerned the information would get to Ledbetter and others before the judge ruled on admissibility. He pushed aside the temptation to convince the Abrams of Robert's innocence.

"Both the Sheriff and Williams believe he had an accomplice. At one time, Talbot suggested they'd actually walked to the park, but that seems unlikely to me. I suspect they're correct about an accomplice." Jack walked around the room as he spoke.

Jerry didn't wish to reveal his knowledge about the three kids who had seen Robert and Kathy at Elm and Ninth. He asked. "Was there anyone who might have disliked Kathy to the point of setting out to scare her and the prank got out of control?"

"No, not possible."

"Or perhaps a boy who was so infatuated with her he couldn't tolerate her relationship with Robert?"

They looked at each other, obviously never having considered the possibility. Janet said, "Not to my knowledge. She never talked about anyone who'd stalked or pestered her."

The Abrams were convinced Robert was the guilty party and nothing would influence them to consider alternatives. Jerry wanted to give them some empathy, knowing they were going through agony over the loss of Kathy, especially under the circumstances. But he didn't want to tell them about his theory and the accumulating evidence supporting his hunch, including the opinion of Fred about the DNA analyses. Then there were those hair samples that might become crucial.

Louise was sitting in her robe, reading the local paper when Fred returned to the motel room after his jaunt to Pineville. He walked over and kissed her.

"I take it things went okay," she said, standing to lean against him.

"I'm more optimistic than I've ever been about Robert's fate." He told her about the analyses and the possibility of charges being dropped at a pre-trial hearing. "We'll know at that point how the Judge is thinking."

"I made reservations at a restaurant tonight. Thought we should get out. Otherwise, what'll people think."

He shrugged his shoulders and grinned. "I'll have a shower and change clothes."

When he came from the bathroom, Louise was dressed in a black and white dress hemmed slightly above the knees. Fred gawked, "Wow, the dress is very nice. You look great."

"I thought I shouldn't lose your attention." She walked closer to him and handed him a box. "This tie will go nicely with your suit."

"Thanks. I haven't bought new clothes for quite some time. Guess they're getting sorta threadbare." He held the tie out for a better inspection.

"I'll help you refurbish during one of these trips."

He continued to look at her. "Sure you don't want to do room service again."

CHAPTER TWELVE

On Monday morning after the Thanksgiving break, Jeff, a doctoral student from Tennessee, stuck his head in Fred's office as he returned the telephone to its cradle. "Dr. Ferriday, here's the corrected draft of my dissertation. You wanted to see it again."

Fred stood to take the thick sheaf of paper. "I'd like to scan through it one last time before the Examining Committee members get it. Let's be sure there are no errors. Sometimes a small mistake gets blown out of proportion and some guy gets the idea the entire research is flawed. Then we spend twenty minutes arguing about nothing."

Jeff shuffled his feet. "I think it's okay."

Fred looked at the young man, dark circles around his eyes. "You must have worked hard over the break?"

"No break this year. I'm trying to finish as soon as possible since the post-doc offer from Texas. I'd like to get there as soon as possible." He grinned. "The stipend is better than an assistantship."

Fred flipped through the pages. "I'll put it on your desk by tomorrow morning. Then you can copy it and give it to everyone on your Examining Committee."

Glancing at his watch, Fred said, "I have to meet Audrey in the conference room. She's practicing her talk for the meetings in New York. Why don't you join us? You might notice things neither of us catch."

205

Jeff nodded. "Okay, but I thought she'd gone through the talk last week."

"She did, but we changed several statements and took out two slides. She had too much material for the time allotted." Most national meetings ran on a strictly controlled schedule with timers warning speakers two minutes ahead of your end and another at the termination of the allotted time. Session chairs broke in to stop your presentation if you ran over, an embarrassment Fred didn't want his protégés to encounter.

Audrey presented her paper as though it was the actual audience, established scientists from all over the nation and hordes of graduate students figuring out how her work impacted their own, at the national meeting. Jeff and Fred sat quietly, listening, making a couple of notes about potential alterations. Fred forced himself to focus, his mind tending to drift to the trial in Pineville, the trial, and his relationship with Louise.

When Audrey finished, precisely at the nine minute mark, the time allocated for the presentation, Fred said, "I like it. You're ready." He clapped his hands softly.

Audrey smiled. "It seems okay, but maybe I'll change one sentence about the conclusions related to the third slide. Let me read that to you again and see what you think."

Audrey repeated the section, then indicated how she might alter it. Fred nodded and looked at Jeff, who added, "Your change is an improvement. Good."

She smiled. "Now all I have to do is live through the presentation at the meeting."

Louise's concerns about their relationship were elevated when Bill Rinehart called Fred on Tuesday inviting him to lunch. They met at their usual table in the Faculty Club. After they ordered the soup and sandwich special for the day, Bill said, "I called Thanksgiving to invite you for dinner on Saturday following, but you weren't there."

"I'd gone to Pine County."

"We wanted you to meet Irma Fessler, the woman I've spoken about. She works with Stella in the library."

Fred said, "That was nice of you to think about me, but I don't know."

"Stella's sure you'll be interested. She describes Irma as nice looking, good personality, and both of you work at the university so there's a common interest." He paused as though letting his argument impact Fred's reluctance, then said, "We'd like to have you Friday, since we missed before."

Fred hated to disappoint his friend, but his emotions were too focused on Louise to think about another woman. "I appreciate it. But the fact is, I'm involved with someone at the moment." He continued to eat soup, not looking at Bill.

Bill stopped eating, grinning. "That's nice, but I didn't know. Who is she?"

"Louise Bull, someone I knew in Pineville."

His face clouding, Bill asked, "She's related to Joshua, this old buddy of yours?"

"His sister. Five years younger."

"How serious are you?"

"Bill, I don't know." He shrugged and grinned. "We've only known each other a few weeks, although she was around when Joshua and I played together years ago."

Rinehart concentrated on his food for a time, obviously thinking about his next statement. Laying aside his fork, he said, "Fred, don't take this wrong. You've known me a long time and understand my feelings about minorities. But marriage or a long term relationship could pose some challenges you've never encountered before. If you think about it, our society is not as accepting of racial mixing as we'd like to believe."

Surprised and disappointed in Bill's reaction, he said, "Louise has said the same thing. She keeps telling me how hard it is for blacks and whites to mix, how hurtful it might become for both of us. But, to be honest, I'm very attracted to her." He scratched his head and chin. "I believe the feeling is mutual. I'm confident we'd be strong enough to live with the problems." He stopped, drinking from the coffee cup, "But it may never get that far."

"My experience," Bill hesitated, as though not sure he should say what he intended, "is most mixed relationships are a disaster. I had these classmates from my graduate class who dated some. He was black and she white. Both were nice intelligent people, but everybody around seemed to resent them being together. I must admit I didn't like it much myself, but I tried not to make an issue of it. Figured it was their business."

Looking up from his soup, Fred asked, "I assume they broke it off?"

"After a year, but they'd gotten to the place they resented each other and everyone around them. She left the program and moved to California."

When Fred didn't respond, Bill seemed to recognize Fred's discomfort with the discussion. He said, "You understand I don't have a personal basis for talking about this issue, but would you talk to Roger Kerr? He's a faculty member in the History department and is married to a Black. They seem happy enough, but they don't socialize a lot. He'll be straight forward with you. As your friend, I don't want you to jump too quickly."

Fred grinned, easing the tension, "Last time, you wanted me to leap pretty fast." He continued, "As I said, it may not work out. Louise is worried I don't understand the implications. Now you're telling me the same thing."

"All the more reason to talk with Kerr. At least, he has some experience with the situation."

Returning to his office across the campus in a swirling wind with flakes of snow, Fred continued to think about Bill's reaction. Bill could be blunt and sometimes overstate the problems, but he'd never given Fred poor advice. Probably a good idea to talk with Kerr. He'd call him for lunch in a few days. Maybe he should meet Irma Fessler. Couldn't hurt anything. During the few days since seeing Louise, he'd realized he'd thought more about females than he had since Martha died. He grinned to himself thinking his dormant biological system had been awakened. He called Rinehart to ask if he could change his mind and have dinner and meet Irma on Friday.

In mid-afternoon, Jerry Preston called to let him know a pretrial hearing had been set for the following Wednesday, the first week of December.

Jerry said, "I'm preparing a motion for dismissal of charges based on the DNA results. That'll lead to an argument over the admissibility of the samples from the scene. I'm planning to call you as an expert witness for the defense."

Thinking about the continuing impact of the case on his own agenda, Fred said, "I'll rearrange my schedule to come. I hope it can be done in one day. My lab is busy now and the end of the semester is close. There's always more work with deadlines for grades, and graduate students defending their theses or dissertations."

"I can't predict how it'll go. It'll depend on how much the County Attorney battles my motion and how much explanation the Judge will demand."

"Let's hope Peabody has an open mind. His denying the use of DNA in a previous trial doesn't bode well, but we don't know the circumstances."

Fred met Roger Kerr at the Club for lunch on Thursday. He'd indicated Bill Rinehart had suggested the meeting when he'd called. Since they didn't know each other, the conversation dealt with teaching loads, research work, time at the university, and weather, while they ordered and waited for the food. Kerr, middle aged, slightly overweight, balding, thick glasses, pleasant and congenial, talked about his research and a forthcoming book on the presidency of Grover Cleveland and asked about Fred's DNA investigations.

As they began the meal, Fred said, "As I said when I called, Bill suggested you could give me advice about a mixed race marriage. He's concerned about me since I'm in a relationship with a black woman."

Roger laughed lightly. "Bill's a worrier, but a good friend. He called me about you." He sipped his coffee, then continued, "Dora and I have been married for fifteen years. We met in graduate school at Berkeley."

Fred waited for Roger to continue. "For the most part, we've been happy together. Our marriage has worked out well. We have two children whom we worry about, but they're too young yet to give much attention to our race differences and their own unique characteristics. And thus far there haven't been problems for them with classmates."

"Bill and Louise, the woman I'm seeing, are both worried about the reactions of friends and colleagues. Louise argues that I'll not understand how people might respond until I've been hurt."

Roger wiped a napkin across his mouth, "She may have seen a side of those relationships we haven't. In some ways, university communities are different, especially a large place like this one. Everyone is accustomed to mixing with cultures and ethnic backgrounds from all over the world. Mixed marriages are accepted more readily than in other parts of our society, particularly in small communities sheltered somewhat from diverse populations."

"Have you felt shunned or ignored or worse?"

"A few times." Roger thought for several seconds while he sipped coffee. "Neither of our families are comfortable with us, even after all the years we've been together and the close associations we've tried to maintain with them. They don't make an issue of it anymore, but you can feel they're always tense. Dora's parents expected her to marry a black and were disappointed when she hooked up with me. My parents' reactions were worse. At first, my father wouldn't speak to me. Took him three years to get over his anger, or maybe he was hurt. We'll never have the same relationship we had before."

"Colleagues?"

"History people are okay with us and they're the ones I deal with for the most part. But, you know," he chuckled, "characters in the social sciences are expected to be odd. Dora is an Associate Prof in mathematics and is accepted as readily as any of her peers."

Roger paused, thoughtful. "It's probably a touch different than being married to a person of the same race, but I don't perceive any reluctance on the part of my colleagues to interact with us. They seem to accept us without reservations. We're invited into their homes and they visit ours. I can't say if it would be different married to a person of the same race, but it might. It's another thing you might worry about. And the way most marriages turn out these days with the divorce rate through the ceiling, it could be a final straw you can't get past."

"You'd do it again. I mean, marry Dora?"

Roger chuckled. "Without a doubt. We've grown closer over the years. I'd be lost without her." He went on, wishing to explain to Fred as many of his feelings as possible. "Where we've received the shuns and adverse reactions have been in society generally. Sometimes in a restaurant, you'll recognize, all of a sudden, everyone at another table is staring at you. Or the waiter will have a strange smirk on his face. Or you're given a table next to the kitchen door when others are obviously available."

He smiled, rubbing a hand across his eyes. "But strangely, the most unpleasant reaction came from people in a small church we attended for a short while when we first came here. We were ignored. No one would sit in the same pew if possible; then no closer than absolutely necessary. It was an unnerving experience. I talked to the minister, thinking he might provide some advice about becoming welcomed into the congregation, only to discover he was no more accepting of us than the congregation. So we stopped going and now attend services at the large Methodist church in Champaign."

Fred grinned. "So much for Christian understanding and acceptance."

Roger laughed and nodded, then said, "My only regret is losing the closeness to my parents, but that might have happened with a different spouse if they didn't like her. Who knows?"

Fred looked at his watch, and picked up the check from the middle of the table. "You've been helpful. Thanks for meeting with me. Any last advice?"

Roger pushed back his chair. "If you really have deep feelings for Louise and she feels the same way, you'll be fine in spite of the minor issues bound to confront you. But I've known several couples who couldn't cope with the little things, ended up blaming each other, and divorced. I suspected they didn't have sufficient commitment to the marriage and to each other. I knew one couple, both rebels of sorts, who I always believed hooked up because it went against the usual practice of our society. I could have been wrong, but I don't think so. They've been together for twenty years and appear to be happy."

On the outer steps, Fred asked, "If I get Louise to visit, would you and Dora be interested in having dinner with us?"

"Sure, we'd like to."

Fred didn't know if the conversation had been useful or confusing as he walked back to his office. But perhaps the Kerr's could become a haven of advice for Louise and him, if this really worked out. He'd been surprised, even a bit miffed, at Rinehart's concern, but had tried to pass it off as a friend thinking about his best interest. But Bill would have not expressed reservation had the female been white, only congratulations and best wishes, perhaps joking comments about sexual relationships. Colleagues less open-minded than Bill might ignore or even object to a mixed couple. At least, he didn't have a potential problem with family.

When Fred arrived at the Rineharts on Friday evening, the Merrys, a couple from the English department whom he'd met with Martha at some university function several years before, and Irma Fessler were already present. Bill took away his coat and introduced him to the others, unaware he knew the Merrys. Fred thought everyone watched for his reaction to Irma and likely hers to him. A short, slim woman, maybe five-two, with dark hair and blue eyes, perhaps mid-forties, Irma returned his smile.

During dinner talk centered around university events, the failure of the football team, the promise of a better performance from the basketball squad, and the issue of a longer drop period for students. In response to Bill's prompting, Fred talked about his research on forensics and the biological sciences. Everyone seemed interested, probably he decided, because none of the others ever dealt with laboratory analyses associated with gruesome crimes or they'd read in the newspaper about the increasing use of DNA in forensics. But maybe they were just being polite.

In the living room with brandy, Fred sat across from Irma and could observe her without attracting obvious attention. She wore a conservative gray dress, black heels. She was a nice looking woman and joined the conversation easily, laughing with the others, injecting ideas and information without forcing. Fred found himself comparing her to Louise. His nerves hadn't leaped at her touch when they shook hands as they had with Louise's.

As the evening came to a close and the Merrys were leaving, Fred talked a few minutes with Irma about her work in the library. She was obviously well informed and able to articulate clearly her interest. She asked about the location of his office and lab.

After a few minutes of conversation with the Rineharts, Fred made his leave without committing to any follow-up with Irma. He thanked Bill and Stella and found his way out. He walked the short distance to his house, although the weather had turned quite cold. He thought he'd gotten past that obligation to Bill in good stead. And he acknowledged Irma was attractive and intelligent. Maybe he'd call her for lunch after he returned from Pineville. So his heart hadn't leaped. The long-term was more important and there'd be no worry about this racial thing. But his feelings for Louise were more than a passing thing. Memories of her face and laugh lingered in his mind. He looked forward to being with her. It was more than a sexual venture, although that part of the relationship was special, too.

Fred called Louise on Sunday morning. As soon as she answered, he started, "I've missed you and wondered if we could get together over the Christmas break."

"I've missed you, too. I'm planning to spend a couple of days around Christmas with Joshua and Robert since they're my only family."

"Maybe we could go somewhere between Christmas and New Years."

"I'd like to. You have anything in mind?"

"I have enough frequent flyer miles to get us about anywhere."

"Such as?"

"One of the Caribbean islands, London, Mexico, as examples. You prefer warm or cold, big city or isolation, sun or snow?"

Louise laughed, but didn't respond immediately to his suggestions, seemingly uncertain or surprised by the choices, so Fred said, "Tell you what. Visit a travel agency in the next couple of days and see what strikes your fancy. If you like, go ahead and make reservations. Just be sure the airline will honor my mileage."

"You're giving me a lot of latitude. When will you need to be back?"

Fred chuckled. "It's your show. Lots of freedom to be creative. Plan so I can be back here by January 2nd for the start of next term."

Fred told her about the scheduled pre-trial and his work for the coming time period. He promised to call again when he returned from Pineville.

As he prepared to hang up, Louise said, "I've thought about us a lot in the past few days. We are comfortable together, more than I thought possible in such a short time. I miss you when you leave and wish you could stay longer."

"Louise, what we have together is special. It's going to be fine." But Rinehart's comments and facial expression at lunch continued to linger.

Jerry had tried to set up a meeting with Gil Brown, but each time he'd been unsuccessful. Earl Sloan had invited Gil for a pizza, but Gil had declined, and told Earl to leave him alone. An attempt to use Donald Payne to arrange something had backfired. As soon as Preston's name was mentioned, Gil turned pale and walked away.

Finally, Jerry called the Brown home and asked for Gil without identifying himself, hoping the woman who answered would assume he was one of Gil's high school classmates. When Gil came on the line, Jerry said, "Gil, I'd like to talk to you sometime about Kathy Abrams. I'm trying to visit with any student who might have known her or Robert Jarvis. Could we get together soon?"

Gil asked, "Who is this?"

Tempted to mislead him, Jerry thought better of his fleeting notion. He said, "I'm the attorney representing Robert Jarvis."

"No. I won't see you. Don't call again."

Jerry injected quickly, thinking Gil would hang up. "So you'd rather talk for the first time from the witness chair?"

Following a pause of seconds, Gil said, "I'll see what my father thinks first." The line went dead.

An hour later, the telephone rang in the apartment. When Jerry answered, a deep voice responded. "It's Harold Brown. You are not to call my son again." Jerry could feel the tension and anger.

"Harold, I'm probably going to call Gil as a witness in the Jarvis trial. He'll be forced to testify. I've offered to review the situation with him, but he's resisted. It might be less stressful if he understands what's coming."

"I don't know what you're up to. He knows nothing about the circumstances, so his testimony will be a waste of time and tax payers' money." Brown's tone changed, almost pleading, begging Jerry to drop the idea.

"Mr. Brown, I'm reasonably certain that Gil and two companions were the last to see Kathy Abrams alive, except for the killer. Their testimony may be important."

"You're guessing. Anyway, I'll not agree to Gil's meeting with you."

Jerry said, "I can obtain a subpoena if you insist."

Brown didn't respond for several seconds, then hung up. Jerry wondered if Gil had told his father about the blood and hair samples. It seemed strange Harold hadn't mentioned it. He recalled Susan's observation that Purcell and Ledbetter had spent more time together since the crime, but he couldn't see any connection, unless the three kids had actually seen the attack. He erased quickly the fleeting notion that the three had tried to rape the girl and in the struggle had killed her, although Scott Little had fantasized about having sex with her. And his tendency to bully others might lead him to do strange things.

Jerry glanced at Fran when a knock sounded on the apartment door at ten o'clock. They weren't expecting anyone, but salesmen often ignored reasonable bounds of time and privacy. He shrugged, pulled on his slippers and shuffled to the door. She looked back to her magazine and cut off the TV.

As soon as Jerry turned the knob and cracked the door, two large men in ski masks charged in, knocking him backwards. Jerry scrambled to regain his balance, yelling, "What the hell?"

The larger man hit Jerry in the face, then in the chest, knocking him down. The second one grabbed Fran as she scrambled from the couch, one large hand across her mouth, the other holding her tightly around the waist and pinning her arms to her body. Her terror intensified as Jerry was kicked in the side, now hurt beyond the point of defending himself. Another kick in the side brought a low moan and unconsciousness.

Fran was paralyzed as she confronted the two. The hold on her prevented movement or yelling for help. While the one held her, the second peered at her through the slits of the mask. He grasped the top of her blouse and ripped it down to her waist. He laughed as the one holding her began to fondle her breasts and shove her bra off.

Pulling her closer, the thug growled, "Maybe we should take turns with her." He nuzzled her neck through his mask.

Surveying her form with his eyes, the second guy said, "Maybe she would like it, but let it wait for another time."

He leaned closer to her face, the strong odor of beer and cigar smoke sickening her. "Your husband has been warned. Stop asking questions about the Jarvis case or it'll be worse next time."

They pushed her onto the couch and vanished through the door.

Jerry remained flat on the floor. She tried to regain her composure, then shuddered when she did. But most of her clothes were intact. Other than the shredded blouse and the scare of her life, she seemed okay, prone on the couch where she'd been flung like a rag doll.

She crawled to where Jerry sprawled. When she put her hand on his head, he moaned and began to move his arms. She brought a wet cloth from the bathroom and wiped the blood from his head and face. Regaining his senses, he moaned, "God, what happened?"

"You've been beaten, out cold for I don't know how long."

Jerry struggled up to lean against the wall. Breathing came in painful gasps. "My side is killing me." He ran a hand down one side. "I think some ribs are broken."

Then as he became more alert, he saw Fran's blouse. He gasped. "Did they do that? What else happened?"

She said, "I'm not hurt, but they scared me to death. I thought they were going to rape me."

Jerry touched her cheek. "Did either ever say anything?"

"Yes," she nodded. "They threatened to come back if you didn't drop the questions about the Jarvis thing."

Fran went to check the lock. A piece of paper lay on the small table near the entrance. A scrawled message: *This is your last warning. Stop poking around in the Jarvis case.*

She handed it to Jerry, still sitting on the floor, leaning against the sofa.

"Those bastards." He started to walk to the couch, but the pain caused him to stop. His face contorted. He groaned.

Fran said, "I'm calling the hospital to send help."

"No, you can drive me there." He struggled to remain erect, fighting the pain in his side. He swiped sweat off his face.

With Fran supporting him, they eased to their car. Jerry flopped into the rear seat. The pain wasn't as intense when he stopped moving.

The doctor in the emergency service ordered x-rays. Two of Jerry's ribs were cracked. After a solid wrap was placed around his torso and sedatives were administered, the doctor came in. "Mr. Preston, you're lucky more damage wasn't done." He showed Jerry the x-rays, pointing out the fractures. "You'll experience some pain for several days, but it will gradually subside. Your ribs should heal completely in a few weeks. The bruises on your face may be unsightly for three to five days. Other than the scare, you'll be okay."

The medic continued, "I'm giving you a prescription to relieve the pain when it becomes intolerable. Only use these when you must."

"I assume I can work."

"No reason not to. Let the pain and your general feelings guide you. Don't push it, though." The young physician said, "You know who did this? Your wife told me what happened."

Jerry said, "I don't know who, but I know why."

"You want the hospital to bring in the Sheriff? Start an investigation? We usually do in these situations."

"No. It wouldn't go anywhere."

"You can't let it pass by without somebody looking for those guys."

"Doc, you wouldn't understand. Not sure I do either, but my hunch is the Sheriff is involved." Jerry wished he'd not blurted out his suspicions, but the damage had been done.

"Good Lord. You can't be serious."

"Never more serious in my life." Jerry weaved slowly toward the exit. "But I want you to keep it quiet for a while." He leaned against the door frame, and looked back at the physician. "If my suspicions get voiced around, things might get worse."

Leaning on Fran, he eased toward the exit and their car, leaving the physician staring with wonderment.

In the apartment, Fran said, "Shouldn't we leave here?"

Sipping water and leaning against the refrigerator, Jerry replied, "We're safe tonight. They'll wait for my reaction, see if I've been scared away."

"You should let the court assign someone else to Jarvis. It's crazy to get killed over this."

Jerry shook his head. "No, I'm going to stick it out. If I give up, they will win and Jarvis will become a victim of the sleazy bastards."

The next morning Jerry called Jim Calloway whose response after hearing of the incident with the thugs was emphatic. "Move out of Pineville. We'll find you a place in Du Quoin, if nothing more than a motel until something permanent can be found."

Calloway continued, "Are you staying with the Jarvis thing? I can assign someone to help, be the front. That is, if the judge will go along."

"I intend to stick it out, but I'm worried for Fran."

"You both could have been killed."

Jerry said, "I don't feel safe, but they're only trying to scare me this time. They were hoping I'd cave and let the verdict go against Jarvis."

Calloway said, "Pack some essentials and come here. I'll have one of the secretaries call around and find a temporary place. You can work out of the office." He paused. "Also, I'm calling the Attorney General and requesting that his office and the State Police begin to look into the Pine County system."

By two in the afternoon, Jerry and Fran were settled into a small furnished apartment in Du Quoin. They had stopped at the firm to get directions and had talked with Calloway briefly.

Jim said, "I spoke with an Assistant Attorney General. As you'd guess, they're skeptical and don't like to get involved in local affairs. But when I persisted and told him about some of the things that have gone on, he agreed to send a couple of people down to snoop around and to be present during the trial."

Fran said, "Jerry needs to get somewhere to be flat for a while. He doesn't like to admit it, but I can tell he's hurting."

"Perhaps he should check into the hospital." Calloway suggested.

Shaking his head, Jerry said, "No, I'll be okay, but I need to take it slow and easy for a few days."

Ross Talbot received a call at his home in the evening. The voice, gruff, "Preston left town around noon. We got to him this time."

"Did you follow him? Where did he go?"

"Followed them for five miles. They were headed toward Du Quoin."

CHAPTER THIRTEEN

Fred arrived in Pineville at nine-thirty Tuesday night to be present for the pre-trial session. Having driven from home after work, a day filled with meetings and deadlines, his body ached with weariness. Travel to deal with the Jarvis case had begun to take its toll on his system as well as on his agenda. He called Jerry Preston to let him know he'd made it okay and was ready for the pre-trial. But the operator cut in immediately to indicate the number no longer existed. Fred dropped the receiver, perplexed and concerned Jerry had given up the battle and ran. Then, he worried Jerry had been abducted by Ledbetter and associates. Not knowing who to call, he decided he had no choice except to show up at the pre-trial on his own. An hour later just as he prepared for bed, Jerry called his room.

Fred said, "I tried calling you. The operator said your phone has been disconnected. I didn't know how to contact you and--."

"We're living in Du Quoin." He told Fred about the confrontation with the assailants. "Bet it was the same two who attacked you."

"Probably, big guys with beards, lots of hair flying around, beady eyes. Acted tough."

Jerry replied, "I don't know. They were wearing masks, plus I was knocked out before I got a good look."

"Did you call the Sheriff?"

"After your experience, I knew it would be a waste of time."

Jerry continued, "The hearing begins at nine-thirty."

Fred was relieved it wasn't earlier. He'd have time to get his thoughts in order without getting up before dawn. But the attack on Jerry disturbed him, remembering the warnings he'd received. He wondered how far these people would go in trying to convict Jarvis. He checked the motel room door again, took a shower, then blocked a chair under the door knob, smiling to himself about his caution.

After scanning background materials about DNA fingerprinting for a few minutes, he dropped into bed and slept soundly in spite of the lumpy mattress and tense nerves.

Promptly at nine-thirty Wednesday, the bailiff escorted the lawyers and witnesses into Judge Peabody's conference room. Peabody arrived immediately and gazed around to be certain recording equipment had been readied. His sweeping glance paused momentarily when he saw the bruises on Jerry's face, but he didn't comment.

Peabody started, "I've called you together to hear statements and arguments on the motion by the defense attorney for Robert Jarvis to admit into evidence findings from samples taken by the police and the Medical Examiner from the scene of the crime. The defense contends that this information is critical."

He paused to look at notes. "Since we're a small number and all are interested in justice, I plan on being informal, but we'll have a record of everything for any who wish to review the proceedings. This hearing is for the purpose of responding to the motion regarding admissibility and is limited to statements by counsels and witnesses on that matter. Any other agenda will be out of order."

Peabody continued, "To maintain some sense of timing and order, I'm going to call one of the Deputy Sheriff's who recovered the body and articles from the scene, then have the Medical Examiner discuss his findings and handling of samples. The defense wishes to have an expert witness, Dr. Ferriday, discuss the validity of certain tests. I'll ask questions of each witness, then allow both the prosecutor and the defense to follow up on anything they believe relevant to the question of admissibility. Agreed?" He eyed the attorneys.

Jerry and Williams nodded consent.

"Then we'll start by calling Deputy John Parsons to the chair."

Parsons, dressed in a starched khaki uniform with badges and working gear in place, came from a side chair to take the seat opposite Peabody. The bailiff administered the usual swearing to tell the truth.

Peabody said, "Mr. Parsons, start by telling us how you happened to find the body of the victim and what actions you took."

Although his facial expressions didn't reveal uneasiness, Parson's voice quavered slightly as he started. "On Saturday, September 19th, the dispatcher received a call from a resident near the park. Her young son and his friend had discovered a body. She hadn't gone to the site to confirm, but had immediately called the office. Deputy Block and I were sent to the scene by the dispatcher."

"We found the victim flat on her back, her head twisted to one side, blood on her abdomen, legs and clothing. Panties were thrown on her chest and were torn." Parsons gulped water from the glass near him on the table. "We called the Medical Examiner's office. When the assistant came, we collected the loose clothing and loaded the body into the ambulance. We searched the site for other evidence. One set of tire tracks near the body appeared to be recent. Several others tracks had occurred before the last rain."

When it became clear Parsons wasn't going to say more, Peabody asked, "You took pictures of the scene?"

"Yes sir. The County Attorney has them now."

"Did you attempt to make impressions of the tire tracks?"

"No sir. We thought it wouldn't tell us anything because of the grassy covering."

"Tell us how you handled the clothing at the scene." Peabody's stare fixed on Parson's face as though he expected confusion.

"I used a ballpoint pen to pick up the panties and place them in a plastic bag. That was sealed and turned over to the Medical Examiner. Deputy Block picked up a sweater from the ground near the body up by the top, what would be the neck or shoulder area, and put it into a larger bag. The M.E. took it, also."

"How much dirt was on the articles of clothing?"

Parsons reviewed notes, and looked up. "None on the panties. The sweater had some dust and pieces of grass, but I wouldn't describe it as dirty."

Peabody broke his own rule about restricting questions to admissibility. "In your judgment, was the crime committed at the park?"

"Didn't appear like it to us. The placement of the panties indicated they'd been dropped after the body was on the ground. The sweater had been thrown aside about two feet away from the body. We figured the victim had worn the sweater but took it off in a car or someone had stripped it off her."

Peabody turned to James Williams, the County Attorney. "Jim, any questions?"

Williams relaxed back in his chair, but asked, "Could you be certain the clothing had not been touched or moved by the kids who found her?"

"There was no way to tell for sure, but they said they hadn't touched anything."

"That's all, Your Honor, "Williams smiled.

"Mr. Preston, what about the defense?"

Jerry remembered the conversation about Peabody's concern of proper handling of samples at the crime scene. He asked, "Were the articles of clothing wet?"

Parsons responded after glancing at his notes. "They were dry. We arrived in the middle of the afternoon, so any dew from the night before would've dried. It hadn't rained in three days."

"You're satisfied the body and the clothing were properly handled so essential evidence would not be destroyed or distorted?" Jerry wanted to look at Peabody, but he focused on Parsons.

"Yes. We followed established procedures."

"Had the body been moved? That is, you didn't observe any signs of it being dragged across the ground, such as crushed grass nearby?"

Parsons considered for about five seconds. "It appeared her feet had been dragged a short distance, maybe eighteen to twenty inches, but there were no marks to suggest the body had been moved after being placed in the position we found her. We didn't observe obvious dirt on the back when we lifted the body onto the stretcher. If she had been pulled along the ground, some dirt would have been ingrained into the clothing. Neither had the grass near her been crushed. We saw none of that."

"You're suggesting that had the body been moved, the clothing would have been much dirtier?"

"Yes. Unless she had been picked up and carefully placed down. That would have taken a strong person or maybe two. We speculated someone had taken her under the shoulders and pulled her along for a couple of steps."

"What made you think the feet had been dragged?"

"Looked like the heels of her shoes had dug into the soil. The tracks looked like shoe marks, like when you scuff your foot through the dirt. Also the heels and backs of the shoes were caked with dirt and bits of grass."

"Describe for us the clothing. What type of garments, shoes, other apparel?"

Parsons flipped a couple of pages in his spiral pad. "I've described the clothes in my notes, made at the scene, as typical high school. Gold sweater with Pine County High inscribed, dark green skirt, oxford type shoes, white ankle socks." He looked up from the pad.

"Was the clothing torn?" Jerry knew he was pushing the boundary of questions relevant to admissibility, but Peabody seemed interested.

"The panties were ripped. Nothing else was torn or ripped."

"Disheveled?"

"The skirt had been twisted around quite a bit. The zipper was out of its normal place, almost in front rather than the side or back"

"But you couldn't make any judgments about what had happened?"

"Not really." Parsons seemed more comfortable with Jerry's easy manner and no longer reviewed notes prior to each response. He volunteered, "I'd guess there had been a tussle, the way the skirt was twisted and the panties ripped, but I'd be speculating some."

Jerry smiled. "Thank you. That's all I have at this time."

Peabody called the Medical Examiner, who went through the same swearing in process as the deputy before taking the chair at the end of the table.

Peabody instructed, "Tell us the condition of the body and the clothing when you received them. Then tell us what you did afterwards."

Henry Neal had done this many times. He approached the task with confidence, a slight arrogance in his voice. "I was called to take care of the body around four on the afternoon of September 19th. As Deputy Parsons stated, the clothing collected at the scene had been sealed in two separate bags. I examined those articles using plastic gloves and replaced them in the bags. Stored them in the walk-in freezer to preserve any fluids. I examined the body carefully and determined the cause of death was a broken neck. A deep bruise indicated she'd been hit a heavy blow across the right side of the neck."

"Are you certain of the cause of death?"

"Yes. The spinal column was snapped between the third and fourth cervical vertebrae. Death would have been instant."

"Any other tissue samples, blood, semen, on the body itself?"

"Blood and semen on the legs and around the vagina. I washed the fluids into plastic containers and put them in the freezer."

"Did you separate blood from semen?"

"Yes. I washed the semen away from the blood as carefully as possible."

"But there might have been some mixing."

"It's possible. But the crime lab will separate the two by more sophisticated techniques than I have here."

"In your opinion, had the victim been raped?"

"I suspected rape had been attempted because of the bruises on her face and shoulders and damage to the tissues near the vagina, but actual penetration had not occurred. It's clear she'd not had sexual intercourse recently prior to death."

"How can you be certain about attempted rape?"

"As I said before, I found a substantial amount of semen near the vagina."

Peabody was searching for something. "Any other evidence? Materials, hair, skin, such things, which might suggest a struggle?"

Neal toyed with his small notebook for a moment. "I found skin under the fingernails of the victim. And I found several strands of hair in her fingers and on her clothing."

"I assume you've preserved those things?"

"Yes."

"In your opinion, have the various specimens, clothing, so forth, been treated in such a manner that accepted testing methods would provide reliable results?"

"Yes, appropriate measures were exercised to avoid contamination and to ensure stability of the samples."

"What samples were sent to the State Crime Lab for analyses?"

Neal squirmed a bit before responding. "The clothing and the fluids washed from the body. Then later, we submitted the hair and the skin samples."

Peabody's face changed color, darkening slightly. "Why didn't you send those when you turned in the clothing and blood?"

"Those were not requested in your order, so I've continued to hold them. But, later, we were told to submit those also. We have done that, but results have not been returned yet."

Peabody turned to face the County Attorney. "Mr. Williams, I'm disappointed you've not taken the initiative to move forward with appropriate testing of all relevant potential evidence. It's rather unusual in my experience to sit on evidence which may be important in determining the truth about a crime, especially one as serious as murder." He stopped, examined his notes, looked again at Williams and then toward Neal. "It may not be important for the motion we're dealing with today, but I want a full written explanation for this negligence within a week. Now I recall it required a request from the defense to get moving with those pieces of evidence."

Neither Williams nor Preston had questions for the Medical Examiner. Peabody looked at his watch. "I'd suggest holding Dr. Ferriday's statement until this afternoon to avoid interrupting him for the lunch break. Let's stop now, but return promptly at one o'clock. I'd like to complete the hearing by normal closing time today."

Fred and Jerry walked down the street to Rosie's Grill and ordered the daily special, thinking it'd be the fastest thing. Jerry asked, after the waitress had taken the orders, "Any surprises? This is my first experience. I wasn't quite sure what to expect."

"It's fairly typical. Peabody is honing in on sample handling. I suspect if there's the slightest inkling of mishandling, he'll dismiss your motion. That seems to be his primary concern."

"Do judges typically not trust this sort of evidence?"

"I'm not sure I'm the one to ask, but remember it's relatively new stuff. No one has much experience, so it's natural to harbor doubts about the validity."

Jerry ran his hand through his hair, wincing when he raised his arm. "What puzzles me is the apparent proper, even cautious, handling of samples, then the failure to follow through with any analyses and attempts to match those results to Jarvis."

Fred placed the chicken sandwich on the small plate. "My guess is the deputies and Neal did their jobs before Ledbetter and his cronies, whoever they are, pressured the system. They believed they could squash the evidence and avoid it coming to light. They wanted to try the case just on testimonies putting Robert with the girl, which pinned the crime squarely on Robert Jarvis."

"Maintain the focus on Robert, thus avoiding any substantial search for additional clues which might divert attention."

"That's how I'd read it. Knowing what we know now."

"Interesting reaction by Peabody when he remembered Neal had sat on some samples until the second court order."

"Yes, but I don't know enough about the legal system to know what he can do about it. Maybe raising a bit of hell is enough to scare Neal and the County Attorney's office." Fred downed the last of the soft drink. "A guy in Williams' shoes can't afford to make Peabody angry or let him believe the C.A.'s office is not interested in justice. Every time he'd appear in Peabody's court in the future, he'd be under suspicion. He'd have to work a lot harder to obtain a favorable ruling."

Jerry thought aloud, "It may be pushing the limits a bit, but I wonder if Peabody would consider obstruction of justice on the part of Williams and Talbot."

"Maybe, I just don't know how all that works. They sure as hell haven't done anything to find the truth, but obstruction, who knows."

As they walked back, Fred asked, "How are you? I can tell you're in pain, the way you're so careful and deliberate when you move."

"Hurts more as the day progresses. But it's getting better each day and I'm trying to wean myself off the pain medication. I've heard you can get hooked on the stuff."

"I'd like to sit down with you and Fran and compare notes on those two guys. Before all this is over, I want to determine who masterminded their little escapades."

"Maybe tonight. Fran remembers more than I."

Everyone was in place when Peabody returned to the conference room as the clock in the dome of the building struck one.

He observed, smiling. "Right on the dot." He turned to Fred and said, "Dr. Ferriday, we appreciate your appearing today. I've tried to find out about your background. It's interesting you were originally from Pine County and now have been called as an expert witness. Strikes me as unusual. Nevertheless, we'll hear your testimony now, following the same guidelines used this morning."

After Fred had taken his place at the table, Peabody said, "For the record, talk about your interest and experience with DNA fingerprinting."

"I've worked with DNA for several years as scientists have tried to understand the basic mechanisms of gene function and how the compound replicates. I'd thought some about its potential in forensics, but hadn't done anything of consequence until the case in England broke. I worked with those scientists for a few weeks to learn their techniques. Since then, I've done experiments on the stability of DNA under various conditions and have consulted with crime labs in the development of their analytical methods."

Peabody said, "Interesting. Tell us about the results of the analyses in this case and what, in your opinion, the data mean."

Looking at Peabody, Fred said, "On the Friday following Thanksgiving, Mr. Neal shared with Mr. Preston and me the information from the State Crime Lab. We made copies for additional study. If you can accept the predominant thinking of several leading scientists about DNA, those results demonstrate without a doubt that Robert Jarvis could not have been the individual involved in the attempted rape. And if he did not assault her, it seems highly unlikely he could be connected to the murder of Kathy Abrams. I'm stating this conclusion because the DNA patterns for Jarvis and the samples of semen and blood taken from the victim's body are quite different."

Williams leaned forward and began to rise, ready to challenge the statement, but Peabody raised his hand. "You'll have an opportunity to ask questions at the proper time, Mr. Williams."

"Explain briefly the procedure employed. I've looked at the comparisons, but I'll admit I don't understand what those various lines and bands mean."

"How much detail would you like?" Fred knew it might take a long time if he started with basic biology and the genetic code, but he wanted to educate Peabody.

"You decide where to begin. If I want more, I'll ask." Peabody smiled.

"DNA is a huge and complicated structure. It's composed of four bases or nucleotides repeated in different combinations hundreds of times and hooked together to make a very large structure. It contains the genetic code for each individual. Every person has a different DNA; that is, the nucleotides are arranged in somewhat different order for each person in some parts of the larger structure. There may be only small differences of configurations within the larger substance, but there's enough variation to clearly identify an individual. The only time you will find matching DNA's is with identical twins.

"In the laboratory, the DNA is placed in a solution and divided into fragments using a biological agent called a restriction enzyme. The enzyme cuts pieces of DNA based on the recognition of specific nucleotide combinations. Because each person's DNA is different, and the sequence of nucleotides vary, the DNA's are cut into different lengths and compositions.

"Those pieces or fragments are separated by an electrophoresis procedure on gels. The fragments migrate at different rates because of size and make-up, thus separating the various pieces on the gel plate. For example, the small fragments move faster than the larger ones and accumulate at one end of the plate. The larger pieces move more slowly. Then the fragments are stained to make them more visible and photographs are taken.

"What you see on the sheets given to us from the State Crime Lab are the photos of the stained gels. The lines or bands represent fragments of DNA. When the lines or fragments from different samples match, we know the DNA came from the same person. When they don't match precisely or correspond to the same position on the gel, we know the DNA's are from different individuals."

Fred stopped, then said, "That's a brief explanation of the process and what the bands on the photographs mean."

"Thank you. That was helpful. But, I'd like to know the possibility of random chance or just happenstance matching of DNA from different people."

"Based on all the evidence presented in the scientific literature, chances of identical matching are astronomical. For example, the changing of one genetic coding molecule will result in different fragmentation of the DNA by the enzyme. So it's virtually impossible to obtain a random match."

Peabody asked, "In your opinion, what are the most important criteria for admissibility of this sort of information?"

Fred pondered the question, one he'd never been asked before. "It's a good question, Judge. In my experience there are two key considerations. First, the reliability and predictability of the tests and analyses in the opinions of scientists working in the field. Second, the proper handling of samples by law enforcement and lab personnel, particularly the latter."

"In your judgment, have those criteria been satisfied in this specific case?"

"Yes. Handling seems to have been properly accomplished at the scene and by the Medical Examiner. I have substantial confidence in the Crime Lab, so I think there'd be no question about appropriate analyses. DNA typing or finger printing is now regarded with respect and confidence by the scientific community."

"I've heard some laboratories do pretty sloppy work. Why do you have such confidence in the State Crime Lab?"

Fred smiled. "Two reasons. I've worked with them a lot and know their techniques are first-rate. Second, several of the people were trained in my lab at Illinois. They do good work."

Peabody chuckled. "So you'd have to express support." He turned to The County Attorney. "Any questions, Jim?"

Williams leaned on the table. "Tell me about contamination of samples. Such as the presence of dirt, grease, etc. Any effect on the analyses?"

"DNA is remarkably stable. Contaminants don't destroy the integrity of the molecule. The usual problem encountered in forensics is cleaning away the gunk, but it's possible with accepted lab procedures, to still obtain reliable data." He didn't volunteer that he was actively researching this question at the present time.

"You will remember Deputy Parson testifying in this case the body had been exposed overnight, probably became wet from the dew, then dried again. Would those conditions alter the analyses?"

"No. DNA would not be affected."

"Mr. Neal testified about separating semen from blood. If this cannot be accomplished, can we rely on the information?"

"It's possible to separate the fluids based on accepted procedures. If for some reason you cannot, and the fluids come from different individuals, the results could be misleading." Fred understood his response might place doubts in Peabody's thinking, but he had no option.

"What if they were not separated cleanly in this case? That might be enough doubt to deny admissibility." Williams had found the flaw he'd looked for.

"Then," Fred said, "I'd go back to the skin and hair samples. DNA from those tissues has not been contaminated or mixed and would serve as a reliable marker."

Williams hesitated as he thought about Fred's recommendation, than asked, "Go back to your first statement about these results indicating without doubt the innocence of Robert Jarvis. Do you hold to that? It's quite a positive conclusion based on a set of photographs of a biological substance."

"I do stick with the statement. Those DNA data don't lie. Samples from the scene and from Jarvis are clearly not a match." Fred paused. "In retrospect, I shouldn't have said that during this hearing on admissibility. I apologize for overstepping the limits established by Judge Peabody. Nevertheless, I'd testify to the same effect during a trial."

"Would results from the scene assist in identifying the real killer or killers if it's not Jarvis?"

"Yes, if you can obtain samples from potential suspects and compare them with the samples from the scene." Fred added. "That's assuming the killer is not a known criminal. As you know, there's beginning to be a national file of DNA scans for some habitual offenders. Matches often identify the real criminal and frees an individual wrongly charged."

"It's fair to assume the blood or some of the blood came from the victim?" Asked Williams.

"Absolutely. Without doubt, some or all of the blood was from the victim. But the semen came from the attacker. My guess is hair and skin are from the attacker also."

"Can you match DNA from blood and semen, two different fluids?"

"Yes. DNA for the person will be the same in all of their tissues or fluid cells."

Peabody interrupted, "Jim, these questions seem to be asking for information already given. Do you have other questions about admissibility?"

Williams reviewed notes on the table, flipping through several pages of a yellow pad. "No, I don't have further queries."

"Mr. Preston?"

"Nothing, your Honor."

Peabody looked at everyone. "I appreciate the manner in which this has gone. We've been exposed to a lot of information related to the biological samples as potential evidence in a trial. I'll want a few days to review the transcript and perhaps consult with others before making a ruling on the motion."

Jerry raised his hand. "Judge Peabody, I'm sure you remember the trial date is less than two weeks away."

Peabody smiled. "I do. You'll know my answer in ample time." He looked thoughtful. "By the way, Mr. Preston, I'd like to visit with you a few minutes if you have time."

Peabody stood, collected papers from the desk, and moved through the rear door without glancing back.

In the lobby of the building, Jerry said, "It seemed to go okay."

Fred responded, nodding. "Think so. We did all we could to convince him to allow use of the biological evidence."

"If you're staying overnight, come have dinner with Fran and me."

He glanced at his watch. "It's not quite three, so I'm going to change my plans and drive home. It'll give me an extra half-day in the office tomorrow." He stopped to lay his briefcase on a chair and pull on his overcoat. "How're the other pieces of the puzzle? Talked to the Brown boy yet?"

"No. I'm stymied with that. You know something I just thought about. It was right after I called Brown's that Fran and I were attacked."

"Who'd you talk to?"

"Mostly the father. He made it clear I wouldn't get to Gil."

"So you'll have to subpoena him."

"I've been considering calling as witnesses all three of the kids who saw Kathy and Robert. They could confirm seeing them at a point away from the place where the body was found. Plus, she was no longer with Robert when they saw her. That testimony alone might be enough to get him off or at the least place some doubts in the minds of the jurors."

"So you'd use that as a way to get them on the stand and then raise other questions."

"Yeah. The problem is the Judge may not allow me to raise enough questions to begin to implicate others. You know if Williams is influenced by Ledbetter, he'd object."

"He's bound to be connected some way or he would have been chasing all the leads."

Nearing the cars behind the building, Fred said, "If Peabody agrees to admitting the DNA stuff, maybe you should file a motion for dismissal of all charges against

Robert. I tried to set the stage for that with my opening statement."

"Williams almost jumped over the table at your comment."

"He knew what I'd done, but it was too late. I'm not sure Peabody understood, but he'll remember if you file a motion for dismissal."

"We'll see what happens. I think I'll hear by Monday."

Fred said, "Back to the problem with talking to Brown. Why don't you see if that teacher could help? I don't know. I'm grasping for a way to get to him without letting the Ledbetter crowd know until it's a done deal."

"You mean Payne. I tried, but failed."

"Maybe Robert's friend could arrange something."

Jerry laughed. "You mean Earl. If he thought it'd help Robert, he'd drag all three of them to some site." He paused, taking a step toward the building. "But I've tried and failed with that approach, too. Those kids are fully alert now and aren't going to meet with anyone from the defense side."

"What about putting Ledbetter and Brown on the stand? They'd have to admit any tinkering with the case or face perjury."

"It could be really tricky, but I'll think about it."

Jerry knocked gently on Peabody's door and stuck his head in. "You wanted to see me?"

Peabody motioned for him to have a chair. "Yes, I've noticed you have several bruises and you're moving very gingerly. What happened?"

"A couple of thugs attacked my wife and me." He reached into his briefcase and handed the note left by the attackers to Peabody.

The Judge looked at the note, then at Jerry. "What's going on here? You told me previously your firm had fired you because of this case. Now this. I don't understand."

Jerry said, "Fred Ferriday was attacked, also, but he fared better than I. We suspect the same two guys were hired by someone to make us give up the Jarvis case."

When Peabody returned the note, Jerry continued, "I should tell you Jim Calloway has called the Attorney General's office about the series of events which have occurred in connection to this case. He's promised to send people to observe at the trial."

"Yes, a clerk from the state office called me," Peabody said. "Should I order the Sheriff to provide you protection until this thing is over?"

"Judge, both Fred and I have informed the Sheriff about the incidents. He passed both off as jokes. In fact, the two who attacked Fred were in custody for a few hours, but were released. To be honest, asking Sheriff Talbot to protect us would be a waste of time." He thought it might get him killed, but he was reluctant to reveal his fears to the judge.

Peabody shuffled a couple of folders on his desk, then looked at Jerry. "This is a different experience for me. I have the feeling, Mr. Preston, you know more about what's going on around here than you've communicated."

Jerry grinned. "I'm working on a theory. I believe it'll come clear during the trial." He paused as if thinking carefully about his next comment. He continued, "I'll probably need considerable latitude with some witnesses. They'll be hostile to my position and to the defense generally."

Peabody stroked his chin. "I can be persuaded to allow you some freedom, but there are limits." He continued to look directly into Jerry's eyes. "Why don't you bring me a list of probable witnesses and a brief summary of your planned query for each? Then I'll know where you're headed."

Jerry nodded. "I'll be glad to. That way you won't be surprised."

Jerry walked through the quiet building, thinking about Peabody's request for a list of witnesses. He might place Ledbetter and Brown on the list with questions to be asked about what they knew from the very outset. And he might call Talbot, if for nothing more than to embarrass him about the treatment and possible ignoring crucial evidence.

CHAPTER FOURTEEN

When the telephone in the small apartment rang at three a.m., Fran jerked awake, mumbled into the instrument, trying to become alert. "Who is it?" But she knew already.

A gruff male voice growled, "We know where you are. Your husband still hasn't got the message—get the hell out of the Jarvis thing or else." With a bang, the line went dead.

Jerry struggled to lean on his elbows, rubbing his face. "What's that about?" He switched the lamp on.

Fran's face was ashen. "Another warning about Jarvis. I didn't tell you, but they've called four times today. The same message each time."

"The same person each time?"

She moaned. "We have to get away from here." Visions of the two thugs tearing her clothes off and killing Jerry had reduced her resistance to the yielding point. She wanted to feel safe again.

Jerry pulled her close, rubbing her back and kissing her forehead. "We'll move and get an unlisted number this time."

"You're going to get killed before this is over."

"No, it won't go that far. They're determined to scare me to the point of caving in." He tried to sound brave for Fran's sake, but he couldn't be sure how far those bastards would go. They didn't like to be crossed and they were protecting someone.

Jerry said, "Maybe you should go to your parents until this is over. I don't want you to get hurt by these idiots."

Regaining some of her usual defiance, Fran shook her head. "No. I'm not leaving without you."

"Let's go back to bed, try to get some rest, and think about what to do in the morning." Jerry walked around the apartment, checking the doors and windows, returned to the bed, but couldn't sleep. He finally went to the couch in the living room and waited for sunrise.

After several inquiries of real estate agents the next morning, they moved three blocks to a vacant unit in a condominium, watching for the anyone who gave attention to them. Both felt like rabbits running from the hounds.

Fred focused on the word processor, his eyes moving back and forth from the scribbled corrections on the draft proposal to the text developing on the monitor. The grant to be submitted to the National Institutes of Health intended to extend the basic work within the lab on DNA replication, an area in which several graduate students were doing their research projects and depending on continued funding. Fred stopped typing for a moment and scanned back three pages to check once again the experimental approach was consistent with the objectives. The slightest flaw could sometimes be fatal in the eyes of nit-picking reviewers and agency bureaucrats. Satisfied with the wording, he scanned forward to the point where he was entering the narrative.

Completing the task, he leaned back in his chair, stretched his legs to relieve the kinks, and glanced at his watch. The night had flown past. Ten o'clock seemed a good stopping point. He felt relieved to have this job behind him. Tomorrow morning, he'd read through the entire document once more, then print it.

He placed the cover over the computer as the telephone rang. He rolled the chair away from the station so he could reach the instrument on the corner of his desk. When he answered, Louise, irritation in her voice, said, "Where've you been? I've tried to call you since noon Saturday."

Fred replied, "Here in the office and lab except for a few hours at home to sleep. How are you?"

"Worried about you. Haven't heard from you since you returned from the pre-trial hearing."

"I should have called, but I've been under the gun with deadlines. Time away for the pre-trial hearing, plus travel, has really cut into my work time. I'm digging in to avoid getting behind."

"Have you heard about Judge Peabody's decision?"

"No. I expected Preston to call, but he hasn't."

"He probably hasn't been able to find you." She stopped, then continued in a softer voice. "He'll call in the morning. I just got off the phone with Joshua. Judge Peabody has issued his ruling to allow the DNA information to be used. I assume that's good news."

Fred, still trying to put aside his thoughts about the proposal, responded. "From my perspective, it should clear Robert. To change topics again, have you been to a travel agent about Christmas?"

"I went the afternoon after we talked to an office near the school. Lots of options, so it's a challenge to select one."

"Did you decide anything?"

"I'd like to try a cruise in the Caribbean. Somewhere warm and sunny. That is, if it'd suit you?"

"Sounds fine, something I've never done. If you'll get the schedule, I'll arrange air travel from St. Louis."

"I have it already." Louise relayed the cruise schedule from Tampa, waiting several seconds after each bit of information so Fred could write it down on a pad on the desk.

There was a brief pause, then in a soft trembling voice, Louise said, "I told Joshua about us. He knew we've been seeing each other, but he didn't know how serious we were." Her voice quivered, "He got upset. I don't like it when Josh and I disagree."

Fred tried to inject a lighter tone. "He doesn't like guys playing around with his baby sister?"

She didn't respond to his attempt to ease the tension. "Fred, it's the white-black thing. Joshua's so sure it won't work, he almost convinced me to call off anything during the holiday."

"Joshua's been in Pineville too long. He doesn't know about other places in the world." He told her about his conversation with Roger Kerr. "I've thought about it a lot because it's a worry for you but I've concluded it's like anything else. It can be insurmountable if you let it, but you can overcome the problems and issues if you confront them head on. Our big decision will be knowing we're truly committed to a long term relationship. Some people have fights about money, others about in-laws, others about a hundred minute issues—the toothpaste tube, dishes in the sink, on and on. We'll know from the outset our difficulties will be about race, not from within us, but from the feelings and actions of people around us." He stopped for a moment. "Sorry, I didn't mean to lecture."

Louise laughed. "That's okay. But you're only partially correct. We'll have those little issues, like toothpaste, plus the race business, not to mention your awful work habits."

Fred laughed in return. "Speaking of work. I have an early schedule tomorrow, but I'll call you in a couple of days."

His mind churning with Louise's worries and plans, Fred pulled on his coat and turned out the lights. He hadn't expected a negative reaction from Joshua and the impact on Louise. He recalled Kerr's comments about his family's attitude. He didn't like the confusing concerns flooding his being. Joshua's feelings were important, but they shouldn't deter Fred's hope he and Louise could find a permanent relationship. But if her brother made it a huge issue, Louise could retreat.

Jerry Preston called at eight-thirty the next morning as Fred initiated the printing process of the proposal. Jerry started talking immediately. "Peabody agreed to allow the DNA evidence, but he won't go along with a dismissal of charges. I talked to him late yesterday about filing a motion, but he let me know quickly he'd turn it down. His position is a murder charge should be heard by a jury."

Fred said, "I'm disappointed. It puts Robert's fate in the hands of a group of locals with all their hang-ups about racial mixing. It's a risk he shouldn't have to face."

"I know, but Peabody wouldn't budge on the issue. Another thing. I've decided to call as witnesses those three boys who observed Kathy Abrams and Robert that night."

"From what you've said, something is fishy there, but it could backfire. Suppose one of them testifies they saw them arguing or struggling. That could really jeopardize Jarvis."

Trying to visualize all the possible pitfalls, Fred continued, "I'm just thinking out loud now, but suppose Ledbetter or Brown organizes those kids to tell the same story, one which implicates Robert. A local jury might believe them in spite of the DNA evidence or anything else to the contrary. They'd put more faith in the three kids, trained to look innocent on the stand, than in biological stuff none of them understand."

"It's a chance I'll have to take." Jerry paused a moment. "It's the only way I can legitimately interview them before the trial. If things seem strange when I talk to them, I don't have to use them or maybe call one of them."

"Maybe the thing to do is not interview them at all, but plan to have them testify. In other words, don't tip your hand. You know basically now what you want them to tell, so you can control their story."

"Only up to a certain point. Williams has the opportunity to get them to muddle what they've said in response to my questions or even lead them another direction." Jerry stopped for several seconds, then added, "I'll think about your idea, but I have to put one of them on the stand. It's important to show Robert and Kathy separated and went in different directions on the night she was killed."

Fred asked. "What about those other samples? When are those results back from the lab?"

"Two days before the trial. If the results are delayed, I'm going to request a postponement."

"Let me know as soon as possible. I need time to schedule substitutes for classes."

"How much time can you spend here during the actual trial?"

"Jerry, it's a dilemma. I'd like to be there all the time, but I can't spare the time away from the lab and office. I'm trying to get ahead, but it's almost impossible."

"Something else. Fran and I have moved again. We kept getting crank calls all hours of the day and night, warning about continuing with the Jarvis defense and the underlying threat of attacks on either Fran or me."

"So Ledbetter's cronies tracked you down."

"This time we've an unlisted number. Let me give that to you in case you need to get in contact." He recited the seven digit number.

"You talked with Talbot about what happened to you and Fran in Pineville?"

"Sure. He passed it off with his usual smirk."

"Not surprising. But you'll be better off away from Pineville."

"That may be true in the long run, but now it means a lot of extra driving."

"Are you still working on Fran's dismissal?"

"I haven't done much. I'm spending all of my time on the Jarvis thing. The teacher's association is pressing the school officials for an explanation. It's not as urgent as Robert's future."

After a pause when neither spoke, Fred said, "Take care of yourself. Let me know the trial schedule as soon as possible."

Three days later, Jerry called again. "Fred, I wanted you to know the trial has been delayed until mid-January."

"What happened?"

"The State Crime Lab called Peabody this morning. Those last samples won't be completed in time for the scheduled trial. After that, Peabody didn't have an open date in December."

"Actually, Jerry, it's a relief for me."

"For me, too. I'll have more time to be a detective. I'm talking formally with those boys next week. Maybe the best thing is we'll have the tests from those other kids by the time the trial begins."

"How'd you manage to get the kids to meet you?"

"I laid my cards on the table with Peabody. He said I could call them in if I thought they might be helpful to the defense, even if I have to get a subpoena. So I requested one."

"Ledbetter and Brown will be upset again."

"Sure, but it's different away from Ledbetter's firm. Like I'm my own person." Jerry paused. "Being with Calloway's group makes all the difference in the world. I feel supported and don't have to sneak around. It's like I dreamed about during law school."

Fred said, "Are you worried about my notion of Ledbetter or someone else influencing the kids' testimony?"

"I've considered the possibility. I'm planning to tape the conversations with them. If their story changes at the trial, I'll have some reason to investigate why it changed. I could scare them with a perjury charge."

Fred waited for Jerry to continue. Jerry coughed, then said, "Another approach is I could obtain a formal deposition, record their meeting with me as though it will be used in lieu of their appearing at the trial."

"That's a safer approach. Then if it seems the stories are changing, you could use the deposition and not bring more than one forward."

Jerry laughed. "Thanks Fred, for causing me to think through the strategy."

Fred said, "I'm treating you like one of my students, but I'm out of my element. I'd recommend you run through your thinking with Jim Calloway or someone in his firm who has experience with trials and court procedures before you fully decide."

Fred concentrated on work for the next ten days, other than an occasional call to Louise. He submitted the NIH proposal on time. Jeff, the doctoral candidate finished his work and experienced a successful defense, always a relief for the faculty member responsible.

Fred spent two or three hours each day organizing lectures and assignments for the large beginning Biology class scheduled for spring semester. Because he refrained from relying on notes from previous years and constantly updated and rephrased his lecture materials, he'd have difficulty keeping up with the class if the trial required much of his time.

Nagging thoughts about Louise and Joshua's comments resisted attempts to submerge them, like an aching muscle demanding attention with every move. He didn't intend to spend the rest of his life worried about people's reactions and having his friends desert him. At one point, he picked up the phone to call Louise and cancel the cruise, but retreated. Several days together among strangers could be a solid test of their commitment and perhaps gauge the reactions of complete strangers to a mixed couple.

A mixture of confusion about the long term relationship with Louise and a growing responsibility to please the Rinehart's propelled him to invite Irma Fessler for dinner. They went to an upscale restaurant, had an excellent meal, found conversation easily and without awkward periods as they shared experiences about the university and their work.

Irma seemed more lively than at Rinehart's, told Fred about her husband who'd died suddenly from a cardiovascular episode, and two grown children now living in distant states. Fred shared his common tragedy of losing a spouse.

At her front door, Irma thanked Fred for the evening. He held her hand momentarily before retreating to his car, a bit relieved she'd not invited him in. He'd enjoyed her company and admitted they had mutual interests, but a vital spark had not been evident. He intended to see her again if worries about Louise didn't subside or worse if they discovered the reactions of others were so potentially damaging neither could abide a continued connection.

After a week in the condo without threats, Fran and Jerry began to feel more secure and not continuously on the alert for those thugs. But the anxiety returned when Jerry left the office at five-thirty and noticed a green van pull in behind him as he entered the street from the parking lot. When the van followed him through two turns, he knew he was being tailed.

Not wanting to lead them to the condo, he drove directly to the police station, parked in front and watched the van drive past. His eyes met those of the front seat passenger, a bulky male with a sneer creasing his features. When the van stopped in the next block, Jerry got out and hurried toward the station.

At that moment a uniformed police officer came out. Jerry said, "I need your help."

The cop looked at him carefully, asking, "What's wrong?"

Pointing to the van, Jerry blurted, "Those guys have followed me for several blocks and I suspect they intend to harm me. I complained several days ago about harassing calls. Those are the people involved."

"I'll talk to them. But it may be nothing."

"Then why did they stop there? Believe me, they're waiting for me to drive on, then they'll follow and discover where we had moved to after the earlier threats."

The cop didn't seem convinced, but he stepped briskly toward the van. When he forced the two men to exit the vehicle, Jerry jumped in his car, did a U-turn and left them staring after him. He had won a battle, but unless the police held those men for an extended period, the war was not over.

The day before the flight to Tampa, Fred took the commuter to St. Louis. Louise met him at the terminal. They stopped for an early dinner at a Chinese restaurant on the way to her apartment.

Later, sitting close on the couch, Louise said, "You look tired."

"It's been a tough period, but I got everything done." He reached over to caress her cheek. "I like to touch your face, soft and warm, nice skin."

"It's good to get the semester over for me, too. Seems like the final couple of weeks are always one crises after another." Her head was resting on his shoulder, his arm around her.

"I've thought about us. Looked forward to this time together." Their feet, resting on the coffee table, touched.

"Let's hope the weather is nice." Louise pulled her legs under her. Fred stroked her knees, becoming aroused.

They kissed, moved apart to look at each other, kissed again. Fred said, "Maybe we should go to the bedroom." She giggled when he picked her up under her back and knees and shuffled toward the back room.

The cruise gave them more time to know each other. In the bright Caribbean sun, they were able to lounge on the deck and share history, desires, hang-ups. She learned about his devotion to exercise when he routinely jogged for thirty to forty minutes around the top deck each day. Then he enticed her to join him in the exercise room on the lower deck with weight machines and treadmills.

He discovered more about her writing and her novel in the works. She asked about the scars on his legs from football. He wanted to touch her all the time. The meals were excessive, but they engaged fully. They went to the late floor shows, then danced before returning to their room each evening. They discovered the pleasure of sleeping together with no alarm clock and no obligation. Fred could never remember a time in his life when he felt so free.

Both were aware of three Black couples on the ship. Neither Fred nor Louise said anything, but both believed they were the only mixed pair. No one seemed to notice or care. Expected snubs or negative reactions failed to appear.

By the end of the cruise, both had begun to experience some boredom and were looking forward to returning to the daily routine of work. As the plane neared St. Louis, Fred said, "We should do this every year. Spoil ourselves for a few days."

Louise laughed, squeezed his hand. "Agreed, but a week is enough. I'd weigh three hundred pounds if we lived this way all the time."

They sat quietly for several minutes, thinking about their time together and beginning to consider the immediate responsibilities facing them upon returning to work.

Breaking the silence, Fred said, "Louise, we should plan to be together on a permanent basis."

"You think about us together all the time?"

"Quite a lot. It'd be wonderful to spend the rest of our lives together."

She hooked her arm through his. "So do I."

"Are you worried still?"

"Sometimes, but not as much as earlier. By now, you should know I worry about everything."

He nodded, smiling. "Why don't you come to my place for a visit. Maybe next weekend."

"I'd like that. See how you live. May be meet people who live near you and work with on a daily basis." She chortled. "Might get a different perspective and discover something I should know before this thing gets completely out of control."

Using the power of the subpoena, Jerry called the three boys for individual meetings in a small conference room in the county administrative building, the space made available through Peabody's assistance. Jerry informed them the conversations were being recorded and made the recorder obvious to them.

Jerry reminded the three of his interest and led them through a series of questions. He didn't learn anything new, although he confirmed Gil Brown had been the driver of the car the night of the attack on Kathy Abrams. All three were reserved, volunteering nothing, responding by yes or no whenever possible.

Jerry reminded them. "I intend to call each of you as witnesses during the trial. It's important for the jury to know you were the last to see Kathy Abrams alive as far as we know at this time. You also saw her after she left Robert."

Gil asked, "Can I refuse to answer questions?"

"You can use your fifth amendment right if you believe your response will incriminate you. But before you do, I'd suggest you talk with your own attorney or Mr. Williams, the prosecutor." Jerry knew they would rely on Ledbetter and Brown. He was reminded of the danger of using hostile witnesses. Fred had made a good point. It would be possible for the three, under the guidance of an experienced attorney, to concoct a story implicating Robert. He'd have to be careful. But he had the tape recording all three stating they'd seen Robert and Kathy separate at the corner of Ninth and Elm the night she was killed, perhaps a slight insurance.

Joe asked in a quiet voice. "What happened to the blood samples we had to give?"

"They were sent to the State Crime Lab for DNA testing."

"Will that be used in Robert's trial?"

"Maybe. I'm waiting until I know the results." He didn't wish to reveal very much, but they'd probably ask Harold Brown what the tests meant. Or maybe they hadn't told Brown, fearful of his reaction.

Dealing with the kids caused Jerry to return to his theory of a conspiracy to cover for the real criminal. He still hadn't been able to figure why Ledbetter was connected and why there'd been such drastic actions taken to block a solid investigation. Maybe he should subpoena Ledbetter and Brown as witnesses. But where would he start to associate them with the focus of the charges against Jarvis? Blind questioning of either might only confuse the jury. And with Ledbetter's apparent control over a lot of locals, members of the jury could be intimidated. Another unknown in the puzzle to think about.

Calloway had been aggressive in seeking positions for Fran, but he'd been unsuccessful to this point. He'd discovered two potential openings as the result of retirements beginning with the next school year, but nothing in the short term. Calloway suggested the firm employ Fran to meet with the parents from West Side and put together their statements about her teaching, since Jerry would be overwhelmed with the Jarvis trial for some time.

Fran had jumped at the possibility when Jerry relayed Calloway's idea. "I could do it. I know the people."

Jerry had been reluctant. "Fran, I'm concerned about two things. First and foremost, your safety in Pineville. Second, the conflict of interest issue. I don't want anything to cast doubt on the legitimacy of those testimonies if we go to court."

When Jerry revealed his concerns to Calloway, Jim agreed. "You're right. It could be construed as a conflict. I was so focused on finding her something, I didn't consider carefully the implications." He stood, apparently ending the conversation, but then said, "I'll make a trade. Let Fran come in and help with some of the office stuff and I'll assign a paralegal to round up the statements."

Within a week, a dozen signed testimonies were completed.

Thinking about Susan Newman's revelation of Ledbetter's telephone call and the delay of the trial easing the pressure, Jerry made an appointment to visit with Superintendent of Schools Clifford Haskins on Monday following the Christmas holiday recess. The offices were in the County administrative building, a suite decently decorated but not plush, metal desks for the clerical staff, several rows of matching file cabinets along one wall. Haskins' office was carpeted in an institutional gray indoor-outdoor. He waited behind a solid oak desk as Jerry entered.

The overweight red-faced Haskins said, "I've been expecting you. Donald Evans called me about your visits."

Jerry said, as he took a chair in front of the desk, devoid of papers except for the stack directly in front of Haskins, "You understand the reason for this meeting."

Haskins nodded, remained silent, waiting. Jerry said, "Just to be certain we're on the same page about our position, we've obtained statements from a dozen parents who had children in Mrs. Preston's class. None complained about her conduct or performance. Nor had they heard of others unhappy with the teacher. That's in direct conflict with Mr. Evans stated rationale for firing her. Frankly, Mr. Haskins, he's not been honest. Now I want your version since I have reason to believe the idea of dismissing her came from your office."

Haskins remained poker faced. "I don't like my principals to be called liars."

Jerry leaned forward, a hand on the front of the desk. "Then maybe you can explain the discrepancy between his story and several parents."

"Maybe the parents didn't understand the situation." He shrugged his shoulders and turned over several sheets of paper on the desk, seeming to suggest the interview was over.

Frustrated and irritated by Haskins demeanor, Jerry wanted to lash out, but restrained his urge to bang the desk.

"Mr. Haskins, your reactions suggest we're not serious about this and you have concluded we'll go away if you stonewall long enough. For your information, the firm of Calloway and Givens has a court order to subpoena the telephone records of your office on the day Mrs. Preston was terminated. I'm reasonably certain we can demonstrate two important calls occurred. One, you received a call from a prominent lawyer in town. Second, you called Evans." He waited a moment. "Then she was fired."

Jerry stood. "Soon you'll be called to testify under oath about the circumstances and contents of those calls. Failure to reveal the truth under oath is serious business." He walked to the door and turned. "Think about the consequences."

He walked out with Haskins still at his desk.

CHAPTER FIFTEEN

By the time the trial began on Monday, January 12, Fred had rearranged his commitments to be in Pineville for a week, but he hoped the trial would be shorter. He'd assigned two post-docs with extensive experience to oversee the research projects. He'd arranged for another faculty to do the lectures in the general biology course for the week, but he didn't want to extend the time and force the students to adapt to a different face and method of communicating the essentials.

The court room filled early the first morning. Several press representatives were present, some from St. Louis papers and television stations, as well as the local paper. As Fred looked around, he saw Joshua near the back of the room, nodded and smiled at him. Several other blacks, probably members of his church, sat with him. Two well dressed individuals took chairs in the second row. Fred guessed they were representatives of the NAACP and the ACLU, since none of the locals talked to them or sat immediately next to them.

Jerry led Robert to a seat at the defense table. The young man, expecting the worst outcome, maintained a somber expression as he walked past the audience, most of whom turned to eye him. Robert had dressed for the occasion, dark blue suit, white shirt, a blue-red striped tie neatly in place. His solid two hundred pounds, six-two physique and his intelligent facial features suggested competence and control.

Peabody started on time with little or no fan fare other than the usual instructions to maintain quiet in the court.

Selection of the jury progressed faster than expected. Jerry Preston focused his efforts on getting jurors who had not been life long residents of Pine County and who had education beyond the high school level. He used three of his peremptory challenges to eliminate prospective members who did not meet those essential criteria. He queried each prospective juror about their knowledge of DNA testing. He rejected two males who said they could not place any credence in biological tests they didn't understand. As expected, Williams sought the opposite experiences, seeking older residents of the county whom he judged would be immune to fancy scientific tests and support the feelings of the community. The final jury consisted of four males and eight females, nine white and three black. Both alternates were white male.

Williams used his opening statement to outline the evidence to be revealed which would convince the jury of the guilt of Robert Jarvis. Well organized and articulate, he made a solid impression on the jury and the audience. He emphasized the relationship between the victim and the defendant and hinted at the racial differences. His seven minute opening revealed nothing new or unexpected to Jerry.

Jerry fought to squash his nerves. He'd never done this before, except in moot court in law school. He'd worked diligently for several days organizing his opening statement and the series of questions prepared for each witness. He walked to the front of the jury box, all eyes on him, waiting for his beginning. Forcing down the quiver in his voice, he started. "Members of the jury, I will present a wide range of evidence. It will demonstrate the innocence of Robert Jarvis. It will point to someone else as the actual criminal. I know you will give close attention to all the testimony. I believe a correct interpretation of the evidence will set Mr. Jarvis free. It will likely result in charges against one or more other individuals." He looked directly at each member of the panel. "Thank you." He returned to his seat. A soft murmur ran through the audience. He'd been successful in capturing the attention of the jury, as well as the spectators, with his statements about evidence pointing to another person. And he'd been brief so that the jurors didn't fall asleep and lose focus on his comments.

The County Attorney called the two deputies who'd been dispatched to the scene. He led them through a set of questions about the scene, the evidence collected, and the condition of the body. He made a point of the heavy dew and the drying that occurred during the next day prior to discovery by the boys.

On cross examination, Jerry wanted to firmly establish in the minds of the jury the possibility the crime had been committed at a site other than the park and a vehicle had been necessary.

"Mr. Parsons, you indicated clues suggested the victim had been killed at another place and moved to the park. I'd like you to explain further."

Parsons looked directly at Jerry. "The way the clothing had been tossed about the body, scuff marks in the ground, and a set of tire tracks near the body led us to that conclusion."

"Deputy, explain a bit more how the scuff marks suggest the body was moved?"

"Her feet had been dragged eighteen to twenty inches." He elaborated by telling the jury about the dirt and grass on the rear of the victim's shoes.

"Would those marks in the dirt and grass be consistent with the body being dragged out of a vehicle? Maybe pulled away from a car a short distance, far enough to drive away without running over the body?"

Williams protested. "Judge, this calls for some speculation by the witness."

Peabody ruled without hesitation. "I'll allow it, nevertheless."

Parsons thought for several seconds, his face blank. "I hadn't thought about it. But yes, it would fit all right and explain why the body had been moved along the ground." He brushed his chin with a hand.

"So she might have been killed somewhere else and transported by car. Or she might have been killed in a car parked at the very spot, then pulled from the car."

"Either would fit with the evidence." His response came quickly, even as Williams rose to object. Peabody allowed the question and the answer to stand.

Jerry made the point with Parsons about proper handling of clothing and other evidence at the scene, although the prosecution hadn't brought it up.

Williams then called the Medical Examiner. Prompted by the C.A., Neal testified about his credentials as a board certified pathologist and his long experience in forensics.

Neal established the cause of death and the fact that the victim had been bruised in several places and rape had been attempted. He agreed with Williams that the hair found on Robert's jacket came from the victim.

On cross examination, Jerry focused on the handling of the evidence. He inquired of Neal. "Please summarize for the jury the evidence found at the scene and brought to your lab."

"The deputies sent with my assistant three articles of clothing which were not on the body."

"Those were?"

"A sweater, shorts, and a pair of panties."

"What other evidence did you discover when you examined the body?"

"Blood, semen, fragments of skin, and several strands of hair."

"Where did you locate the skin and hair?"

"The skin was under the fingernails of the victim. I found hair on her clothing, specifically her sweater, as well as several strands tangled around her fingers."

"You reported to the Sheriff and the County Attorney the finding of those pieces of evidence?"

"Yes, as soon as I completed the routine examination."

"What were you told by those officials?" Jerry walked to stand at the corner of the jury box.

"To hang onto those samples, not release them to anyone." Jerry nodded while gazing at members of the jury.

"Go back to the hair found in the fingers of the victim. What was the color and texture?"

Neal looked down, then glanced in the direction of Williams, apparently trying to decide how he should respond.

When the pause became noticeable, Judge Peabody broke in. "Mr. Neal, your response."

Neal hunched his shoulders as though gaining strength. "The hair was light brown, almost blond."

Still standing at the corner of the jury box, Jerry smiled and asked. "The color is very different from that of the defendant. Would you agree?"

Quietly. "Yes."

"Have efforts been made to match the hair with another suspect?"

"Not to my knowledge."

"From the bruises, the skin under the nails, and the hair around the fingers, would you agree that the victim struggled fiercely with the attacker?"

"I'd agree with your statement."

"Let me return to your holding of all these samples. How long did you retain those?"

"Until just before Thanksgiving."

"Or until the defense was able to obtain a court order for their release to the State Crime Lab for analyses?"

"Yes." Neal shifted in the chair.

"Mr. Neal, you're an experienced public official who's been involved with many, many cases. Have you ever known the County Attorney and the Sheriff to insist you retain samples without obtaining an analysis from a scene before?"

Williams shifted in his seat, leaning forward as though he were about to stand. Then he settled back as Neal said, "No."

"Why is this case different?"

"The Sheriff and the prosecution were convinced they had sufficient evidence without those things."

Jerry turned so he could observe the jury, but glancing toward Neal. "Yet no attempt was made to locate another person whose hair might match that found in the victim's fingers. Did it ever occur to you that perhaps they were covering up something?"

Before Neal could respond, Williams was out of his chair and shouting. "Objection. I resent the accusation, Your Honor." Several members of the jury sat up straighter. The audience shifted collectively in their chairs.

Jerry smiled at the Judge. "I'll withdraw the question. But it does cause one to wonder, doesn't it?" A scattering of murmurs among the audience.

Williams was on his feet again, sputtering in his fury and frustration. "I resent the inference again."

Peabody looked directly at him. "So noted, Mr. Williams. But you must admit the handling of the evidence went against the usual process in determining the facts of the situation."

Next, Williams called three high school students who had observed Kathy and Robert leaving the stadium the night of the crime. Jerry let all pass on cross. Their testimony was straight forward and there was no reason to try to refute anything they stated. Earl Sloan, Robert's friend, agreed the two had walked away together.

Then a young man, Jonathan Still, was called. Jerry had been notified he'd be a witness, but he wasn't certain about his potential testimony or impact. The appearance of Still was a concern. Jerry had called Earl Sloan about him and his relationship to Robert and Kathy, but hadn't gained much information. Earl knew Still because he played football and basketball, but couldn't guess why he would appear for the prosecution. Earl thought Still, six-three in height, might be the best basketball player in the school.

Williams asked, after Still's full name and address had been recited for the record, "Jonathan, did you understand the relationship between Robert Jarvis and Kathy Abrams?"

Dressed in a brown sports coat and matching tie, his brown hair neatly combed, Jonathan came across as poised, confident. "Yes. They were very close friends."

"Were they often together at school?"

"Yes."

"Did you observe them in classes and other events, assemblies, other things?"

"Yes."

"Tell the court how they acted when together." Jerry started to object, but decided to let the boy respond.

"They sat together on the team bus to away games. I saw them holding hands several times."

"Would you describe them as a steady couple? If that is the correct terminology in your age group." The audience tittered a bit.

Jonathan smiled. "Yes, I would."

"Was Robert Jarvis jealous of other boys who gave attention to Kathy?"

"Yes."

"On what basis do you make such a conclusion?"

"I saw him hit another boy about Kathy." Jonathan maintained a steady look at Williams, his eyes not wavering.

"Where did this occur?"

"While a group of us were waiting for the bus after a football game." A light dawned in Jerry's memory. He flipped back through his notes to find his conversation with Robert about the incident.

"In your opinion, could Robert Jarvis have become so enraged with jealousy, he would have killed Kathy Abrams?"

"Yes." Still continued to focus closely on Williams.

The response was out before Jerry could object. He said, "I must object. The witness has no training or experience on which to draw such a conclusion.

Williams grinned. "I'll withdraw. Your witness."

Peabody turned to the jury. "You are to disregard the last question and answer." But Jerry realized some damage had been done. He decided to confront Still directly, based on information Robert had given him about the argument. Jerry was guessing, but it likely wouldn't damage anything if he was wrong.

Jerry walked to the witness box, as near to Jonathan as he could be, and looked directly at his face. "Were you the person who Robert hit?"

Jonathan flushed, not anticipating this aggressive approach. He mumbled, "Yes."

"In fact, didn't his action follow three of you pinching Kathy on the buttocks, grabbing her, and generally causing her anguish?"

"I suppose."

"And hadn't she asked you to stop—several times?"

"Yes." He looked steadily at his feet, his confident manner disappearing.

"But you persisted in spite of her protests?"

Jonathan's face was dark, his eyes downcast. He didn't understand how this lawyer knew what had happened. "We were only playing around."

Jerry moved away from the box a few feet. "What occurred when Robert suggested you stop?"

Jonathan reddened, sweat appeared on his face. "I told him to bug off. It was none of his business."

"Didn't you in fact swing at him?"

The answer was very soft. "Yes."

"And that's when he knocked you down?"

"Yes." He maintained his stare at the floor.

"Would it be fair then to characterize his action as protective of Kathy?"

Jonathan glanced up and shrugged. "I suppose you could."

Jerry turned to face Peabody. "No further questions, Your Honor." He returned to his chair, feeling relieved. His hunch had been correct.

Williams stood and said, "This concludes the case for the prosecution, Your Honor. We've established the victim being seen with the defendant, the presence of his hair on her clothing and vice-versa, and a probable motive. I remind you the victim was not seen by anyone else after she left the stadium that night with Robert Jarvis. She did not arrive at her home. There are gaps, but we believe the evidence is sufficient to support the charge against the defendant."

Peabody said, "We've made remarkable progress today and since it is now thirty minutes short of the normal closing, I'm going to recess until tomorrow morning. At that time, the defense will begin its presentation." He rapped the gavel once and walked out the door to his chamber.

Jerry and Fred were staying at the Pineville Motel. Jerry had made the choice of remaining overnight in Pineville rather than spending time driving back and forth. Since the incident with the van, they'd not been harassed. Fran convinced him she'd be safe with other occupants in the condominium complex within range of her voice.

They stopped for drinks at a small lounge a block from the motel after leaving the court house.

Fred said, "It went well today. You made good points with the cross examination of Neal."

"I don't know how the jury will react. I didn't want to embarrass him. Some of the jurors probably know him, may even be a friend who would hold it against the defense if Neal were made to look bad. But I did want them to understand this case was treated differently for some reason."

"I liked your cross of the last witness. How'd you know he'd been the one Robert hit?"

Jerry smiled. "I'd talked to Robert who told me about the incident, but I didn't know it was Jonathan Still. I guessed after he was on the stand. Pays to do your homework and have good hunches." He paused, twisting the martini glass, then added, "I could have asked Robert, but I didn't want the jury to know I'd been surprised."

"It could be over by tomorrow's closing."

After several sips of their drinks, Fred asked, "How's Robert? He should have made a good impression on the jury today with his dress and manner."

"He seems fine. You know, he may not understand the potential consequences."

"He does, based on my conversations with Joshua. He's somewhat fatalistic about it, taking for granted he'll be found guilty."

"Maybe his opinion has changed as events have unfolded. He knows about my discussion with the high school kids as I'm sure Earl tells him everything."

Fred drained the last of the Scotch and soda. "Let's drive out to that restaurant on the west side of town."

"Okay, but I want to return early. I need to review my notes for tomorrow. And I want to check on Fran."

At the door, Fred said, "I thought Williams would make some reference to Robert's color."

"He's letting the jury figure it out for themselves. Remember, he made some slight reference to their differences in his opening. He might hammer at it during his closing argument."

Fred walked the six blocks from the motel to the court house on Tuesday morning. Jerry had gone earlier to get his arguments and background papers in order. Fred would be the second witness for the defense.

After the usual opening by Peabody, he called on Jerry to begin his defense. Jerry called Joshua Bull to testify about the time Robert had returned home from the game the night of the crime. Dressed in his best brown suit, maybe his only suit, Joshua's hands betrayed his nerves as he took the oath, but he answered in a clear baritone voice, demonstrating confidence in his responses, looking at his grandson who smiled at him several times during his testimony. The jury noted the exchange, realizing this was the first time Robert had revealed any emotions.

Williams challenged Joshua's estimate of the time, but Joshua didn't waver in placing Robert at home by eleven p.m. "I had the television on. The eleven o'clock news had just come on when Robert came in. He had a drink of water and went straight to bed."

Then Jerry called Fred to the stand and led him through the statements about the validity of biological testing of samples and the reliability of DNA typing, essentially the same set of questions and responses presented during the pre-trial, but this time for the jury.

"Dr. Ferriday, you've compared DNA patterns from the defendant with samples from the victim's body. What are your conclusions?"

Fred looked more toward the jury than to Jerry. "Actually the samples from the scene are from two sources. Blood from the body compares precisely to the victim, thus there's no doubt the blood came from Kathy Abrams. Semen samples found on the body do not match samples from anyone implicated to this point. Clearly the DNA from the semen does not correspond to DNA of the defendant."

"What about the skin and hair samples?"

"I've examined the results of those analyses. The hair does not match either the victim's or the defendant's. To start with, the color of the hair found in the fingers of the victim is a dead give away that's it's not from the defendant. You don't require further testing or comparisons to make that conclusion. Then, the DNA tests prove it's not from either the victim or the defendant."

"Your conclusion?"

"The hair came from a third person."

"And the skin from under the nails?"

"I didn't have an opportunity to observe the pigmentation of the skin, so I can't comment on that. However, DNA tests were run on the skin taken from under the finger nails of the victim."

"And?"

"DNA of the skin is identical to DNA of the semen and to the DNA of the hair. Thus, skin, semen and hair came from a single individual, neither the victim nor the defendant. My conclusion, after reviewing all of the DNA patterns is that a person, unidentified to this time, struggled with the victim, probably intending to rape her, and was likely the killer."

The statement produced a ripple of exchanges throughout the audience and an exchange of looks among the jurors. Three of the blacks in the audience clapped. Two individuals hurried from the room, probably to file a story with their paper or television station in time for the noon newscasts.

Jerry said, after quiet had been restored, "Your witness, Mr. Williams."

Jim Williams stood with several pages of notes in his left hand. "That's a very conclusive statement, Dr. Ferriday. How much faith do you really have in this DNA stuff?" His tone was an attempt at a put down or cast doubt.

Looking primarily at the jury, Fred said, "I have great confidence." When Williams hesitated, Fred continued, "As I pointed out in my explanation earlier, every individual has a distinct DNA pattern. So when three samples produce identical results, there's only one conclusion to be reached."

"Is it possible for the analyses to be flawed, for mistakes to be made by laboratory workers?"

"Of course, as there is in every endeavor undertaken by humans. But the State Crime Lab has an excellent reputation for sound, reliable work."

"Samples taken from the crime scene were exposed to overnight conditions of heavy dew and rapid drying under a hot sun the next day. Could those conditions have influenced the results?"

"If you recall the testimony of Deputy Parsons, conditions were quite mild on the night in question. Nevertheless, DNA is a very stable compound. The structure is not damaged by most contaminants, including water, dirt, air, etc."

"What happens if you get a mixing of blood samples?"

"Mixing could pose a problem. You'd get a different pattern representing a combination of the two, or whatever number of different DNA's happen to be in the mixture."

"Suppose I gave you samples from a thousand different people. How many of those would be identical?"

"None, unless two of the samples were from identical twins. Even samples from fraternal twins would be different."

"In your opinion, is DNA as accurate as finger prints in the identification process?"

"The two are equally reliable. DNA is relatively new in forensics and people are adjusting to this type of evidence. But in time, everyone will accept and depend upon such data."

"Most lay people, members of juries for example, don't understand all this biological stuff and tend to disregard it. Why should this jury give much credence to your conclusions?"

Fred looked directly at the jury, shifting his gaze from one member to another as he said, "It's true DNA fingerprinting is not yet understood by most people in our society. But we don't understand many principles of nature and we don't ignore those. How do we think? How do we remember things? These are mysteries of the brain, and someday, we'll understand. DNA typing is commonly accepted by courts throughout this land, the world for that matter. In fact two states now have established data banks of DNA taken from criminals so they can go back and match if the person if ever charged again. I'd hope a jury in Pine County would be as open to new ideas as juries in other places."

Williams shuffled the pages in his hand. "That's all I have at this time."

Jerry said, "I call to the stand, Joseph Dobbs."

Williams and his assistant looked at each other, wondering what was coming, although they'd known the three boys would be called. Fred noticed Ledbetter lean over to another man, dressed in a suit and tie, and mutter something. Ledbetter pointed a finger and talked rapidly into his companion's ear. The calling of Dobbs apparently raised a concern.

Joe Dobbs, dressed in a dark blue suit, his face chalky white, his hands trembling to everyone's observation, as he was sworn in by the bailiff. He took the witness chair, clasping his hands firmly together, his knuckles white.

Jerry said, "I know this will be painful for you, Joe, but I ask you to give close attention to each question, and answer as briefly as you wish." He smiled at the youngster, hoping to communicate support and understanding.

"Start by telling me your address and how you know Kathy Abrams and Robert Jarvis."

His voice quivered, but Joe looked at Jerry. "I live at 222 Nugent Street. Kathy lived next door. I've known her since we were small children. I've known Robert since I started high school. I know him mostly because he plays football and other sports."

"Were you a friend of Kathy's?"

"We talked sometimes when we walked home from school at the same time."

"Did you like her?"

"Everybody liked her." Joe was looking at Jerry, trying to avoid the eyes of others.

"Did you ever have a date or go out with her?"

"No. I'm a year younger and not in her classes at school."

"Do you know anything about her relationship with Robert Jarvis?"

"They were together a lot at school. Sometimes he walked with her to the corner of Ninth and Elm. Then he'd continue out Elm toward his home. Kathy would go on Ninth to her house."

"To your knowledge, did he ever go to her home?"

"Kathy told me he did once or twice, but her parents didn't like her to be with him. I know she got grounded once when he walked to her house with her. After that, he didn't anymore."

"Now, this is important. Be sure you're correct in your response. Did you ever see Kathy and Robert holding hands, kissing, doing things suggesting they cared for each other?"

Joe's voice dropped a bit more, almost a whisper. "Yes."

Judge Peabody glanced toward the jury to be certain they were hearing. The jurors were attentive, even eager to hear from this slight young man.

"When did you see them holding hands?"

"When they walked together along the street, when they thought no one else would see them."

"Did you ever see them kissing or hugging each other close?"

The audience was so quiet everyone could hear Joe's soft response. "Only time I saw them doing that was the night she was killed." Robert had been staring into space, but now he focused on Joe, intensely interested.

"Where were you when you saw them and where were they?"

"They were at the corner of Ninth and Elm. I was in a car half a block away."

"Parked on Ninth Street?"

"Yes."

"What happened after they kissed?"

"They talked, hugged, kissed several times for maybe five minutes. Then Kathy came along Ninth, and Robert started down Elm toward his house."

"Thus, Joe, on that fateful night, you saw Robert leave Kathy before something happened to her?"

"Yes."

"Were you by yourself in the car?"

"No. Two other guys were with me."

"Did you watch Kathy all the way to her house?"

"I'd rather not say more." Jerry thought if he pressed, Joe would either come apart or recall he could plead the Fifth.

"Will you tell us who was with you in the car?"

"I'd rather not tell."

Jerry looked at him, trying to understand his desperation. "I won't press you to reveal your friends at this time, but I may wish to call you back again. My last question. Did you willingly provide a sample of blood for DNA testing?"

"Yes, I did." Fred saw Ledbetter lean toward the man next to him who grimaced and shrugged. They hadn't known about the blood samples.

Jerry turned to Williams. "Your witness."

Williams stood. "Your Honor, I'd like to reserve the opportunity to cross examine at a later time." Williams had been surprised by Joe's admission of seeing Kathy and Robert on the fateful night, maybe minutes before she was killed, and had no counter. He didn't want to press Joe Dobbs or challenge his testimony.

Peabody announced the noon recess, requesting everyone to be back at one-thirty.

Fred caught up with Joshua on the front steps of the building. "Want to get lunch with me?" They shook hands. "Haven't seen you very much."

They walked quickly to McDonalds, three blocks away. As they moved along together, Fred said, "It's going okay. Jerry has raised so many doubts, the jury's bound to find Robert not guilty."

Joshua growled. "Don't trust Pine County juries." Lines of concern creased his face.

They suspended conversation while in line at the counter and found seats at a small booth in the rear corner, not yet crowded for the lunch period.

Fred said, "Louise said she'd told you about our relationship"

"She did." His face revealed nothing.

"You okay with it?"

Joshua shook his head. "Don't matter what I think. Both of you are grown people."

"Joshua, level with me. Louise said you were upset."

"I am still. I'm worried what'll happen to both of you." He chewed a bite of burger. "I was upset when she told me, but I've thought about it a lot. You're my good friend and Louise is the only sister I have. It'd be wonderful to have you together, except for worrying you'll both get hurt and take out your frustration on each other. Louise couldn't stand that. Maybe you can't either, but I know her better."

"She's never told me, but has hinted at having been badly hurt in some previous relationship. She worries about our future."

Joshua had finished his sandwich. He leaned back to sip his soft drink. "I'll tell you, but you have to promise not to tell her what I said. She went with this guy in St. Louis for a long time. I thought sure they'd be married. She talked about him a lot. He was a big wheel at another college and she'd met him at some meeting. She finally broke everything off. Never saw anyone seriously since then, until you came along."

"Why did she terminate the relationship?"

"Once we were talking about it. Louise said she couldn't love him. She tried and tried. For a while she considered marrying him anyway and hope it'd work out. But each time he pressed her, she'd retreat. Finally, he gave up. He married someone else within a few months."

"Was he white?"

"Yeah."

"So that's the basis of this concern she talks about?"

"Partly, but there's more. Two of her friends married whites. Neither marriage worked out and ended in divorce. Louise thinks they couldn't stand the pressures from friends and families about the race stuff."

Joshua shoved the container aside. "One was a teacher in her department; committed suicide. Louise has talked about her often. She blames the husband for caving in to his narrow-minded family."

Fred stood as they prepared to return. Outside the restaurant, walking together, he put his hand on Joshua's shoulder. "Josh, I don't know if it'll work out for Louise and me. But I have strong, good feelings when I'm with her. I miss her when I'm not with her. In my mind, it's serious."

"She says the same thing, but don't dare tell her I told you." Joshua snickered. "Divorce is one thing. Killing a brother is another."

"We'll know in a few weeks. Louise may decide she's better off without me. I hope not, but I can't predict. If she does, I'll not pester her."

"You both have to be strong. You have to love each other above anyone or anything else or this pressure will do you in." He stopped walking and Fred stopped to look at his face, somber, serious. "I don't want you to hate each other because of what other people do. And you know, some can be devilish."

They resumed walking, almost to the front steps of the court house now. Fred said, "We're both strong enough to stand the pressures."

"You are, but I don't know about Louise. She acts tough, but she's fragile. Little things get to her, wear her down emotionally."

"She wanted to be here for the trial," Fred said, "but she couldn't get free of teaching responsibilities."

Joshua said, "I understand. I'll call her tonight."

Fred held the door as Joshua went in ahead. "We'll see what happens, but I think it'll work out okay for us."

Joshua's frown expressed his doubts and concerns.

CHAPTER SIXTEEN

As the afternoon session began, Jerry called Gilbert Brown, a tall, slightly built youth with dark black hair, dressed in a brown suit and striped tie. Again, murmurs swept across the audience in reaction to this unexpected witness, and again Ledbetter leaned forward to say something to a man in the row ahead. Jerry led Brown through the same set of questions he'd posed to Joe Dobbs. Brown's responses were similar when asked about knowing Kathy and Robert and their friendship. The jury and the audience now realized that everyone in the school acknowledged the relationship.

Jerry stopped, looked at the jury, then back at Brown. "You were driving the car the night you and Joe Dobbs observed Kathy and Robert. Am I correct?"

Gil sat erect in the chair; a slight tentative smile. His eyes darted around the audience. He rubbed a hand across his face. "Yes, it's my father's car."

"Did you see Kathy and Robert hugging and kissing?"

"Yes, we all did." The quiver in his voice had disappeared as he became more comfortable with the questions and the environment of the court room.

"What happened after they stopped?"

"They talked for a short while, then she came down Ninth toward her home. He continued walking along Elm."

"Were you able to hear their conversation?"

"No. We were too far away."

"What happened when Kathy passed your car?"

The court room was deadly silent. Gil looked down, biting his lip, his face becoming ashy. "I'd rather not reveal anything more." Jerry had thought about this question a lot, but had never posed it with any of the three previously. He was not surprised at Gil's reaction.

"Can you tell the court who else was in the car, the third person in addition to Joe Dobbs?"

"I'd rather not." A deep frown was on his face, the smile gone, his shoulders sagging.

"I'm going to ask you a very serious question now. Did the three of you do anything to Kathy Abrams? You were probably the last to see her alive."

"I'd rather not answer." Standing close, Jerry could see beads of sweat on Gil's brow.

"Did you willingly provide a sample of blood for DNA testing?"

He hesitated, then said, "I did under a court order."

Jerry waited several seconds, scanned through several pages of notes, then asked quietly. "When did your father learn about the crime?"

Gil looked stricken. His face contorted, he stared at the floor, clasping his hands together. He muttered softly, "I'd rather not answer that question." A buzz of talk floated across the court room.

Jerry continued to look at him for several seconds, then turned to the jury. "That's all I have for this witness, but I reserve the right to recall him."

Again Williams passed without cross examination.

Jerry turned to the Judge. "I call to the stand Scott Little."

Scott, dressed in gray slacks and an open collar white shirt, lumbered to the witness box, a scowl on his face, his brownish hair falling over the left side of his face. He brushed it back from his eyes as he swore to tell the truth. Jerry led him through the same opening questions, then moved on.

"Were you the third person in the car that night?"

"Yes." He glared at Jerry as though he wanted to leap from the witness chair and swing at him.

"Why did you stop to watch them?"

"Just wanted to see what'd happen."

"Tell us what you remember after Kathy and Robert separated."

"He walked off down Elm. She came along Ninth, past the place we were sitting in the car."

"Let me go back a bit. How well do you know Kathy and Robert?"

"I play football with him. I knew her at school. She was in lots of things and we had some classes together."

"Did you ever date her?"

"No." He looked at the floor. Jerry could hear his feet shuffling on the floor.

"Had you ever asked her for a date?"

Scott reddened, and rubbed the hair away from his face. "Yeah, a couple of times."

"She refused?"

"Yeah."

"Would you say you're a friend of Robert's?"

"No. We're on the team together, but we've never done anything else together."

"Were you jealous of Robert and his relationship with Kathy?"

He looked at the floor, then mumbled. "Didn't like it."

"Any specific reason other than she seemed to like him, but wouldn't go on a date with you?"

"Don't like blacks mixing with whites. It's not right." A scattering of soft whispers in the audience at the first open admission of the racial divides in the town. Peabody looked up and the murmurs subsided quickly.

"Now, think back to the car and the night she died. Did the three of you do anything to her, grab her as she passed, speak to her, anything like that?"

Quickly he said, "No." His eyes were focused on his hands, twisted together in his lap.

"One last question. Did you willingly give a sample of blood for DNA testing?"

"I did under court orders." His eyes raised to glare at Jerry.

"Are you afraid of what it might prove?"

"I'm not going to answer that."

Jerry smiled at the jury. "No further questions."

Williams passed on cross again.

Jerry stood. "Judge Peabody, I'd like permission to make a brief statement and then a motion. I know this is an unusual request, but it will serve justice, move us toward a solution of this crime, and bring this trial to an end."

Peabody looked at the County Attorney, anticipating an objection.

Williams stood. "Judge Peabody, this is a bizarre request. I don't believe it's proper, nor will it serve a useful purpose. Further, I suspect it's nothing more than game playing by the defense counsel."

Peabody gazed across the audience, scanned the jury. "It is uncommon but not unheard of in courts. Let's take a fifteen minute recess, but I'll ask the prosecutor and the defense counsel to discuss the proposed statement in my chambers."

Five minutes later, Peabody, Williams and Jerry Preston convened around a small conference table in the judge's suite. Peabody looked to Jerry. "Let's hear your ideas. Then I'll hear comments from Mr. Williams and consider carefully any requests or motions."

Jerry said, "Judge Peabody, there's sufficient evidence to support a motion to dismiss charges against Robert Jarvis. The DNA evidence, the color of the hair in the victim's hand, plus the testimony of those three kids, all of whom stated under oath Robert and Kathy separated at the corner of Elm and Ninth, and she walked past their car on the way home is compelling. My motion would request dismissal of charges."

Peabody turned to Williams. "Any objections or observations regarding the motion to dismiss?"

Williams hedged. "Judge, I'd like an opportunity to review the transcript and talk with those boys again before I agree."

Jerry said, "Judge, Mr. Williams has had ample time to meet with the boys. He's known for three weeks I intended to call them as witnesses. He should have known what their testimony would be. But if he insists, the DNA analysis, failing to match the blood of Robert with that recovered at the scene, alone is sufficient to support my motion. In addition, there's the matter of the hair recovered from the victim's hand. The coloration should have resulted in no charge being levied against Robert Jarvis, but for some reason, the Sheriff ignored that piece of crucial evidence."

Williams countered. "I'd like to have a jury verdict. First, I'm not so caught up with the biological tests. Second, the people deserve an opinion of peers."

Jerry was concerned Peabody might cave in. He remembered his earlier motion to dismiss and Peabody's decision to let a jury hear the case. Trying again to persuade the judge, he said, "I believe the DNA is irrefutable. There's no suspicion about the handling of the samples, other than the long delay caused by the prosecution's failure to seek the facts of the case. If there was agreement to admit those tests, there has to be acceptance of the outcome. And that proves Robert Jarvis could not have committed the crimes for which he's charged."

Peabody was silent, thinking about the conflicting statements. "Before I decide, let's hear your idea about a statement."

Jerry considered carefully the phrasing of his next comment. "Judge, you recall your court order to have the three kids provide blood for DNA testing?" Peabody nodded.

Williams injected, "And remember I objected on the basis of no solid rationale. It was a shot in the dark."

When Peabody ignored Williams' comment, Jerry continued, "The DNA analyses incriminate Scott Little. DNA from the semen, and skin taken from the victims fingernails, match his blood. Also, his hair matches the color and texture of that in the victim's fingers."

Peabody and Williams looked at each other as if stunned. Jerry took advantage of their silence. "In addition, I'm reasonably sure I can piece together how the three boys were involved and why there's been a concerted attempt to cover up the evidence in this case. I'd be willing to do that after your ruling on the motion to dismiss."

Rising to his feet, Williams almost shouted, "Good God, what a bunch of crap. You really have the gall."

Peabody continued to look steadily at Jerry. "I assume your statement will incriminate several individuals."

Jerry nodded somberly. "Yes, it will. Further, it should lead to charges against those people who interfered with the justice process." He paused, making sure he made his next point correctly, then said, "Or, I can recall Fred Ferriday who will testify about the matches of Scott Little's DNA from his semen and hair to that of his blood sample. Then I can force those kids to talk about events started by Brown's father to cover up the facts. If necessary, I could call Harold Brown to the stand and unravel the entire scenario, but that would take a lot of court time because I don't have all the necessary information at this time." He stopped when Peabody raised his hand, shaking his head.

Peabody walked to the window, and stood for a few minutes, staring into the court yard. Finally he turned back to Williams and Jerry. "Let's do it this way. Make your motion to dismiss and I'll rule in favor. Then I'll allow your revelation about Little and the other two. But let's hold the cover up business until tomorrow. I'll meet with the two of you again and review your tale." He smiled at his use of the word.

Williams said, "Are you going to call a witness about the DNA tests? It would be the proper way to introduce evidence."

Jerry responded, "I could recall either Mr. Neal or Dr. Ferriday. Both have seen the results and are capable of interpreting the information."

Peabody advised, "Use Ferriday in case there are questions of a technical nature." He also remembered Neal had sat on significant evidence until forced to release it.

Peabody ordered the court back in session. When everyone had returned to their seats and the jury had returned under the guide of a bailiff, the Judge announced. "I've agreed to allow Mr. Preston to make a motion. After I've ruled on his motion, he has permission to recall a witness." He turned toward the defense table. "Mr. Preston."

"Thank you, Your Honor. Based on the testimony of three witnesses who observed Robert Jarvis leave Kathy Abrams at the corner of Elm and Ninth, and the DNA patterns of samples taken at the crime scene and from the blood of Robert Jarvis, I move that charges against Mr. Jarvis be dismissed." He sat down, and reached over to place his hand on Robert's shoulder. The murmurs in the court room, not yet entirely subdued since the session had reconvened, erupted into a steady hum.

Peabody waited until the noise subsided. "I've considered the evidence presented yesterday and today. I've concluded charges should never have been levied against Mr. Jarvis from the outset, although there was some circumstantial evidence pointing to him. A cursory investigation by the prosecutor and the Sheriff would have resulted in his early removal as a suspect. Charges are dismissed. Mr. Jarvis, you are free to go. Any record of those charges will be erased from the record. Further, I apologize to you and your family on behalf of the entire law enforcement system of Pine County and their failure to properly handle this episode."

Robert stood, a huge grin splitting his face. He found his grandfather in the second row of the audience and hugged him, then sat by him in the middle of the crowd, as others shifted seats to make room for him. The audience, stunned for several seconds, broke into animated conversation.

Peabody banged his gavel several times, restoring order and gaining the attention of everyone. He turned to the jury. "Ladies and gentlemen, I thank you for your good service. Even though you were not placed in a position of making a judgment, I'm certain you would have done your duty as informed and responsible citizens. You are dismissed with our gratitude."

He banged the gavel again as a few people stood, believing the session was over. Peabody elevated his voice to gain attention. "During our discussion in chambers, I agreed to permit Mr. Preston to recall a witness. The usual rules of questioning and cross-examination will apply. Mr. Preston."

Jerry stood and said, "I recall Dr. Fred Ferriday to the witness stand."

As Fred found his way up the aisle to the box, he was glad Jerry had warned him this might happen. Jerry said, "I remind you of the samples of blood taken from the three young men who observed Robert and Kathy and their testimony about providing those samples. Have you had an opportunity to review the results of those tests?" Jerry handed copies of the tests to Fred and to the clerk as official evidence.

"Mr. Neal, the Medical Examiner, and I examined the results together."

"I'd like you to share your interpretations with the court."

"When I compared the photographs of the three plates, representing the three witnesses, with the plates from the crime scene, the patterns of DNA match precisely for one of those youngsters."

"And the name of the individual?" The audience leaned forward.

"Scott Little." A low rumble of whispers broke the quiet.

"In your opinion, did Scott Little murder Kathy Abrams?"

Fred paused for several seconds, considering his response. "The skin taken from the victim's fingernails and semen samples are definitely from Mr. Little. Based on those matches, I'd conclude without any reservation that Mr. Little was the individual with whom Kathy Abrams struggled as he attempted to rape her. Less certain, but highly probable, is if Mr. Little attempted rape, he was also the killer." The court room remained absolutely quiet, stunned and waiting.

Jerry turned to Peabody. "I have no further questions, Your Honor."

When Williams indicated he had nothing on cross, Peabody said, "Mr. Scott Little will be held for questioning pending placement of charges against him. Furthermore, Mr. Joseph Dobbs and Mr. Gilbert Purcell are to undergo further questioning related to their activities on the night of the crime. They are remanded into the custody of their families, but are not to leave the county without permission of the court."

He banged his gavel firmly. "This session of Pine County Court is dismissed." As pandemonium erupted in the court room, Judge Peabody walked out. Reporters charged from the room.

Fred waited for Jerry to gather up his notes and discuss for a moment the situation with Robert. Throughout the trial, Robert had remained a stolid figure, never showing emotion, but looking steadily at each witness during their responses or the lawyer who had the floor. Fred had tried to catch his eye several times, but Robert's gaze never departed the scene of the witnesses. Fred couldn't tell what he was thinking, but he seemed to make a favorable impression on the jury, dressed today in a gray suit and maroon tie, neatly knotted and snubbed securely in place.

As they walked out of the court room into the hallway, Ned Ledbetter was standing against the wall in deep conversation with the man to whom he had said something several times during the trial. They were glaring at each other, both red-faced and hands waving excitedly to emphasize their obvious disagreement.

Suddenly aware of Fred and Jerry, Ledbetter pivoted toward them, glaring at them angrily. He said loudly, "Those two bastards caused this problem."

Bystanders in the hall were attracted by the loud voice. Fred and Jerry glanced at each other and continued to walk toward the outer door. Ledbetter followed and began to scream profanities. His companion tried to pull him back but Ledbetter knocked his hand away.

When he called out, "Ferriday, you nigger lover!", Fred stopped and turned, facing Ledbetter, almost bumping into him.

Trying to restrain the emotion in his voice, Fred said, "Haven't you done enough harm already?"

Ledbetter, out of control, thrust his face almost into Fred's. "You heard me. There's no place for the likes of you in this county."

Fred turned to walk away. Ledbetter grabbed his shoulder and jerked him around. "Don't do that when I'm talking, you sorry bastard."

"I suggest you cool down. Go somewhere and think about your comments before you do something you'll be sorry for."

Ledbetter took a step toward Fred and swung his fist, a roundhouse, telegraphed well before the action. Fred stepped back, the intended blow missing widely.

Fred turned to Ross Talbot, standing in the background. "Sheriff, I want to you to stop this foolishness."

Talbot, the usual smirk on his face, didn't respond, but Ledbetter prepared for another thrust. As the wild swing passed close to his face, Fred moved away, then stepped forward and hit Ledbetter a short, chopping left in the midsection. Ledbetter doubled over, gasping for breath, sinking to his knees. Fred grabbed his shoulders to prevent him from collapsing to the floor.

At that moment, Ross Talbot stepped forward. "I saw what you did. I'm taking you in and charging you with assault."

From the back of the group, now twenty or more, came a stern voice. "I don't think so, Sheriff."

A tall heavy-set man in a gray suit stepped out of the group. "I'm Bill Phillips with the State Police." He flashed a badge at Talbot. "I observed what happened here. This man had to defend himself, after you refused to stop Ledbetter."

Talbot felt compelled to stand his ground in front of the hometown crowd. "And just who gave you the right to interfere in the affairs of Pine County."

Phillips said, "The State Attorney General. He detailed us here to keep an eye on this trial and the related activities around here. He suspects there's been an attempt to thwart justice. And from what we've seen, he's probably correct. So there's not going to be a charge against Dr. Ferriday. However, you'll have to explain to my boss why you didn't stop this melee when asked."

By then, Ledbetter had regained his breathing and was struggling to stand. Fred and Jerry assisted him in regaining his feet. Fred said, "I'm sorry if I hurt you, but you gave me no choice." Ledbetter leaned against the wall.

Fred turned to Phillips. "Thanks for intervening. I'm pleased your office has become involved with this whole episode. I'm sure you'll discover irregularities in the way the Jarvis investigation and trial have been handled. And I'll be pleased to give you my take on the entire episode."

Jerry and Fred walked out the door, a sigh of relief escaping their breaths. Fred said, "If Phillips hadn't been there, I'd be in Talbot's jail tonight."

"Where'd you learn to punch like that?" asked Jerry. "I'm impressed."

Fred laughed, his nerves beginning to return to a normal state. "If you've been around athletes much, you learn to defend yourself. A few of them always want to prove everything in a physical manner."

"Well, I bet it'll be a cold day before Ledbetter swings at anyone else."

"He lost control of his senses. You had punctured his balloon with your defense. When he saw us, he wanted revenge, any way he could exact it."

When they were at the motel, Fred asked, "Who was the guy with Ledbetter when we came out of the courtroom?"

"Harold Brown. He's one of the partners."

"And Gilbert's father?"

"Yes.

Fred walked into Jerry's motel room for a minute. "There's the person they've been covering for. Somehow they knew Gil was connected to the murder of Kathy Abrams. Maybe Ledbetter and Brown thought Gil did it. That'd be enough. Now I know why you asked Gil that question about when his father knew."

Jerry grinned. "We know he had the father's car and the three boys followed Robert and Kathy, then parked to watch them. But when I asked if anything happened after Kathy and Robert separated, all became flustered and
300

refused to answer. My theory is they grabbed her, drove to the park and Scott tried to rape her and accidentally killed her or maybe became so frustrated with her resistance, he broke her neck out of sheer rage. Maybe there was blood or other evidence in the car which made Harold Brown suspicious. He assumed his son had done the dirty deed or had been involved. Maybe Harold confronted Gil and the boy told his father what had happened. Harold likely called Ledbetter for advice or help. Right now, I'm guessing, but it all fits."

"I tried to watch both Ledbetter and Brown after the reactions to Joe Dobbs' testimony. They were more than concerned the kid had ratted on his buddies."

"Let's think about this line more while we find dinner."

In the car, Fred asked, "How far were you able to get the boys to go in their private conversations with you before today?"

"About what they testified to."

"Did you suspect more?"

"Not at first. I was probing, grasping for any clue that might lead away from Robert. I kept going back to my discussion with Scott and his revelation he'd been with Gil and Joe the night of the crime. Just his voicing of his dislike of Robert and his frustration with not being able to get close to Kathy suggested he might do something rash. Then you suggested testing their blood samples for DNA matches."

"You think Scott did it by himself?"

"Don't think so. They were all in cahoots. A car was necessary. Scott could have borrowed the Brown car and was the only participant, but I don't think so."

"If Scott was the only one who attacked her, where were the other two?"

"I don't know yet. Maybe watching. Maybe holding her down. Maybe Scott made them leave Kathy alone with him. They're both afraid of him."

"That's makes all three guilty of something, accessory to murder, I suppose."

"Correct."

Jerry said, "If Peabody hadn't given me some flexibility, it could have been much more difficult to prove anything. I figured all three would take the Fifth Amendment and refuse to reveal anything about the events of that night."

"Peabody wasn't thrilled with your request to spell out the string of events. But I don't know how he reacted in chambers."

"He was unaware I was going request such a thing." Jerry turned the car into the parking area. As they walked toward the restaurant door, he said, "You know, Peabody is a cool character. Most judges would've thrown me out of the court for offering such an idea."

"Weren't you jeopardizing your case with him?"

Jerry chuckled. "I didn't think so. We've sort of hit it off. Two outsiders in Pine County. He didn't like the way those specimens from the scene were held so long. He realized those would have never come into play except through his court order. In short, he was pissed. That's when he began to suspect something wasn't right in the way Williams and Talbot had handled the situation. Also, he learned about the attacks on you and on Fran and me and Talbot's refusal to do anything."

During the coffee and dessert,. Jerry said, "Peabody is meeting with Williams and me tomorrow. I've promised to sketch out for them my theory of what occurred, both the crime and the cover up."

Fred shoved aside the cheesecake, leaving about a third of the slice. "Should be interesting. You think it'll lead to additional charges."

Jerry grinned. "Maybe. I'm after revenge because I suspect Ledbetter, Brown and Talbot, probably even Williams, were involved. I'd like to embarrass all of them. And I hope they can be forced to identify and charge those thugs who attacked us. And if I'm right, there should be charges placed against all of them."

"It's a temptation for sure."

"You're right. It'll be interesting."

"I wish I could be here to see their reactions."

"I'll let you know how it goes."

CHAPTER SEVENTEEN

When Jerry appeared at Peabody's office the morning after the trial, Williams was already there, sitting quietly and sober faced in the waiting room. Jerry said, "How're you doing? Glad the Jarvis thing is over?"

Williams nodded without responding verbally. His face remained impassive.

After several minutes of waiting in the outer office without a word between the two, their thoughts running through the trial and the pending fall out that could pose disaster for several prominent citizens of Pineville, both were startled when Peabody stuck his head out of his private chamber, saying, "Come in."

As they settled into chairs around the small conference table, Peabody opened. "Well, to the business of this get together. Mr. Preston, you suggested you'd be able to reveal the sequence of events leading to the crime and then to the so-called cover up. So, let's have it."

Jerry leaned forward, placing his arms on the table. "Judge Peabody, please recognize what I'm going to say is based on speculation in part. Much of my thinking is based on my discussions with those three boys and other people, plus those threats and attacks on those involved in the defense of Robert Jarvis."

When Peabody nodded, Jerry continued. "I learned Scott Little had been somehow associated with the observation of Robert and Kathy when a friend of Robert's set up a session with a group of high school students. Scott's demeanor at the session tipped me off that he viewed Robert Jarvis in a perspective different than the others and his failure to participate in the sharing of ideas. Later I met with him and he probably inadvertently revealed the other two. I suspected those three boys were more deeply involved because of their reactions when I talked with them individually. All three were open about the events of the evening up to the point Kathy and Robert went their separate ways. Then they refused to say more. I think Joe Dobbs would have told me what happened, but he's afraid of Scott Little. Gil Brown has been protected and guided by his father, so he'll likely not talk to anyone and would probably take the Fifth Amendment if placed on the stand again. Thus there's no doubt the three were together when Kathy Abrams was killed. All may have all been involved in the attempted rape, but I'll have to dig some more to prove what really happened.

"My theory fits in a reasonable sense what we already know from the trial. The DNA patterns prove beyond any question that Scott Little was the actual attacker and he probably killed Kathy Abrams. I'd speculate now, if you pressed me, that the three were together in the car, watched Kathy and Robert at the corner of Ninth and Elm, then grabbed her as she came along Ninth. Maybe they were planning to play a prank, scare her, who knows. We know Gil had his father's car, the vehicle essential to transporting Kathy from Ninth Street to the park. That vehicle may contain evidence, although I'm sure it's been thoroughly cleaned. Both Gil and his father likely know but won't volunteer any information.

"It's clear Robert Jarvis was not involved after he and Kathy separated. Everybody I've talked with is firm in their belief he would have fought for her. No one would have done those deeds unless they killed Robert first, so the three had to wait until he was out of sight and sound."

Peabody looked at Williams who sat quietly, then asked, "And the cover up you've suggested? You have ideas about it? "

"The demands of Ledbetter toward me made me suspicious from the beginning. There was no apparent reason for his interest in the crime or his threats that I not mount an aggressive defense. When I didn't cave in, he fired me and probably pressured the School system to terminate my wife's job. My suspicion is that Harold Brown somehow learned Gil was associated with the murder of Kathy and he and Ledbetter set out to protect Gil. My guess is Harold discovered blood or other stains in his car or Gil told him what had happened.

"Then the lack of a real investigation by the Sheriff's office to clarify how the body got moved from Ninth Street to the park added to my belief that something fishy was going on. Failure to seek out the source of the hair in Kathy's fingers represents an outright failure, probably a deliberate act, on the part of the Sheriff. Talbot's reactions to the attack on Fred Ferriday and on Fran and me added more fuel to my hunch something was not right in Pineville. My bet is that Sheriff Talbot directed the attacks, but I don't know with any certainty. Talbot, Ledbetter, and Brown were partners in a cover up. Thinking back through the chain of events, each time someone pushed hard to discover the facts, they were threatened, attacked or fired.

In my mind there's sufficient evidence to charge them with obstruction of justice."

Jerry looked at Williams, sitting straight in the chair, his face revealing no expression. "In addition, Mr. Williams had to be connected, or he would have mounted a more assertive effort to discover the facts or he would have caused the Sheriff's office to do so. I can't believe the Medical Examiner didn't tell them about the hair and other evidence from the scene. In fact, you remember Deputy Parsons had doubts at the very outset and probably shared those with the Sheriff." Williams reddened, but did not respond, choosing to stare at the floor.

Jerry concluded, "That's as much as I know now."

"So where do we go from here?" Peabody was solemn, looking at the two of them.

Jerry glanced at Williams. "Under normal conditions, the County Attorney and the Sheriff would be swift to start a full-scale inquiry, in addition to flushing out any additional evidence around Scott Little and the other boys. But frankly, Judge, it won't happen because they're all involved. Mr. Williams never pushed for additional evidence for some reason and that likely means he wouldn't now."

Williams stayed quiet, stone-faced, still staring at the floor. Peabody waited several seconds, looking at him.

Finally, Peabody asked, "Mr. Williams, do you have anything to say? These are pretty severe allegations."

"I'm not prepared to respond at this time," Williams mumbled, his head down. "I want to review the situation and my options."

Peabody shrugged and turned to Jerry. "Mr. Preston, I've thought about this case a lot in the past few weeks. I suspect you're correct about the participants in the cover up. After yesterday's court session, I called the State Attorney General to discuss alternatives. He'd rather we solved it locally if possible." He walked to the window, his place for thinking through issues. Jerry had seen him do this several times.

When Peabody returned to the table, he said, "Mr. Preston, I intend to appoint you as a special prosecutor to solve this thing. You know more about the details than anyone else, so you'd not be starting from ground zero. And the Attorney General will provide some assistance in running down leads or doing other essential background work. I'll make an official announcement so everyone understands your authority to probe into the situation."

Jerry, caught by surprise at the idea, said, "I'll need to clear it with my employer."

Peabody smiled. "I've talked to Jim Calloway. He's willing for you to take on this assignment. And the county will reimburse Calloway's firm for your time and any expenses."

"Maybe he'd rather I not screw up things around the firm." His eyes lightened, then his face turned hard. "But seriously, Judge, I have to be assured Talbot, Ledbetter, and others will not interfere. I'm not willing to risk further personal attacks on me or my wife."

"The State Police are prepared to step in if you encounter difficulties of any kind. I'll make it clear to Talbot and everyone else concerned that interference will not be tolerated. In fact, Talbot has been placed on administrative leave until all this is clarified for his failure to intervene in Ledbetter's attack on Ferriday after the trial yesterday. The County Administrator will appoint an acting Sheriff and has agreed to make resources in the Sheriff's office available for investigative work."

Williams finally joined the discussion. "The County Attorney's office will help if you wish. But I promise personally to stay on the sidelines."

Jerry wanted to trust "Red" Williams, but was reasonably certain he'd been caught up in the web of local politics and power struggles. He didn't know if Williams could free himself from those tentacles. He said, "It'd be better if you stand aside. But I'd like to reserve the option of calling on you. You may understand pieces of this puzzle because of your perspective as the prosecutor."

Peabody stood. "Okay. Let me know how things go And, Mr. Preston, keep me informed, especially if you encounter resistance."

Following his session with the Judge, Jerry met with Fred, Joshua, and Robert for lunch at Grady's restaurant south of town. While they waited for their table, several well wishers gathered around Robert and Jerry. Fred watched, thinking how quickly people's behavior changed when suspicions were lifted. He said to Joshua, standing close and watching, "The outcome must be a relief for you."

Joshua put his hand on Fred's shoulder and grinned. "Oh, yes, bless the Lord it turned out okay. But if you hadn't come here, Robert would have ended up in prison. For something he didn't do"

By the time Fred was able to speak to Robert, the group had been seated at a table in the corner of the dining area. "Now you can turn all your thoughts to completing high school and deciding on a university for next fall. Remember my offer to help if you are seriously considering Illinois."

Robert, an expression of delight and relief on his face, said, "I'm scheduled to visit week after next with the football coaches there. They've promised a scholarship. I'd like to see the facilities and discuss their expectations of me, both for the football and the academic side. I want to get a solid education and hope the demands of the coaches won't prevent that."

Fred asked. "Are you visiting other schools?"

"Michigan is still calling, but I'm leaning toward Illinois. If things look okay, I'll likely cancel with Michigan. It's hard to decide about schools."

"Give me a call when you're there. Sounds like everything is under control, but if I can help, let me know." More than he liked, the Athletic Association called for his advice about prospective student-athletes, particularly those whose academic performance in high school had been borderline. More often than not, Fred recommended against offering scholarships to those not likely to graduate from the University. Sometimes he called the high school coach and a guidance counselor to get a better handle on the academic potential of the eighteen year-old.

Fred said, "Jerry, it turned out well, better than we could hope for. You did a fine job."

Jerry wiped his mouth with the napkin. "It did, but I've you to thank for getting me back on the right track. If you hadn't pushed and prodded, I might have caved in to Ledbetter."

"I pushed a bit, but you were confronted with an unusual situation."

"I met with Peabody this morning," said Jerry. "He's appointing me as a special prosecutor to follow through on my suspicions."

Fred asked, "When did the Attorney General become interested? I was thinking about the presence of the state policeman yesterday."

"Guess I never told you. Calloway phoned them after we were attacked. Couple of their people have been around asking questions, showing up at the trial."

"Are they planning to do anything formally?"

"Peabody told me this morning the Attorney General wanted the local court to solve the issue if possible, but the state office will provide investigative help."

Joshua said, as the waitress moved away, "This is the first time in a long while I don't feel pressure. No more worries about this trial thing." He grinned, a couple of broken teeth showing in his dark face.

Robert touched his shoulder. "I know, Grandpa." His face turned grave. "But I'll miss Kathy for the rest of my life."

He glanced at Fred, "I know you'll call Aunt Louise, but I want to tell her first about the trial." He grinned, "She'll be glad, especially after she sent me those two new suits."

An hour later, as they walked through the front door of the restaurant, Fred said, "Good luck. I've got to get back but I'll see each of you soon. Jerry, keep me informed about the outcome."

Louise arrived in Champaign via commuter flight early Friday evening. Fred met her in the airport and retrieved her luggage from the carousel. As they stopped in the driveway at Fred's house, she said, "You okay with my staying here? Won't upset your neighbors?" She surveyed the large brick structure that must have four bedrooms and spacious living areas.

"It'll shock them. Old Fred shacked up with a beautiful, sexy woman."

She giggled and hugged his arm.

He led her through the living room, a dining room and kitchen, showed her several photographs on the wall of the den, the door into the garage, then upstairs where one of the four bedrooms had been converted into an office. "I haven't changed many things since Martha died, but if you come, we can rearrange it to suit your desires."

Sober faced, Louise said, "It's a big place. We'll work on it together." She paused as she thought about how to suggest a change, then said, "The only thing I'd really like is a space for my books and where I can write, set up my computer and printer."

They spent most of Saturday walking around the university, Fred's office and lab, the huge library, partially submerged under the famed Morrill corn plots, the student union. Toward the end of their meandering, Fred said, "Well, you've seen where I live and spend my time."

"It's a very big school."

"It is, sometimes overwhelming. The down side is you never get to know many of the faculty, only those in your department and those you happen to serve with on committees."

Fred said, as they returned to the house. "We're meeting the Rineharts and Kerrs for dinner. They're looking forward to meeting you."

"You should have warned me. I would have brought a different dress. I want to impress your friends."

"Don't worry. You'll be fine."

When she came out of the bedroom later, he walked closer and turned her around in mock inspection, the gray wool dress complementing her figure. "You'll be more than fine."

At the restaurant on the outskirts of Champaign, Bill Rinehart shook Louise's hand, and looked into her face. "I can understand why Fred finally got out of the lab for a while."

She laughed. "But it's hard to keep his attention. He loves that place with all that strange equipment and the exotic fumes."

Roger Kerr inserted. "His colleagues tell me he's always there, but my guess is he'll change his habits now."

Louise asked about their work and families, seemingly comfortable with people she'd just met. Fred watched her interchanges with his friends, pleased she was at ease. And so were the Kerrs and Rineharts.

Back at the house, as they removed coats and wraps, Louise put her arms around Fred's neck. "It was a nice evening. I liked them."

"They're good friends and you wowed them. I was proud to have them meet you. Now they're thinking how did this dull old codger attract such a wonderful woman."

"You're saying that to soften my resistance for your scheme for the rest of the evening."

Fred pulled her close. "Maybe. But you usually seem willing enough."

When Fred woke on Sunday morning, Louise was no longer beside him, but he couldn't hear anything. He tugged on his robe and walked into the living room. She was sitting on the couch, looking through an album of family pictures.

"I didn't know when you got up."

"Thirty minutes ago. Looking at these, others who've shared your life."

"Not many people. Parents, no siblings or children. Martha."

"You are a loner, aren't you? Nobody but you in the Ferriday clan."

"That's true now. Neither of my parents had siblings. I was an only child. For some reason Mother didn't want other children."

He laughed softly. "Maybe I was too difficult. But you're correct. When I go, the line of Ferridays will disappear."

"I didn't know you'd been in Vietnam."

"Served a year after completing my B.S. degree here and received a commission through the R.O.T.C. program."

"Does that explain some of the scars on your legs and back?"

"Only one. Others are from football."

"There are a lot of photos of Martha. You loved her very much, didn't you?"

"We were very close for a long time. I've missed her terribly at times."

Louise looked into his face for several seconds, then asked, "Are you sure you're ready for another person in your life?"

"When Martha died, I figured I'd live alone for the rest of my time. A couple of my friends, like the Rineharts, have encouraged me to become active in the social scene and seek another spouse, but I've been reluctant. I'd found comfort in work and associated activities until they made me think about it. When the house felt empty, I'd go to the office." Fred took her hand. "Then you came along and changed my thinking."

She stood. "I'll make coffee if you'll show me the things."

They made breakfast together, then scanned the newspaper while they finished coffee. At mid-morning, they dressed in heavy coats and walked around the neighborhood. Louise put her arm through his as they meandered through the quiet subdivision, neat yards. huge oaks and elms, not many residents stirring on the quiet Sunday morning.

At one point she asked, "What do you usually do on Sundays?"

"Go for an early jog, read the paper, maybe a few household chores. Often go into the lab to do some work."

"Ever go to church?"

"Not in years. Martha always went, but I lost interest and gave it up."

"Would you go with me if I moved here?"

"I'd consider it." He put his arm around her shoulders and looked into her eyes. "Is that a proposal?"

Louise chuckled, pressing her body closer to his. "Maybe of sorts."

"I wanted to be sure before I promise anything so dramatic as returning to church."

Although the sun was bright, temperature in the twenties with a slight wind made them pick up the pace. After two more blocks they returned to the warmth of the house.

She said, as they hung coats, "This feels good."

Fred touched her face. "Your nose is cold." He touched her cheek with his lips. "How serious were you back there or did the cold get to your brain?"

She gazed up at him, her hands on his arms. "I've thought about us quite a lot since our trip at Christmas. You remember what you said on the plane coming back?"

He nodded. "And, what's the verdict?"

Louise turned away to the window, her back toward him. "Our discussion this morning made me realize how alone you've become. Now I'm thinking I'll fill a vacuum in your life. We certainly don't have problems relating. We're comfortable, maybe too much so." She returned to stand by him. "We seem accepted here okay. That is, as far as we know."

"I hope I meet your need, too. I've suspected there's a void in your life as well."

Louise was quiet, her hand pressing his. "Yes, at times it's been difficult living alone."

Fred said, "I'd like us to be together. There's more than a feeling of ease and comfort. There's passion. I care about you in ways I don't remember feeling about another person for a long time. I want to touch you all the time, to know you're with me."

She grinned. "You're almost a romantic."

"Oh, no. I'll never qualify as that type."

She looked at her watch. "We'd better get going or I'll miss my flight."

Having Louise for the weekend erased any reservations Fred had about the long term relationship. There might be thorny issues at some point, but he couldn't envision anything they couldn't deal with.

CHAPTER EIGHTEEN

Six weeks after the trial ended with Peabody's ruling to dismiss the charges against Robert, Fred received a call from the clerk of Pine County court. "Judge Peabody wishes to talk with you. Please hold for a moment."

Fred leaned back in his desk chair to stretch his legs while he waited for Peabody to come on the line. He could hear conversation in the background and the receiver being shuffled from one hand to another. While he waited, he idly flipped pages in the biology text, looking for a specific short section the students seemed not to understand.

Thirty seconds later, Peabody said, "Dr. Ferriday, we're reviewing fallout from the Jarvis case this Friday. I'd appreciate your coming to Pineville in the eventuality there are questions or concerns about the DNA evidence."

Fred let the chair tilt forward so he could locate his calendar. "Is this a formal hearing or just a consultation?"

"The latter for which we'll pay your expenses and a small honorarium. I expect we can wrap things up in a day. Mr. Preston has pulled together an interesting scenario related to the crime and associated events."

Fred said, "I'll clear my schedule and come on Thursday afternoon." But he wondered why the Judge wouldn't rely on the local Medical Examiner. May be he no longer trusted Neal after the sample screw-up.

He called Louise at her office suggesting she meet him in Du Quoin Friday night. They could spend some time with Joshua and Robert over the weekend after the conference with Peabody and others.

When Fred arrived at Peabody's conference room at nine on Friday morning, Jerry Preston and Sam Redmond, an investigator from the Attorney General's office, were waiting. Peabody entered simultaneously with Fred. Jim Williams ambled in five minutes later.

Peabody, eager to get started, said, "Well, Mr. Preston, how're things? Bring us up to date."

Jerry pulled out a sheaf of notes from his briefcase. He looked at Redmond sitting next to him. "We've learned a lot in the time we've had. Some surprises, but I believe the puzzle is complete. After I go through this, I'll be interested in your reactions. Maybe there are holes neither Sam nor I see at the present."

He flipped several pages of the pad. "First, I'll outline the actual crime based on conversations with Gil, Joe, and Scott. Both Gil and Joe talked freely. Of course, Scott is reluctant and his counsel guides him, but he's confirmed some important details. We believe this is what really happened or as close as we're likely to get. Of course, you will understand I've created some of their conversation based on their memories of that night."

The three boys hadn't intended their prank to turn out the way it did. It began on a whim with no thought of the potential consequences as they cruised along Elm street after the Friday night football game between Pine County High and Highland, passed Robert Jarvis and Kathy Abrams. The street lights, located at each street corner, provided ample illumination for the boys to see. Robert and Kathy were holding hands as they walked slowly, enjoying their time together and not wanting the evening to end.

Gil Brown, the organizer of the group and the driver, said, "Look at ole Robert. I bet that black boy is making out with Abrams."

Joe Dobbs, in the back seat, but leaning over the front so he could hear everything, added, "I see them together a lot, but they don't know. I live next door to her and see them walking from school."

Gil asked, "Does he go as far as her house?"

"No. Her dad would raise hell if he knew they were seeing each other."

The third member, Scott Little, had been quiet, thinking. A member of the football team, Scott had a reputation for a lot of bluster and bullying. As Gil reversed their route by turning into a driveway and started back along Elm, Scott said, "Why don't we scare them a little?" His voice quavered slightly with excitement.

Joe said, "What do you mean, scare them?" He never trusted Scott's impulses. More often than not someone was knocked around and hurt by the bully.

Scott responded, "You know, stop, maybe yell at them. Or maybe even threaten them. I don't like that black boy messing around with Kathy."

Gil chimed in. "You better think twice before you take on Jarvis. He's a big guy."

Scott persisted. "He can't take all three of us." But he had doubts. He remembered Robert Jarvis running over him in football practice.

Joe suggested. "They'll separate at the corner of Elm and Ninth, the street she goes along to her house. Robert won't go closer than that corner. Go around the next block and park on Ninth. We'll talk to her after he's out of the way."

Gil pushed his reservation. "What do you mean? I'm not sure any of this is a good idea."

"Shit, don't be such a damned chicken," declared Scott. "Maybe we'll grab her, take her for a little ride. Threaten her if she doesn't stop seeing that nigger."

They tacitly agreed to do it. Neither Joe nor Gil wanted to challenge Scott. Gil pulled the car under the large oak trees into a vacant space not occupied by residents of the street a half block from the intersection. They watched as Kathy and Robert stopped at the corner, the street light and full moon spotlighting the couple. Robert and Kathy held each other closely, his arms around her waist, hers around his neck. He leaned over to her and they kissed for a long time. The watchers were aroused, wishing they were in Robert's place. She was a beautiful and sexy girl, long blond hair, blue eyes, all the alluring curves of a maturing young woman. Scott, especially, had visions of a sexual relationship with her, but she would never agree to date him. Her rejections irritated him deeply. He didn't understand how she could turn him down, yet be involved with this black. That wasn't right.

At the corner, Robert and Kathy stood for several minutes, talking, holding each other closely, kissing. Scott said, "I bet he's into her pants when he gets her alone."

Joe said, "That never happens."

Scott said, "He'd find a way. I would."

Gil, who had been watching closely, said, "Hey, they're breaking up. He's walking away. She's coming this way. Stop talking until she's near."

Scott, now taking charge, leaning forward in anticipation, said, "When she gets close, Joe, we'll grab her and I'll hold her in the back seat. Gil, you drive away from here, maybe to the county park on the other side of town."

There was not sufficient time for the others to object or change the plan. Kathy, walking rapidly, was getting close. As she passed the car, Scott leaped out, grabbed her around the waist with one arm and covered her mouth with the other. She struggled, but he was a big, strong boy. With little assistance from Joe, Scott pulled her into the back seat as the car starting moving. Joe jumped into the front. Gil avoided the main part of town and kept on the side streets. He didn't want any attention.

In the back seat, Scott continued to hold Kathy tightly, but released the pressure on her face. He didn't want to suffocate her. He became sexually excited with her body pressed against him. He could feel an erection starting. He relaxed his arm around her waist, but held her on his lap. His free hand explored her stomach and breasts. He wanted to strip off her clothes.

Finally, Kathy mumbled, "What're you doing? You'll get in big trouble if you don't let me go." She was scared out of her wits, but didn't want to show her fear. She knew all of them, but didn't like what was happening. She hated Scott's hands all over her.

Scott said, "We're warning you to stay away from Jarvis. It's not right you making out with that coon."

"What Robert and I do is none of your business."

"We're making it our business." Scott was rubbing one of her legs and knee and his lips brushed her neck. Kathy tried to remove his hand, but her actions seemed to encourage his exploration as he moved his hand up her thigh. She had always been afraid of Scott Little. She had turned him down several times when he'd asked about dates. She knew it made him mad, but she couldn't stand being near with his eyes ogling her body.

Kathy was surprised at the presence of Joe Dobbs who lived on her street and was a year behind her in school. He was a quiet kid who avoided attention. She yelled, "Joe, why are you mixed up with these guys? You'll be in trouble with your parents when they find out."

Scott interrupted, "They won't find out. If you tell anybody, we're going to get that black buddy of yours."

"None of you have the courage to face Robert. He'd break your heads."

Gil steered the car into the back part of the isolated park, twenty yards from Pine Creek. Under the bright moon nothing was visible except a few picnic tables scattered through the area now covered with brown grass and weeds. Families used the park in the summer months, but now, late at night and with cooler weather, it was quiet and empty. Gil braked to a stop and switched off the motor and lights.

Scott, thoroughly aroused by his caressing of Kathy's breasts and legs, said, "You guys take a walk. I'll talk to her. She'll get the message."

Joe was eager to get away, but Gil turned to say, "Don't do anything you'll regret." He didn't trust Scott and knew he intended to have sex with Kathy, but didn't dare challenge him.

Scott grinned. "Just go. I'll call you when I'm through. Maybe you'll want a turn with her."

As the two slammed the doors, Scott tried to kiss Kathy on the mouth, but she twisted her face away. "I think we'll have a little fun," he growled, as he pulled her sweater free and tossed it into the front seat. He jerked up her skirt and began to tear at her shorts and underpants. "I should be able to do the same thing ole Robert does."

Kathy struggled to get out of his clutches, but he was too strong. She knew screaming would be useless, but she cried out anyway. They were too far away from any house. And the other two wouldn't challenge Scott. She yanked at his hair, tearing some out. He retaliated by slapping her across the face, almost knocking her out. He ripped away her shorts, ripped her panties in his frenzy, and jerked her skirt up above her waist. She kicked out at him, but the confines of the back seat prevented a solid blow. He rolled on top of her, his weight pinning her firmly against the seat.

Scott unzipped his pants to release his engorged penis. He tried to force it into her as she struggled and scratched at his face. He swiped at a bit of blood caused by the scratches near his left eye. Frustrated by her resistance, he tried to punch her face, but hit her in the neck with his fist. She cried out, then moaned softly and went limp.

The frustration and fighting had destroyed his ardor. He couldn't function, but continued to lay on top of her. He realized he had ejaculated. This hadn't worked out like he planned. He lay sprawled on top of her for several minutes, losing track of the time, but becoming concerned. She hadn't moved since he hit her.

Scott gathered his senses. He tried to locate a pulse in her wrist, but wasn't successful, not certain he was pressing the right place. He shook her shoulders, but there was no response. She sprawled across the seat like a rag doll. He scrambled out of the car, getting his pants rearranged, and called out, "Hey guys, come here!"

Gil and Joe trotted back from the edge of the creek where they had been standing. As Gil looked into the back, he saw Kathy limp and still, her clothes ripped, naked from the waist down, blood on her legs. He screamed, "What've you done? You crazy bastard!"

Scott grinned. "Just a little fun. She's okay. Just passed out."

Gil reached in to take Kathy's wrist. After a few seconds, he stepped back, his eyes wide with fear. "There's no pulse. You've killed her!"

Joe didn't want to look. He wailed, "Oh Jesus, what we'll do?"

Scott, still not believing she could be seriously hurt, grabbed her under her arms and pulled her out of the car. When she remained limp, his concern mounted. "I didn't hit her hard. The bitch was scratching and clawing. I just wanted to stop her."

Gil grabbed him by the shirt collar. "You dumb jackass. You've killed her."

"But I didn't mean to hurt her. I just wanted her to stop clawing my face."

Gil and Joe glanced at each other, both knowing they had a big problem, and beginning to think about how to escape. Scott, still holding Kathy's sagging body upright, couldn't think. The three stood looking at her, dazed by the turn of events.

After several seconds of silence, Scott said, "Let's just leave her here. No one will ever know we were involved."

"We can't just leave her here," muttered Joe, "maybe she's still alive. We should take her to the hospital."

Gil nodded agreement, but Scott stormed, "Hell no, let's get the fuck out of here. There's nothing else to do."

Neither Gil nor Joe had the nerve to fight with Scott and they wanted to vacate the scene, so they silently went along. Scott dragged her away from the car and placed the body down gently, straightening her clothes as best he could. He tossed the shorts and panties on top of her. He threw the sweater from the car and it landed on the ground two feet away.

They were quiet as Gil drove away. Near Scott's house, Gil said, "I'll drop you off at the next corner."

Scott said gruffly, "Remember, no one talks. You do, you got me to deal with." He banged a huge fist into the palm of the other hand.

Joe said nothing when Gil dropped him off in front of his home. He wobbled into the house, hoping neither of his parents would be up. The image of Kathy being dropped on the grass wouldn't go away. He thought he would be sick.

Gil carefully parked the car in the garage and stole into his house, certain his parents would hear him come home, but wouldn't question him unless he made noise. He hadn't looked into the back seat of the car again. The reality of Kathy's death overwhelmed him.

Jerry stopped and looked at the group. "As I said, we are confident of the scenario." He glanced at his notes. "Much of what I've told you came from revelations by the kids. Obviously, I've embellished the conversations a bit, especially the thoughts that must have been running through Kathy's mind. No one will ever know the depths of her fear and loss of control."

When no one commented or asked questions, Peabody said, "Dr. Ferriday, perhaps you can review the DNA evidence again. I want to be sure we're on solid ground before Little goes to trial."

Fred spread across the table several photographs of DNA analyses. "Mr. Neal brought these by the motel this morning. I've examined the photographs to become familiar with them again." He pointed to the arrangement. "Here are the samples taken from Robert Jarvis. In this next row are the samples from the crime scene, hair, skin and semen. Note all the DNA fragments or bands match. All came from one individual." He pointed carefully to each one, standing and moving away from his chair, giving the others an opportunity to peer at the photos before continuing. "Then you have blood samples from Gil Brown, Joe Dobbs, and Scott Little. If you'll move them around so certain photos are side by side, it's clear the blood DNA from Little matches all the ones taken from the victim's body."

Jerry said, "And coincides with the statements."

Fred nodded agreement and continued. "No doubt Scott left skin, hair and semen at the scene. In my opinion it's irrefutable evidence proving he tried to rape Kathy Abrams. It fits with the scenario just revealed by Jerry."

Peabody asked. "And nothing from either of the other boys?"

"Nothing," Jerry said. "Perhaps they left hair in the car, but it had been cleaned before we got to it."

Peabody looked around the group. "Any questions or differences of opinion?"

Everyone looked at each other, but no one challenged the evidence. Peabody turned back to Jerry. "Now, what about the cover up? Any progress?"

Redmond, a tall, middle-age, man who'd been with the state agency for fifteen years, took the lead. "That's been more difficult, but we've done a lot of work. Harold Brown has been reasonably open after we pressured him a bit and discovered a residual stain on the back seat of his car. But Ledbetter has resisted at every turn. We've obtained some telephone records which helped. Gil Brown added some revealing things."

Jerry said, "If you wish, I can tell you what we know." Peabody nodded, giving permission.

Jerry grinned as though he enjoyed his task. "Let me start by revealing a conversation between the two Browns." Again he flipped through his notes. "This is based on our discussions with Harold and Gil and follows Harold discovering blood stains on the back seat of the family car the Saturday afternoon, the day after the crime. When he heard the news about Abrams death and the speculation a car had been involved, he became suspicious and challenged Gil about the coincidences."

Harold found Gil watching a college football game on television in the downstairs family room. He asked, "Gil, did you guys see Kathy Abrams last night?"

Gil's face turned ghostly white. He couldn't look at his father. "Why are you asking that?"

"She was apparently murdered after the game last night." When Gil continued to avoid his eyes, Harold said, "The deputies believe a car was involved. I found blood on the back seat of the car when I cleaned it this afternoon. I must know if there's a connection."

Gil put his hands to his face. "It was an accident."

"What in God's name do you mean?"

With his voice quivering, his body trembling, Gil told his father the story of the boys following Kathy and Robert, then grabbing her. He choked out the resulting action in the park.

Harold walked around the room, trying to remain calm and think through this disaster, looking at his son, usually a sensible, dependable kid, now accessory to murder and rape. It might even be more, once the full story came out. After five minutes, he said, "Don't tell anyone what you've told me. You understand. Keep it quiet."

Gil nodded, understanding and accepting, but not sure what his father intended.

Harold said, "I'll talk to some people as soon as I can find them. Keep quiet and make sure your buddies keep quiet about this. All of you could spend a long time in prison if the wrong people discover what happened."

Jerry stopped. "Now a second conversation becomes important to our understanding. The pieces came from the senior Brown after we'd reviewed his telephone records for the Saturday and Sunday in question."

Harold walked upstairs to the room he used for an office and called Ned Ledbetter, his long time friend and law partner. "I'm lucky to get you. I figured you'd be out tonight."

Ledbetter heard concern in the voice of his friend. "What's wrong?"

Quickly, Harold revealed the series of events culminating in the death of Kathy Abrams. "I need advice. I don't want Gil to do jail time for this. He swears he did nothing wrong."

Ledbetter was silent on the other end of the line for several seconds. "I'll call Ross Talbot and Jim Williams. They owe me some favors. I'll let you know their reactions. It may be Monday before I get back to you, but it'll be okay. Just sit tight and make sure those kids don't panic and talk. Not even to each other. Don't even let them get together."

Harold Brown's worries subsided when he heard on the late night Saturday news that Robert Jarvis had been charged and arrested for the crime. Jarvis would remain in custody of the Pine County Sheriff pending formal arraignment and establishment of bail terms.

Jerry interrupted his reading of the transcript. "Ledbetter intervened to help his partner and his partner's son and saw an expeditious way when he found out Jarvis was black. He intended to sacrifice Jarvis using the old fears of racial hatred. Maybe he would have tried in any case, but Jarvis being black made it easier to sway the Sheriff and perhaps the County Attorney. Mr. Williams may have been an active participant, or he may have just gone along with Talbot and Ledbetter. Ledbetter almost successfully manipulated the justice system by influencing my appointment as the defense attorney, and then attempting to limit my activities to using only the information provided by the prosecution. In retrospect, several officers of the justice system and prominent citizens have some guilt to bear in what almost became a miscarriage of justice."

Jerry continued, "I thought something was amiss when Ledbetter made such an issue of my asking for an examination of the samples from the scene and my questioning of high school students about the relationship between Robert and Kathy Abrams, but I was intimidated and drifted along for a while. Then Fred Ferriday appeared at the request of Joshua Bull. Fred immediately challenged me, threatening to bring in the Attorney General if I didn't shape up. I knew Fred was right. I wasn't doing what a defense attorney should do. That's when things began to change."

Williams had sat quietly during Jerry's recitation, but now said, "It all makes sense. Ledbetter and Brown didn't care who paid the price, just so the Brown boy remained out of the picture. They didn't care about Scott Little, but couldn't risk an inquiry into the kid's actions for fear it would include Gil. And I'd guess there was concern about the fall out damaging the law firm."

His face darkened. "I admit I was used by Ledbetter. He called me and demanded that I take the case forward on the basis of the evidence the Sheriff had collected from Robert and the testimony of the kids who saw them leaving the stadium together."

Peabody said, "Well, I admit being hooked in by Ledbetter. I honestly believed he was trying to serve the County by offering one of his junior people for the defense. Many firms shy away from those duties because of the loss of time and revenue by the appointee." He laughed.

"Henceforth, I should remember the saying if the deal looks too good to be true, something must be wrong."

Fred asked, "But how does Ledbetter control or influence the Sheriff's office?"

Williams responded. "I'm not sure, but he probably has something on Talbot. Maybe Ross owes him money. That's where I'd start to look."

Jerry continued. "And what about yourself?"

Williams reddened slightly. "Ledbetter is a strange bird. In my case, he never threatens, but he doesn't hesitate to remind me he controls the party politicians who, in turn, can make sure I'm not nominated for another term." He rubbed his forehead and wiped his glasses with the bottom of his tie. "I'm susceptible to the threat of losing my position, one I enjoy very much."

Peabody observed. "Like all politicians, so-called public servants, we are easy prey. Jim is no different."

Everyone was silent, thinking about their own situation. Peabody broke the quiet. "Jerry, are you able to move forward to a trial with this case now?"

Jerry rubbed his face. "You know Judge Peabody, there's more than one charge to be placed."

"You mean the assault and murder, plus obstruction of justice."

"I'm willing to take on the case against Scott Little for murder. But I prefer not to be involved with the issues against Ledbetter and Brown. In fact, I'll be called as a witness." He glanced at Fred. "So will Fred be called to testify. Both of us were assaulted by hoodlums acting on the orders of Ledbetter or Talbot. That needs to get into the record as part of the obstruction."

Peabody stared at his notes, sipping from the glass of water. "Perhaps I should discuss it with the Attorney General's office. Maybe with the Illinois Bar. But, Mr. Preston, I want you to follow through for the crimes against Kathy Abrams."

Louise arrived late afternoon at the motel where they'd stayed during the Thanksgiving holiday. Fred was scanning a manuscript when he heard the key and the door open.

Accommodating to the different scene, she smiled. "Always working."

Fred moved to her and pulled her close. "Trying to keep my mind off you."

"You mean what you hope will happen when I got here."

Fred tipped her face up and kissed her gently. "It's predictable."

She responded by dropping her coat across a chair and hugging him close, her lips finding his.

Afterward, as they were stretched across the bed, Fred said, "We're meeting Joshua and Robert for dinner at Raymond's."

"Are you ready to tell them about us?"

"Joshua is expecting something. But the question is how much do we reveal?"

Louise laughed and rolled on top of him. "Well, there are limits."

Fred caressed her back and tousled her hair. "I'm ready to tell him we're getting married and stopping these weekend trysts."

Louise scrambled off the bed, and pulled her robe from her bag. "You're serious, aren't you?"

"It's time. We've both considered all the implications. We both know it'll be a wonderful relationship. Our feelings for each other will only get stronger."

She said, "I'm ready to say yes. But we haven't talked about the future. Maybe you've assumed I'll move to your place and become a lady of leisure. But I want to continue working professionally."

Fred said, "I've thought about it and made some contacts. In fact, the English department has essentially promised a position for you beginning next fall."

"How'd you swing that so fast?"

"Louise, several of the faculty in English know about your writing and your empathy with students. They're eager to have you come." His plea hadn't been hurt by his knowing the department head for several years dating back to their joint service on a university committee on grade inflation. And he knew English, a faculty overwhelmed with teaching hundreds of undergraduates each semester, seemed always to have vacancies.

"I don't know if I should be flattered or feel used."

"Be flattered." Fred pulled her close. "Also, I told the dean if he couldn't work it out for you, I'd start looking for a place where we could both have positions."

She touched his face. "So you threatened."

"Blackmail. They like the money I bring in through grants and contracts."

As they were dressing for dinner, Fred said, "I've thought also you might like to be free of jobs and concentrate on your writing. We've talked several times about your wanting to do that someday. This could be your opportunity."

She turned away from the mirror. "Now you're bribing me."

"Maybe, but you should think about it." He walked closer to her. "We could set up an office for you in one of the spare rooms. The university has a wonderful library should you need to research for background materials. Your time would be free of any other responsibilities. And, my salary will keep food on the table."

Louise straightened his tie. "What else have you thought about? You've covered every angle in breaking my resistance."

Fred reached into his briefcase and retrieved a small box. He took her hand and placed a large diamond ring on her finger. "I've thought of this, too."

She looked at him. "You think of everything." Tears appeared in her eyes.

"We'll let the evidence tell Joshua our plans."

At the restaurant, Robert and Joshua were exuberant when told the plans of Louise and Fred to be married. Robert said, "I've accepted a grant-in-aid to Illinois. We'll all be in the same place except Grandfather."

"I plan to remain as the stable member of this family," Joshua grinned. "Keep a place where you all want to come to reconnect with your roots."

Fred reached across the table to shake Robert's hand. "Good news. It's a good school. You'll get a fine education, and have fun playing football in the Big Ten."

Robert, more open and animated than Fred had ever seen him, said, "Dr. Ferriday, according to Grandfather, I owe you a lot. He says if you hadn't come here, I'd have been found guilty."

Joshua chimed in. "It's true, Fred, don't deny it. Even Jerry Preston admits you caused him to get moving on the case."

Fred said, "Don't know how much credit I'm due. I suspect Jerry would have done the right thing. Maybe I pushed him to move faster, but he's a fine young man. He'll do well, especially since he's moved to Calloway and Givens."

Louise had been sitting quietly, observing the interchange. "Fred seems to finish what he starts. He's much more aggressive than you'd think."

Fred laughed. "Let's talk about the future. It looks wonderful from my perspective."

CHAPTER NINETEEN

Three months later, Jerry Preston called Fred as he pushed through the door from the garage into the den, arriving home after a long day in the lab and office. "Fred, it's Jerry. How're things?"

Fred dropped his briefcase on the floor in the den and sat on the arm of the couch. "Going well but busy. The semester is coming to a close and there's always the rush of exams and grades. How about you?"

"I called to let you know the outcome of the hearings and trials centered around the Jarvis affair. First, on a personal note, when the Illinois Teacher's Association threatened a suit about Fran's dismissal, the School Superintendent caved in. He admitted Ledbetter had pressured him and then he bulldozed the principal into suspending Fran. The system paid Fran fifty thousand dollars for damages and anguish—settled out of court, so to speak."

"They should have made Ledbetter pay. So does Fran have a new position starting in the fall term?"

"Yeah. Calloway's efforts paid off, plus support from parents in Pine County. At Calloway's suggestion, a delegation from the Pine County PTA met with the superintendent here. So she's all set to teach the same grade level she had in Pineville and is looking forward to being with the kids. She's going to love the place, a new school with up-to-date equipment and from all accounts the kids are bright and eager."

Jerry caught his breath and continued. "On another topic. After all the evidence was revealed, charges were placed against all three of the boys involved in the crime. Scott Little was found guilty of aggravated assault and murder. Actually, the technical charge was criminal homicide. He was sentenced to thirty years in the state prison, but likely can be paroled in twelve years, if he doesn't screw up. In a way I feel badly for him. He's made a mess of his life, but he committed a terrible crimes and must pay his due to society."

"Don't feel too badly for him. Remember he destroyed a vibrant young woman with a promising future. What about the other two? They were unwilling accomplices, weren't they?"

"In the strictest sense, they were, but neither did anything to prevent Scott from his act. Deep down, they knew he had this thing for Kathy. Both admitted Scott intended to force Kathy to have sex, but they didn't regard it as rape, but as some form of seduction. Of course, they hadn't counted on her being killed."

Again Jerry paused. "Both arranged pleas bargains with lawyers from a law firm in St. Louis acting for them. Their records will show accessory to assault and murder. It's probably the right decision. They were in some ways bystanders, too intimidated by Scott to do anything. Rather than try to stop him, they walked away until Kathy had been killed. Maybe if they'd intervened at all, even yelling and screaming at Scott, Kathy would have survived."

"Will they serve any time?"

"Not unless they commit a crime during their probation. Both received sentences of ten years with prison time suspended. Peabody went soft with them. I suspect he felt sorry for them."

Fred said, "Maybe they'll learn something about responsibility."

"But at a steep price for Kathy Abrams and her family." Jerry continued. "Their lives will never be the same and neither will those boys. I saw Joe Dobbs' mother several days ago in a local pharmacy. She told me he has nightmares, has lost weight, and his school performance has dropped off. He's headed for long-term psychological treatment but will be haunted by the episode the rest of his life."

"What about Gil Brown?"

"Haven't talked with anyone close to him. My guess is he'll shove it aside and go on okay. He seemed less shaken by the events than Joe. But who knows at this time. It's bound to have some impact."

Fred sat on the couch, slipping off his loafers. "I'm interested in what happened to Ledbetter and his buddies. I've been expecting a call to testify at their trial."

Jerry laughed. "I've never seen so many guys cave in so easily after they realized their usual bluster and threats were not going anywhere. Deals were struck to avoid trials in every case. Bottom line, Ledbetter and Brown lost their licenses for ten years, so the firm is in trouble and will probably fold from what I hear on the street. But I've also heard that Kline may return for a short while to provide leadership until the organization has found its bearings again. Nevertheless, I feel badly for the younger people in the firm. They'll be contaminated although they knew nothing and were never involved. I've heard a lot of long-time clients have moved to other firms. In fact, three came to Calloway and Givens and I'm their primary attorney now."

"So Ledbetter and Brown may never practice law again."

Jerry responded. "That's true for all practical purposes. They'll be able to request reinstatement, but their reputations and client bases are destroyed. They could hook on with a large firm somewhere and disappear into the library doing background work. Maybe even do small civil cases, but I'd guess they'll simply withdraw and live off their investments."

"And our friend Talbot?"

"He pleaded guilty to obstruction and was hit with a stiff fine. He admitted he acted on Ledbetter's orders, who held the mortgage on his house and a small farm. At one time Ledbetter had co-signed a loan with Talbot, but Ross couldn't make the payments. Ledbetter bailed him out, but always used him for dirty tricks. By the way, Redmond and I have pieced together from tapes one conversation between Ledbetter and Purcell followed by a call from Ledbetter to Talbot that's quite revealing. Let me play it for you." Fred heard the instrument being placed down, then Jerry came back on the line. "Here it is. It starts with Brown going into Ledbetter's office."

"Ned, this thing with Jarvis is coming apart." A deep sigh followed by a muttered oath could be heard.

Ledbetter, calm voice. "What makes you think so?"

Movements, a chair scraping on the floor or bumping against the desk. "Jerry Preston called the house, wanted to talk with Gil. He either knows or suspects Gil and his buddies were the last to see Abrams alive. He's figured it out. Somehow he knows what happened."

Ledbetter, still calm. "Ah, he's bluffing. How the hell could he know?"

Again noise of movement, then Brown's voice. "Gil says Preston talked to Scott Little and Joe Dobbs."

"They wouldn't admit anything after the warnings we've given them. I still say he's shooting in the dark, hoping someone will break."

Brown's voice and an audible sigh. "Should we do anything?"

"No, but you're right about keeping Gil away from Preston"

Jerry broke in. "Apparently as soon as Brown left with his spirits raised, Ledbetter called Ross Talbot. Here's that part of it."

Ledbetter's voice, stern, demanding. "Ross, we're continuing to have problems with Preston. See what you can do to head him off."

Talbot coughed. "Any suggestions?" When Ledbetter waited, he said, "He's pretty determined. Those scare tactics didn't work."

"Maybe you haven't used enough persuasion."

"We tried it on Ferriday and it backfired. He's after my butt now for not charging those guys who rammed his car." Talbot stopped, then continued, "He was mad as hell when I released them. If I hadn't been the Sheriff, Ferriday would have clobbered me. I knew the matter wasn't over. He accused me of being part of a cover-up and threatened to alert the State police."

Ledbetter's voice elevated several notches in volume. "Ross, either we get Preston sidetracked or this thing's coming apart. Now, get on the goddam ball. Do something to stop him. I don't care what, but make sure he gets the message." The phone slammed down.

Fred heard the recording hum, then Jerry's voice again on the phone. "Redmond and I pieced the thing together. Talbot was worried and frustrated because Ledbetter used him to do the dirty work. Efforts to derail us had failed. Ledbetter was demanding he go beyond anything he'd contemplated when Ledbetter got him involved immediately after the crime. Covering evidence had been one thing. Stopping my investigation would take drastic action, either have me killed or injured so badly I'd have to drop out of the case. He apparently settled on having those thugs knock me around and threaten Fran, figuring if her safety became an issue, I'd cave in and run. And you know, I thought about doing that, but Calloway saved the day by letting me work from his offices."

Fred asked, "When did that happen?

"After I'd called the Brown's home to talk to Gil. Later, Harold called me, telling me to lay off trying to get to Gil. My call to Brown initiated the response from Ledbetter, then Talbot and his hired thugs went into action. Brown and Ledbetter were getting desperate. I was getting too close to the truth. But I didn't know it at the time."

"Who recorded those conversations?" Fred asked. "It's hard to believe anyone would leave those around or even tape things like that in the first place."

"Susan Newman helped us locate the tapes. She knew Ledbetter kept records of conversations, either callers or visitors to the office, when there might be the potential for using a statement against someone. In fact, when I met with her, she told me he taped some things, but I didn't give it much thought then, knowing I couldn't gain access to the tapes. Ledbetter worked on a lot of deals where he would gain control of people and then use them for his own purposes. He always recorded those conversations to use against the person if he balked or failed to obtain results."

"I'm surprised he didn't destroy them when things started coming apart."

"So were we," said Jerry. "But remember Nixon—he decided to bluff his way and Ledbetter tried to do the same. Also, Peabody granted a subpoena relatively soon in our investigation of Ledbetter and Brown for us to search his private office and he probably didn't have time to get rid of things. Our probe moved faster than he'd expected or he believed he could talk his way out of any suspicions."

Fred said, "Back to Talbot. Did those two thugs of his escape punishment?"

"No. Talbot gave them up. They were charged with three counts of assault and sentenced to a year of jail time."

Fred asked, "And what about Jim Williams? Did he stick with his statement he made to Peabody during the discussion after the trial?"

"He accepted responsibility for not pushing the Sheriff's office for a more intensive investigation, and acknowledged Ledbetter pressured him to take a passive position. Jim promised Peabody he'd not seek reelection at the end of this term. So it's a cost to him but it could have been worse if the court had held him responsible for obstruction and shielding evidence."

"So with all that behind you, how's life with Calloway and Givens?"

"It'll be great when I can finally settle in there. Truth is, I've spent most of my time wrapping up those things in Pineville. Calloway has been more than understanding and supportive and keeps telling me I'll earn my salary. I have a case for them starting next week and am looking forward to that. And by the way, Susan Newman is taking a position with Calloway as secretary to three lawyers, including myself. She was glad to leave Ledbetter after all the ruckus."

Fred said, "If you've talked to Joshua, you probably know Louise and I are getting married this summer. We're looking at a date in mid-August. I'll let you know about our plans."

"Joshua told me. I bumped into him at the food mart a few days ago. He's really pleased, but I got the feeling he didn't want to admit his pleasure."

Fred laughed. "He's always been like that, even as a kid."

"I assume you'll be living in Champaign-Urbana?"

"We will. Louise has decided to focus on completing the novel she's worked on and other writings rather than taking a position at the university. I tease her about hitting a best seller and we'll retire to the Caribbean."

Fred stood from the couch arm to stretch his legs. "You and Fran must come visit this fall. I'll round up tickets to a game and we can watch Robert perform unless they redshirt him his freshman year."

"We'd like that." Jerry laughed. "Fran gives you credit for saving my career, but you were sort of a bastard in doing it."

"No doubt I was." Fred's laugh trailed off. "I'll let you know specifics about the wedding and a game this fall."

"Good. Fred, take care—and thanks."

Robert's nerves were on edge as he rang the doorbell of the Abrams home on the last Sunday in July. He'd responded positively to a telephone call from Janet Abrams three days earlier inviting him to lunch. She'd indicated they wished to talk to him about Kathy, but he wasn't certain that was their real intention.

Jack Abrams responded to the bell. "Come in Robert. We're pleased you could come." He led Robert toward the dining room where Janet was putting the finishing touches on the table setting. She stopped placing silverware and came to shake Robert's hand, saying, "Robert, thanks for coming."

Robert remained on edge throughout the lunch, making sure he used the soup spoon correctly and didn't scatter crumbs from the sandwich. The conversation centered around recent events in Pineville. They asked about his plans for college and seemed pleased he'd accepted a scholarship to Illinois.

After lunch they moved to the den and suggested a chair for Robert while they huddled close together on a couch facing him.

Jack Abrams took the lead. "Robert, the reason we wanted to meet you was to get a better understanding of the relationship between you and our daughter. Please tell us about that if you don't mind."

Robert looked at the two, then said, "I'll be honest and direct and trust you can accept my feelings as well as those of Kathy. We had become quite close and both of us wanted to be together for a long time. As you might imagine, we were frustrated by the limitations placed on us by people in the town, including the two of you. Kathy didn't wish to disobey you and thus we were limited in what we could do openly. We loved each other, although we accepted that we were young and not experienced. We intended to go to the same university and continue our relationship to the point we knew without doubts we were bound to each other or that we would go our separate ways. From my perspective, we would have lived our lives together forever."

Staring at his feet, Jack said, "One thing we wished to tell you today is we're sorry for our actions in keeping you apart. While there's no real excuse for how we acted, you understand the feelings of the people in the town about racial mixing and the pressures your friends place on you. Nevertheless, we want to say we're sorry for the way we acted toward you."

Robert didn't know how to respond. He sat silently for several seconds remembering the frustrations he and Kathy had experienced because of her parents. Then he said, "I can understand your feelings because of the things that happen to my Grandfather almost every day. I'm sorry too we could not have talked about things before Kathy's death."

Janet entered the conversation. "We've thought a lot about the night Kathy died." She paused, wiped her eyes with her hand. "We have come to believe had we not made such a fuss about your walking her home, she would still be with us."

Robert nodded. "I've thought about that too. If I had been able to escort her to the front door, those boys would never have done what they did. They wouldn't have grabbed her had I been there. I would have defended her with all my being."

Jack stood. "We know that now. And it only makes our loss so much more difficult because we could have prevented it."

Robert stood to shake Jack's hand. "I know, but I recognize you were doing what you believed was the right thing to do. I hope you can accept I had deep feelings for Kathy and I will miss her the rest of my life."

Janet stepped to Robert and to his surprise, hugged him close. "Good luck, Robert. When you are home during breaks, please come by to see us."

The wedding took place in Pineville on the second Sunday of August, a warm sunny day causing participants to stay inside the air-conditioned building. Joshua escorted Louise down the aisle. She looked happy and beautiful, the white dress matching her radiant smile. As he and Louise stood in front of the altar of the small church, Fred experienced a feeling of coming home and finding his roots again. The minister, a large figure in his white robe, of Joshua's church smiled wisely as he pronounced them husband and wife.

During the reception in the fellowship hall of the church, Fred and Louise were congratulated by three of Louise's colleagues from St. Louis, close friends of Joshua's from the church, Robert, the Preston's, the Rinehart's, and three graduate students from Fred's research group.

Robert beamed as he hugged Louise in the reception area and shook Fred's hand. "I'll see you at the university. Maybe you can guide me in choosing a major." He turned away before Fred could respond as a young woman led him toward a corner of the hall.

After the receiving line had ended and people began mingling, Fred and Joshua found themselves standing on the fringe of the group as people filled plates from the table, sampled the cake, and sipped the punch, Fred said, "Weddings bring together people who will never see each other again."

"True," said Joshua, "and sometimes even families."

"Joshua, we've come a long way to finally make connections again. Let's not lose track of each other again."

"No danger of that." He laughed. "Louise will make sure everybody's in touch from now on."

THE END

ABOUT THE AUTHOR

S. J. Ritchey began writing fiction after retirement from Virginia Tech. He has short stories in magazines and in two collections published by Blue River Writers. His detective/lawyer series has four books in print and his series about the adventures of a biology professor has two published manuscripts.

The author lives with his wife, Elizabeth, in Blacksburg, Virginia. They spend summers at her family cottage on Lake Couchiching near Washago, Ontario, Canada.